A MOM, A WAND, AND A MISSION

A MOM, A WAND, AND A MISSION

CASE FILES OF AN URBAN WITCH™ BOOK 8

MARTHA CARR

MICHAEL ANDERLE

This book is a work of fiction. All of the characters, organizations, and events portrayed in this novel are either products of the author's imagination or are used fictitiously. Sometimes both.

Copyright © 2021 LMBPN Publishing
Cover by Fantasy Book Design
Cover copyright © LMBPN Publishing
A Michael Anderle Production

LMBPN Publishing supports the right to free expression and the value of copyright. The purpose of copyright is to encourage writers and artists to produce the creative works that enrich our culture.

The distribution of this book without permission is a theft of the author's intellectual property. If you would like permission to use material from the book (other than for review purposes), please contact support@lmbpn.com. Thank you for your support of the author's rights.

LMBPN Publishing
PMB 196, 2540 South Maryland Pkwy
Las Vegas, NV 89109

Version 1.00, September, 2021
ebook ISBN: 978-1-68500-424-8
Print ISBN: 978-1-68500-425-5

The Oriceran Universe (and what happens within / characters / situations / worlds) are Copyright © 2017-21 by Martha Carr and LMBPN Publishing.

THE A MOM, A WAND, AND A MISSION
TEAM

Thanks to the JIT Readers

Dave Hicks
Jackey Hankard-Brodie
Diane L. Smith

If we've missed anyone, please let us know!

Editor
Skyhunter Editing Team

From Martha

*To everyone who still believes in magic and all the possibilities
that holds.*

To all the readers who make this entire ride so much fun.

*To Louie, Jackie, and so many wonderful friends who remind me
all the time of what really matters and how wonderful life can be
in any given moment.*

From Michael

*To Family, Friends and
Those Who Love
To Read.
May We All Enjoy Grace
To Live The Life We Are
Called.*

CHAPTER ONE

The Silver Griffins' office was dark, quiet, and still, the only movement a swirling of dust motes around the outlet from the air conditioning system. Lucy Heron walked between the desks, watching for any sign of activity, any shifting of shadows that could've shown her that someone was around.

This was uncanny. The office was never this deserted. There were always witches and wizards around, logging cases, sifting evidence, preparing to rush out and hunt down rogue magicals. Gnomes were always pottering back and forth with armfuls of papers as they filed, archived, and did all the mundane yet precise administrative tasks that kept the office going. There were always pigeons, scattering feathers as they hurtled through the upper reaches of the office with mission briefings for field agents strapped to their legs. The office couldn't possibly be this quiet. It defied all logic.

She ran a finger across a desk. It came away dusty. Lucy knew dust. She was a mom with a good-sized house and three kids to chase after, none of whom were as handy with a duster as she would've liked. She knew what it looked like when the top of a cupboard or an out-of-the-way ornament went untended for too long. This wasn't that sort of dust. This was something darker, with a greasy texture. When she wiped the finger on her leg, it left a coal-black stain down her wedding dress.

Wait, why was she wearing her wedding dress? That made no sense at all. The dress was carefully packed away in the attic of the family home, as it had been for the past decade. She and Charlie had gotten it out once to indulge in a moment of pure nostalgia not long after Ashley was born, but had kept it safely boxed up ever since. No way she would be wearing it in the office.

Why *was* she in the office on a Saturday night? She felt like there was something she had to do, but she wasn't sure what.

Her wand hand tingled. Although the wand wasn't there, sparks of magic gleamed in her palm, stinging her. Their sharpness cut through the fog in her mind, and suddenly it all became clear. This was a dream.

She sighed in relief, sat at her desk, and spun in her chair, letting the dress spin out with her. If she was asleep, she might as well relax.

Except that something was moving in the shadows, and she didn't think it had come to give her a goodnight kiss.

She got to her feet and peered into the darkness. Now that she looked more closely, she realized that it wasn't a movement within the shadows: the shadows themselves were in motion, swirling, churning, and oozing across the floor like a dark tide.

She looked across her desk, but there was no sign of her wand or anything else she could use to defend herself. She yanked open the top drawer, but the only things inside were toys belonging to Eddie, her youngest kid. Most of them were plastic robots or dinosaurs. She slammed the drawer shut and stood protectively over it, glaring at the shifting shadows.

"You can't have this." She laid her hand on the drawer.

"I don't want that." The shadow spun into a dark gray pillar of smoke, tinged with metallic blue and putrescent yellow. Its voice was a croak as if it was choking on itself. "I've come for you, Lucy Heron. I'm going to have my revenge."

Lucy coughed. The air stank of car fumes and burning plastic, with a hint of something even worse. Tendrils of smoke reached for her. She raised her hand to counter it, but she didn't have her wand, and she couldn't punch the smoke.

"You're gone," she said to Blight. "We destroyed you."

"You could never destroy me. Not while the filth of your cities remains."

Streams of smog reached for Lucy. She stepped back, tripped over her chair, and fell on her back. The pollution kept advancing. She twisted over, the dress ripping as she trod on a section of the hem, then scrambled to her feet and ran.

She dashed down a corridor, away from the main office floor and into the depths of the Silver Griffins' L.A. offices. She couldn't escape the stink of pollution or the taste of toxins in her mouth with every breath. She couldn't get away from the rasping, wheezing noise of Blight. Still, she ran because it was all that she could do and because the corridor seemed to stretch on forever, mile after mile of featureless concrete. Her friends Jackie and Sarah appeared on either side of her, dressed in their running gear.

"Mustn't be late," Sarah said. "Ellis is waiting."

"And of course," Jackie said, "the future of the world is at stake."

Then they both dashed off down side corridors that closed behind them, leaving Lucy all alone.

At the end of the corridor, she stumbled into the pigeon loft. The birds all stopped their cooing and pecking to look at her. Lucy leaned over and propped her hands on her knees, trying to catch her breath. She'd left the smoky odor behind, but something else didn't smell right here. It was a different sort of stink, lower and more earthy but equally unpleasant.

Tar ran down the walls and oozed across the floor. It dripped from the ceiling, coating the pigeons' feathers and sticking their wings to their sides. They made sounds of distress, and some tried to take flight but fell to the floor with sickening *splats*.

An orange figure lumbered from between the cages at the back of the room. His flesh rippled above his shorts. Large, frog-like eyes stared at Lucy.

"Zero," Lucy whispered. "I saw you die."

"The devil offers the best deals," Zero replied. "I'll give you a way out of this in return for your soul."

"I'm not selling my soul to you!"

"Fine, your children's souls then. They won't need them."

"I'm not selling you my children!"

"I can offer a fair price." Zero opened his hand and gemstones tumbled out. "Well, fair for me, at least."

"How many times do I have to say no?"

"All right then, if you won't give me anything, I'll take it from you." Zero waved, and a swarm of tiny black creatures appeared in the air around him. "Go get her, my pretties."

As the swarm of magical mites hurtled toward Lucy, she turned and raced away, back down the corridor. Except that it was a different corridor, a lower level of the Griffins' HQ than she'd been on before. The swarm buzzed after her, ready to descend and devour her if she paused for even a second. The world filled with their buzzing, the hammering of her feet against the floor, and her pounding heartbeat.

"Wake up, wake up, wake up," she gasped to herself. "I have to wake up."

Although she pressed her nails into the palms of her hands, she could barely cling to the knowledge that she was asleep, never mind escape into wakefulness.

The corridor ended, and she emerged in the transport room. Someone had set out a row of desks in the middle of the floor where they brought prisoners for magical travel to Trevilsom Prison.

Many magicals sat at them, including witches, wizards, gnomes, dwarves, and elves. A Willen at the front wore a particularly sour look on her face, and the human sitting next to her in the sleeveless hoodie looked like he wanted to punch the whole world. At the front of the class stood Meredith Womack, witch and con woman, waving a slim black wand bound in dull iron.

"Today's lesson, class, is dealing with the authorities," Womack said. "It's going to be a practical lesson."

She waved her wand. A bolt of ice flew toward Lucy, who dove to the floor. The ice magic froze the wall behind her. She rolled over and sprang to her feet, the dress now thoroughly torn and dirty.

The whole class was staring at her. Each of them had magic shining around their fingers or the tip of a wand.

"Come on, come on..." Lucy tried to will her wand into her hand. After all, this was a dream, and hers had some special power when it came to those. That should count for something, right? Regardless of how hard she strained, it still wasn't there.

"On my mark." Womack pointed her wand. "Three, two, one..."

Lucy dashed off down the corridor again.

"Go!"

Magic flew all around Lucy, fireballs and glue spells and freezes spattering the walls. A chorus of footsteps told her that the class was hot on her tail. She didn't dare look back. She kept running until a steel bulkhead slid aside ahead of her and she stepped into the familiar surroundings of the Special Equipment and Weapons lab.

"Jenkins!" she shouted. "Jenkins, are you here?"

In the shadows at the far end of the test range, she glimpsed a lab coat.

"Thank goodness," Lucy said. "I need a weapon, any weapon, something to defend myself with. Or a wand. You have the new ones down here, right?"

Someone walked out of the shadows, but instead of having Jenkins' ginger hair, they were bald, their head smooth and pale. The lab coat fell to the floor, revealing a black suit on a slender, sinister frame.

"Mr. No." Lucy glared at him. "I should've known. Who else could be giving me nightmares like this?"

Mr. No laughed, and the sound was like a knife blade rasping over a whetstone.

"Oh, this isn't me, Agent Heron. How could it possibly be me? You defeated me, remember? Just like you defeated them..." The crime school burst through the door behind her. "And them..." Zero and his swarm stepped out of a shadow. "And him..." The cloud called Blight swirled down from the ceiling. "And so many more."

Other old opponents appeared, from a glowing businessman in a white suit to a graffiti artist with spray cans floating around her head. "So many of us, all gone. Still, you can't defeat what's on its way. The end time is coming, Lucy Heron. It's coming for you."

Mr. No took another step forward, and a shadow fell across him. The same happened to the artist, the businessman, the crime school, and the loan shark. Even the smog seemed to be drenched in shadow, becoming deeper darkness that set a wave of terror racing through Lucy. They closed in on her, all these enemies coming at once, but none of them themselves. They merged as the darkness closed in, about to engulf her. She desperately wished for anything to fight them with, some slim thread of magic.

Then she felt cool wood in her hand. She raised her wand and cast a spell.

"Lumen!"

There was a flash of light, and Lucy woke up in her bed. She sat bolt upright. The wand was in her hand, and the fading afterglow of the light flash filled the room. Beside her, Charlie rolled over and rubbed his eyes.

"Are you okay?" he asked.

"I think something terrible is coming." Lucy clutched her wand tight. "But I have no idea what."

CHAPTER TWO

Deep under L.A., so far down that even the cockroaches found no comfort, the Shadow Men stirred. By the light of old and dripping candles made from rancid fat, they peeled themselves off the walls of caves that had been ancient when the dinosaurs roamed the land above. Their flat forms folded through the world as they followed old ways through the close, cold confines of the world below. It was time to gather. Their leader had news.

The Shadow Mage waited in the largest of the caves they called home. He was taller than the rest, but like them, he existed only in two dimensions. He could be the darkness cast across the wall behind an unknowing innocent or a strange presence in his own right, so thin that he became invisible when viewed from the side.

His ancestors had cast him at dusk, a time that had stretched him out to tower above his minions. It had filled him with the magic of that shifting point when day faded into night, and tough predators became vulnerable prey. He was the greatest of his people, their leader, and the source of all their power. Still, the world he walked through when he emerged from the caves didn't suit him. It was a world made for solid people, for people of the light.

The Shadow Mage set down a crystal ball in the middle of the cavern. It glowed with a pale and sickly light, one that did little to chase away the smaller dark patches around the Shadow Men. That was how they liked it.

"That is the object you gained from Zero," the Shadow Sentry said. It was his duty to be watchful, observe the shapes and patterns of the world, and look for anything that might threaten the Shadow Men. The object was unusual, magical, and forged from light. That made it the sort of thing the Shadow Sentry was cautious about.

"It is." The Shadow Mage brushed dust from the sphere's surface while more Shadow Men filed into the cave.

"It cost us dearly," the Shadow Steward added. He guarded the fortunes of their kin, calculated their power and counted their losses, keeping it all in his dark ledger. "Brothers captured in the fight against those youths and the Silver Griffin fighting with them. The books were balanced, but the price was higher than it should have been."

"It was a price worth paying," the Shadow Mage said.

"I could have found it." The Shadow Stalker was the hunter, the seeker, the one of them who most often went out into the world. He pursued targets that might be a person, an object, or simply an idea, to be retrieved or destroyed as the will of the darkness dictated. He scowled, an expression that no one but another Shadow

Man could have seen. "I should have been the one to find it."

"But you didn't," the Shadow Mage said. "So we made a deal because this matters more than your pride, or our ledger balance, or a few shadows lost to the light."

The others hissed.

"How can you say that of our brethren?" the Shadow Sentry asked. "Who have you been listening to? What light-sider ideas have infected your mind?"

"I don't need the light-siders to recognize the value of this orb, even if your eyes cannot see it, or the Steward cannot count its value, or the Stalker cannot hunt it down. I have been studying it for months, and what I long suspected has proved true. This is the Stone of Dusk."

Whispers ran through the cave. They would've been excited whispers if the Shadow Men were capable of such a bright feeling. Instead, they were the dry whispers of fall leaves rattled by the wind, dead sounds from desiccated tongues.

"Are you certain?" The Shadow Sentry ran a hand over the orb.

"He's right." The Shadow Steward stared at the orb, and greed tinged his voice. "Now that I've seen it; I can't unsee it. The stone. It is time."

The Shadow Mage nodded, then stretched his arms out to push the others gently but firmly away from the stone.

"The time has come." He raised his voice so all the Shadow Men could hear. "In the beginning, our ancestors held the Stone of Dawn. It showed them how the world began, a ball of light emerging from a great shadow and bringing us with it. That world's destiny was to become another true world, like the shadows from which it first emerged, but light captured it and held it hostage by powers that seek the brightness of illumination instead of the comfort that darkness brings.

"The Stone of Dawn showed the doom that has fallen upon us, but it also held out a promise. It told our ancestors that one day, darkness would come. Magical forces would align, and we would have a chance to save this world from the light, to plunge it back into shadow so our people can spread across the Earth. The Stone of Dusk's arrival would presage that time."

He held the orb aloft, and every face in the cavern felt the touch of its cold, faint light, the sort that didn't illuminate a path but highlighted the darkness around it. They sighed in a shadow of happiness.

"Now, it is our turn to carry out the rituals of foretelling," the Shadow Mage said. "It is time to unlock the vision of the Stone of Dusk and see the future promised to us. To see how many more generations must pass before this world is ours."

The Shadow Men spread out around him, forming two rings. The inner ring, made up of the most powerful Shadow Men, circled clockwise around the Shadow Mage, while the outer ring circled counterclockwise. They moved with the strange unfolding and refolding steps of their kind, and they chanted as they danced.

Each Shadow Man had a chant, passed down by his ancestors. No two were the same, but each became a thread in the spell that the Shadow Mage was weaving, and each played a crucial part. The voices flowed together, and order emerged from the chaos of sound.

The Shadow Mage raised his hands. He was the silence to their sound, the shadow to their light, the death to their life. Magic flowed from his hands and filled the cave. The chanting and the movement of bodies stirred it, shifted it, reshaped it into new patterns, ones that none of them could've created or even foreseen alone. Threads of shadow twisted and turned, tangled and knotted, turned from simple darkness into something infinitely more complicated: a map to the future.

The Shadow Men stopped moving. They kept chanting, their words carrying their power to feed the magic as it grew through the cave. All around them was something wonderful. Somewhere inside it was their hope for the future, one stripped clean of the solid, light-living creatures that dominated the world, a future made for them. Still, most of them didn't have the sophistication to understand what they were looking at, to unpick those strands and read what lay ahead. Only the Shadow Mage could do that.

He lowered his hands and looked around. The prophecy surrounded him, a vast web of potential futures. The trick was to find the right one, the path they needed to follow for victory. The way that would set future generations on their course.

When he found it, he couldn't believe it. The path was so much shorter than expected. Complicated still, full of small details they would need to get right, and it would involve a great deal of effort from the Shadow Men. Still, there was no denying it. The day they lived for was coming and far sooner than he'd thought.

Barely able to contain his excitement, he plucked at the

threads, drawing them to him to take a closer look. He examined every tiny detail, committing them to memory. This was the only way to do it. When the spell ended in a few minutes, this vision would fade, and there would be no going back to it. He'd prepared for this moment his whole life, mastering techniques of memory and understanding, engraving channels of magic through his mind. He read the patterns, and they became his.

Then he stepped back and raised his hands. The rings of Shadow Men moved again, rotating in the opposite direction from the way they'd gone before. Threads of dark power unraveled, returning to the shadows they'd spooled from. The Shadow Mage stood triumphant in the middle of them.

The chanting faded. The dance ended. The light dwindled in the Stone of Dusk, then vanished entirely. The orb cracked and fell to the floor in two jagged, uneven halves. Most of the Shadow Men stared at it in shock, but not the Shadow Steward, who'd seen its imperfection from the start. He'd known, as the Shadow Mage did, that this could work only once.

Once was enough.

"It is done," the Shadow Mage announced. "I have seen the future, and our time is coming."

The Shadow Men nodded solemnly.

"Ours," the Shadow Mage emphasized. "Yours and mine, not merely a time for our distant descendants. The time for victory is almost upon us."

Crackling whispers ran around the room.

"Soon, the human world will end. By our hands, the Shadow Time will arrive. The world will be cleansed of the bright, burning light and return to the state of darkness from which it was born, the state of nature. We will stride a world made for us, by us."

The whispers rose to excited chatter, and the Shadow Mage did nothing to stop them. His people deserved this moment.

"Hard work lies ahead of us," he shouted over them. "Hard work and sacrifices. In the end, we will triumph because we are the shadows, and the light can never stop us."

The Shadow Men cheered. One of them started singing, more joined in, and others began dancing. Their celebrations filled the cave.

The Shadow Time was coming.

CHAPTER THREE

Lucy took the roast out of the oven and carefully carried it through to the dining room. Bowls of potatoes, peas, and beans were already sitting on the table, along with Yorkshire puddings and gravy. It wasn't the best roast she'd ever made, thanks to the distraction of the previous night's dream, which kept gnawing at her mind, filling her with a vague, unnamed dread. However, a roast was still a roast, and she could think of nothing more comforting to eat in a time of stress.

Plus, she knew the kids would gobble it up without a fuss.

"Dinner's ready," she called.

Feet thundered as her children stampeded through from the living room. First came Dylan, twelve years old and starting to shoot up. He'd always been tall for his age, but now he was really growing, and Lucy didn't think it would be long before he was taller than she was. That was a crazy thing to consider when it felt like only yesterday that he'd been a tiny pink creature waking up every three hours to howl for food.

Next came Eddie, the opposite end of the household age spectrum, and the explanation for why they were so loud. The three-year-old was currently in the shape of an elephant, although at least an infant one, having learned to control his size better since a recent giant animal incident in the back yard. His elephant feet pounded the floor and made the table shake, knives and forks rattling as they bounced up and down.

Last came Ashley, less desperate for dinner than the boys. She didn't look up from the tangle of silvery threads in her hands, the string robots she'd been working on perfecting all summer. Now fall was coming, and while the days were shortening, her attention span wasn't.

At eight years old, the household science genius remained undistracted by dolls, clothes, boys, or any of the other things that would come within the next few years. Lucy almost wished she could keep her this age, her nose constantly in a science project, but then she wouldn't get to meet the extraordinary young woman her daughter would one day become.

Ashley managed to take her seat without looking up from her robots, which she was contorting into structures that Lucy couldn't even pretend to understand. In the seat next to her, Dylan was already reaching for the potatoes.

"Charlie!" Lucy shouted. "It's time for dinner, sweetheart." She turned back to the table. "Eddie, you know the rules. No animals at the dinner table."

Eddie's trunk uncurled from around the back of his chair. He pointed at Buddy, the family dog. The dachshund had come into the room with the kids and was waddling around the table on his little legs.

"You know what I mean," Lucy said. "No kids transformed into animals at the dinner table. Real animals can stay as they are."

The air around Eddie shimmered, and he turned into a little boy, his t-shirt crumpled and his hair sticking out in every direction.

"Not fair." He pointed at his sister. "She's doing science."

"He's right, Ashley," Lucy agreed. "You know the rules."

Ashley got up from the table, took a slip of paper off the sideboard, scribbled her name on it, and put it in a jar bearing a label that said "MAGIC."

"We should change the label." Ashley returned to her seat. "I'm not doing magic."

"All right, next time we empty it, I'll change the label." Lucy raised her voice again. "Charlie, for the third time, it's dinner, and now we're waiting for you."

A door banged open, and her husband hurried in, wiping oil from his hands onto a rag.

"Sorry. We're trying to develop a new part for the green car conversions, and I didn't want to leave the thing nearly done."

"Hands." Lucy pointed at the kitchen sink.

This hadn't been a problem when Charlie's sole occupation was IT support, but now his business making the cars of magicals run more cleanly was starting to pay off. It was great for the environment but not so great for his available timing or the house's cleanliness.

"I made some veggie sausages," she said. "For those looking to eat less meat and reduce their carbon footprint."

"Thanks, honey." Charlie returned from the kitchen and kissed her on the cheek. "You're the best. You know that?"

"I do, but you can keep saying it."

At last, everyone was in their seats, ready to eat. Everyone except for Buddy, who stood by one corner of the table. He reared up on his hind legs and waved his forelegs in the air.

"Buddy dog," Eddie said. "What you doing?"

"He's trying to rest his paws on the table so he can join in with us," Dylan said. "Like he used to do, before..."

His voice trailed off. Poor Dylan would probably never stop feeling awkward about turning the family bloodhound into a dachshund, even if it was by accident. Lucy liked to think that he'd learned a valuable lesson from the incident and would be more responsible with his magic for the rest of his life. However, a few incidents since showed that lessons sometimes needed to be reinforced.

"Fill your boots." She gestured at the food. "There's plenty to go around."

Eddie peered at his feet for a minute, then shrugged, took off a sneaker, and started stuffing it with peas.

"No, no, no!" Lucy reached out to stop him. "That's not what I meant."

"You said fill."

"It's a British thing," Dylan said. "She means you should have as much as you want."

"Okay." Eddie held out his shoe, ready to tip the peas over his plate.

"You get new peas." Lucy took the sneaker. "I don't think anyone should eat these."

She set the shoe down next to her plate and took a

forkful of gravy-soaked Yorkshire pudding before she noticed that Ashley still didn't have any food. In fact, Ashley had pushed her plate aside to make room for the string robots.

"Ashley, you need to eat some dinner."

"Yes, Mom." Ashley reached absent-mindedly for the potatoes, one hand still manipulating the strings.

"You also need to put another slip in the magic jar now."

"Oh." Ashley put the robots down and went to add another IOU to the jar. Someone would be doing a lot of chores when they emptied the jar.

While Ashley was away, Buddy hopped up onto her chair and rested his forepaws on the table.

"Sorry, lad, but Ashley needs that space. Down, boy," Lucy commanded.

Buddy gave a disappointed whimper, but he did as ordered and jumped to the floor. Ashley took her seat again and finally loaded her plate with food.

"So, who's turn is it to do the quiz?" Lucy asked. "Charlie, you keep the schedule."

"Hm?" Charlie looked up from where he'd been scribbling on a scrap of paper. "Sorry, honey, I had an idea about how we can alter the spells around the exhaust pipe. What were you saying?"

"What happened to no magic at the table? That was your idea as well as mine!"

"I'm not casting magic, only talking about it. We talk about magic all the time. Otherwise, how could we talk about your work or how smart Dylan's getting?"

"Working on a design for your cars is not the same as talking."

"Let's put it to a vote."

"All right. Dylan?"

Dylan chewed thoughtfully for a moment. "He's not casting spells or making anything," he said once his mouth was empty. "I think it should be allowed."

"Eddie?"

"Let daddy draw."

Lucy could see that she had lost this one, even without all the votes in.

"Fine, the maths is against me. No punishment for your dad."

"There's only one math, mom," Dylan said.

"Well, back home we have multiple maths. Hundreds of them, wild maths running through the forests, being hunted by the royal family."

"Silly mummy." Eddie grinned.

"Thank you, I think. What is that sound?"

They peered around the end of the table. Buddy was jumping up and down, trying to reach a height where he could see them all. Each time he fell short and landed back on the floor with a *thud*, then tensed his legs and got ready to try again.

"Poor lad," Lucy said. "You miss being bigger, huh?"

Buddy looked at her with a confused expression, his tongue hanging out.

"Tell you what, let's give you another option." Lucy went to the kitchen, then came back in with a folding chair, which she set up at Buddy's end of the table. "You can come up on here and see what we're doing, but no climbing onto the table, understood?"

She was pretty sure that he didn't understand, but

Buddy knew a good thing when he saw it. He jumped onto the seat and sat up, looking around at the family with a big doggy smile.

"Good Buddy." Eddie reached across to pat the dog on the head, spilling peas across the table in the process. As they rolled off the edge of the table, Buddy leaned over and gobbled them up.

"One more reason to let you join us." Lucy's smile turned to a frown as she saw what her daughter was doing. "Ashley, I've told you twice already, no robots."

"Daddy's working on his machines. Why can't I?"

Lucy put her head in her hands. "Charlie, sweetheart, this is your doing. You can explain it."

Charlie looked up from his diagram.

"Sorry, what was that, honey?"

Lucy sighed. Maybe, with the kids getting older and their own lives changing, it was time for her and Charlie to re-examine some of the household rules. They might not need to change them, but they needed to think about how they enforced them and how the kids responded. The logic of "because I said so" wouldn't hold anymore.

"I give up," she said. "For tonight at least. Eddie, I think it's your turn to quiz us. What animal have you been learning about?"

CHAPTER FOUR

The next morning, Lucy headed into work early. It wasn't strictly necessary, but she felt like Charlie needed a gentle reminder that even their wonderful children took some energy to manage. Nothing would remind him of that like getting them ready and doing the school run on his own.

At a local Starbucks, she got herself a cup of tea in her Wonder Woman travel cup, then headed for the back of the coffee shop. When no one was around, she tapped her wand against a hidden spot in the back wall, then walked through it onto the stairs down to the magical subway. There was a separate platform down a tunnel with a security gate for trains to the Silver Griffins' L.A. HQ. That was the train she caught, sitting in the comfortable but old-fashioned carriage with a pair of chattering wizards while they steamed along bending tracks and swayed up to the HQ station.

Normandy, the gnome station master, was on duty as he always seemed to be. The brass buttons gleamed on his smartly pressed uniform, which he kept as immaculate as the station.

"Do you ever go home?" Lucy asked when she reached his office.

"Of course," Normandy said. "But not when someone might need me."

"How do you know when that is?"

He shrugged. "We all have our talents, Agent Heron. Mine are station maintenance and timekeeping, although my pottery is also improving. Yours are magic and baking."

"I can't argue with that. Speaking of baking..." She took a tub of homemade cookies out of her Batman backpack. "I was stressed out yesterday, so I did a lot of baking to try to relax. Peanut butter biscuits with chocolate on the top."

"Thank you. They smell delicious." Normandy handed her another plastic box, spotlessly clean. "From the muffins you gave me last week. You're very generous."

Lucy shrugged. "Least I could do. This seems like a pretty thankless job."

"Are you making a joke, Agent Heron? A job like this is a reward in itself! Not just station master, but station master for the Silver Griffins. My family is so proud."

"Bless, that's so sweet." Lucy stuffed the empty tub into her bag. "I'd better go. See you later."

She headed up a tunnel, then a spiral staircase, and out through a secret door into the Griffith Observatory. The Observatory wasn't yet open for the day, which made it much easier to get through the building to yet another hidden door into the Silver Griffins' reception.

"Wand, please." The receptionist pointed at a box on his desk.

Lucy pressed her wand against the box. Holding it made her think about her dream from two nights before and the feeling of dread that had followed her out of it. Something wasn't right. She could feel it in her guts. But what?

A light on the side of the box went green.

"Thank you, Agent Heron," the receptionist said. "You can go in now."

Lucy hesitated, one hand on the door to the main office. She couldn't escape the feeling, absurd as it was, that the office would be as barren as in her dream with dark forces lurking in the shadows. Was her wand trying to warn her about something? Or was she getting paranoid, the years of battling magical villains finally making the world seem darker than it was? It didn't matter. One way or another, she had to go in.

She opened the door, then sighed in relief at the sight of a messenger pigeon striding back and forth on top of a desk divider. The world couldn't be too dark with such creatures around.

"Have you got a message for someone?" she asked and held her hand out to the pigeon. It hopped onto her hand and peered at her palm, probably hoping to find worms. There was no slip of paper tied to its leg. "Looks like you've escaped from your cage. Guess I'd better put you back."

Lucy carried the pigeon down the office and dropped her backpack off at her desk. Roger Applegate, the regional manager, was already in his office, with his PA Sam sitting outside. Lucy waved hello, then headed down a corridor to take the pigeon home.

The pigeon loft was always one of the noisier, more

distracting parts of the office. For all the great work that the gnomes did keeping it clean and the inhabitants well cared for, hundreds of pigeons were always going to make fuss and mess. That fuss rose when they saw a witch or wizard come in. After all, these were the people who took away the pieces of paper tied to their legs and turned those messages into handfuls of plump, tasty worms. Any chance of that treat was worth getting excited about.

Lucy checked the tracker ring on the pigeon's leg, then used that to locate its cage. She put it away and handed it a few seeds from a feed bag. The pigeon still looked disappointed, but seeds were better than nothing, and it was pecking at them by the time she left.

When Lucy got back into the main office, a few more people had arrived, but the place was still mostly empty. Later in the day, that would be a sure sign of a crisis, but this was Monday morning, and no one rushed to end the weekend.

"What's up with the boss?" Lucy asked Sam. "He's never normally in this early."

Roger Applegate was good at his job, but he was good because he delegated as much work as possible and didn't crowd the office with his presence any more than his contract told him to. To see him in before nine on a Monday was almost unprecedented.

"There's going to be an announcement later," Sam said. "You'll see then."

"Blimey, sounds serious." Lucy raised an eyebrow. "Is it bad?"

Sam hesitated. "Opinion will be divided."

"Mysterious." Lucy handed over a couple of cookies.

"Sounds like you have a busy day, so hopefully these will help you through."

"Thanks, Lucy. You're a star."

Lucy settled down to catch up on her paperwork. There were no messages on her phone from Charlie, which meant that either everything was under control or he was too busy to message. Either way, she could focus on her work.

An hour later, Jackie Kowal and Ellis Ellis walked in. Ellis was hard to miss in his usual outfit of dark suit, bright red sneakers, and matching tie, but it was Jackie's voice that carried.

"How many times do I have to explain this? That's not how Ultimate Magical Fighting works. There's no point to it if everybody can't use their talents."

"It doesn't seem fair," Ellis said as they approached the desk. "That shifter was twice the size of the Willen."

"That Willen has beaten trolls and ogres before. It's not about size. It's about how you use it."

"Since when do you two watch sports together?" Lucy asked.

"Sarah's trying to get us to bond," Jackie said. "Last weekend they made me sit through some sappy rom-com with that floppy-haired English guy and some chick in an impractical dress. This week we had some proper entertainment."

There was a *clack* of stiletto heels, and Kelly Petrie approached. She nodded at Ellis and held a folder out to Jackie but didn't even look at Lucy.

"From that lunatic Jenkins," Kelly said. "Apparently, you asked for the details on some new tech out of Mana Valley?

That pasty-faced assistant of his wanted to bring it to you, but I told him to stay in the lab where he belongs."

"Aren't you a ray of sunshine today?" Jackie took the folder.

"I have to work with idiots. That doesn't mean I have to pretend that they're not idiots."

"Good morning, Kelly," Lucy said with forced brightness.

"Good morning," Kelly said in a tone of voice usually saved for death threats and oaths of vengeance. Without looking at Lucy, she stalked away.

"She's still mad about that trial, huh?" Ellis asked.

"It's absurd." Lucy shook her head. "The help I gave Gruffbar helped the right side to win. Even Kelly's husband accepts that, and he's the one who lost the trial, but she's still mad at me for helping Max's opponents."

"Kelly always needs to have a stick up her ass about something," Jackie said. "No point caring about what it is."

A sudden sound made everyone look up. Roger Applegate was banging a stapler against Sam's desk. Once silence had fallen across the room, Applegate stopped and turned to face them all. With his chest puffed up beneath his vest, his hands clasped behind his back, and a broad smile on his face, he looked like a jolly philanthropist out of a costume drama, come to raise the wages of everyone at the cotton mill. Lucy wondered what he was feeling so pleased about.

She glanced around the crowded room. Sam had summoned the admin gnomes, the lads from the lab, and even the receptionist to hear the announcement. This must be big.

"Thank you all for your attention," Applegate said. "I

won't keep you from your work for long. I wanted to let you know that I'm stepping down from my position as regional manager and will be leaving as soon as the directors and I find a replacement. It's been a great honor to work alongside you all, and I look forward to hearing about your future adventures, but for me, retirement calls.

"There will be an email from the directors filling you in on the details, including the application process for anyone hoping to take my place, and I dare say we'll have some sort of celebration to mark my departure when it comes. Until then, keep up the good work, and thank you all for your excellent service and even better company."

He gave a small nod. Someone started clapping, and others joined in. Within seconds, the whole room was applauding. Whatever his flaws, Roger Applegate was well-liked, and the thought of him enjoying his retirement was a pleasing one.

Once the applause was over, and people had returned to their workstations, Jackie leaned over the desk.

"Are you going to go for it?" she asked.

"Go for what?" Lucy asked.

"The regional manager job. You took that management training course, and you're one of the most experienced agents here. It has to be yours."

"She's right," Ellis added. "You'd make a mighty fine manager."

"I don't know." Lucy pondered the power and responsibilities the post would involve. "I've been thinking about promotion as this theoretical thing sometime in the future. I'm not sure if I'm ready now."

"You certainly aren't." Kelly had appeared at the end of

the desk. Now she was looking at Lucy, and that look could have frozen the Sahara. "But I am. I'm going to make sure I get that job, and once I have it, I'll make your life a living hell."

She spun and stalked away.

Lucy groaned and Ellis frowned, but Jackie laughed.

"What a drama queen," she said.

"She could really get it!" Lucy said. "She has the same training and experience as me. Do you want to wind up working for her?"

That wiped the smile off Jackie's face.

"Let's get on with some work," she said. "If every single one of us has to take that interview to stop Kelly from getting the job, I want to make sure our résumés look good."

CHAPTER FIVE

Ten minutes after Applegate's speech, the phone on Jackie's desk rang, showing the number for reception.

"I keep forgetting that people still use these things." She picked it up. "Hello, this is the twenty-first century. How can I help?"

"Hilarious, Agent Kowal," the receptionist said. "I only hear that one fifty-seven times a day."

"If you want me to stop mocking you, maybe you should tell me what you want?"

"Your sidekick's here in reception."

"You mean Twylan? Surely her wand gets her through security by now."

For the past few months, Jackie had been showing Twylan, a teenager from the Underfoot Brigade, what working for the Silver Griffins was like. Jackie sometimes felt that she gained more from having Twylan around than Twylan gained from her haphazard tour, given the teenager's intelligence and impressive magical power. She was certainly going to be an asset once she was old enough to join the Griffins.

"It's not her wand that's the problem. It's the woman with her."

"I am the chief of the Tolderai," a voice announced near the other end of the line. "I won't stand on attention for you, little man. Now let me in."

"Is that Heather?" Jackie asked.

"Is your name Heather?" the receptionist asked.

"I told you so already."

"I don't think—"

"I'm on my way." Jackie slammed the phone down hard in hopes of distracting the receptionist. The last thing she wanted was to break up an unnecessary fight between two magicals who were both equally stubborn in their ways.

She hurried to reception, where Twylan and Heather Fields were waiting. Here in a safe magical space, Twylan had taken off her dark glasses to reveal the magic glowing from her eyes. She stood awkwardly to one side, glancing back and forth between Heather and the receptionist, who were glaring at each other. With her flannel shirt and solid boots, Heather looked as different from the smartly suited receptionist as she could, but they had found something in common: an unwillingness to back down.

"Heather, what brings you here?" Jackie asked.

"The subway," Heather said. "I came with Twylan."

"I got that. I meant why are you here."

"I have a meeting with Roger Applegate."

"You couldn't let her in for that?" Jackie asked.

"She wouldn't tell me who she was," the receptionist said indignantly. "Or the details of her appointment."

"None of that is your business," Heather snarled.

Jackie sighed. "I hate to admit it, but here, that is his business. In fact, it's his sole and entire business, which is why he's so damn picky about it."

"Hey!"

"Picky can be good."

The receptionist narrowed his eyes. "Yeah, right." He tapped the box on his desk. "Wand, please."

With a little encouragement from Jackie and Twylan, Heather pressed her wand against the box. The receptionist typed a few words into his keyboard, and an imp hopped from a door in the side of the box, then presented Heather with a guest pass.

"They've upgraded the kit." The receptionist put air quotes around "upgraded." "Apparently this is more secure than the old version. Anyway, you can go in now. Have a nice day."

To his credit, he almost managed to keep the hostility out of his final words.

Jackie led Heather and Twylan into the office.

"It's good to see you, Jacks," Heather said. "I'd hoped you might be here."

"Good to see you too." Jackie forced herself not to laugh. There was something endearing about how the mighty chief of the Tolderai struggled to cope with even basic interactions once stuck in an office setting. It was understandable for a nature witch in such an unnatural environment but still entertaining. "What's this meeting with Applegate? Have you come to congratulate him on his retirement?"

"Retirement?" Heather frowned. "He'd better still have

the authority to negotiate."

"I'm sure he does."

They'd reached the desks where Jackie and her friends sat.

"Hi, Heather," Lucy said. "Want a biscuit?"

"No. Thank you."

"Howdy." Ellis gave a tiny wave of greeting.

"Hi. Where's Applegate?"

"Heather Fields?" As if by magic, Sam had appeared. "Come with me, please. Mister Applegate is expecting you."

Sam led Heather away, and Jackie relaxed into her seat. It wasn't that she didn't enjoy seeing Heather, far from it. Combining her with this place made everything feel at odds.

"How come you two came in together?" she asked when Twylan wheeled up a spare chair.

"I've been helping out a lot with the underground forests," Twylan said. "So have all the Underfoots. It's becoming a big thing for us."

"Good for you, kid." Jackie opened the folder Jenkins had brought her. Inside were pictures of a device Jackie hadn't seen before. "You want to see some cool new things out of Mana Valley?"

"Should we be talking about that?" Twylan glanced around. "I mean, isn't it bad luck?"

Jackie snorted. "Just because they've had an accident or two. That's going to happen if you have a whole community experimenting with new magic tech. Would you rather have a world without magic apps or wand updates?"

"I don't really use those."

Lucy leaned across her desk. "Hey, Jackie, I have

someone I want to go question. Are you up for riding along in case I need backup?"

"What do you think, kid?" Jackie reached for her wand. "Want to get out into the field?"

"Sorry." Sam had appeared again, darting into the conversation with impeccable efficiency. "Mister Applegate needs you, Jackie."

"Bureaucracy over action?" Jackie shook her head. "The sacrifices I make for this place." She looked at Twylan. "I'm a lost cause here. You go without me."

"Actually, I'd rather stay with you. Especially if it involves Heather. It might affect the Brigade."

"Well then, let's go brave a meeting."

They headed into Applegate's office. As Jackie looked back over her shoulder, Lucy and Ellis were heading out the door. It was all right for some.

Then she remembered that Heather was involved, and the meeting didn't seem so bad.

"Agent Kowal." Applegate beamed. "And your splendid sidekick. Please have a seat."

"How can we help?" Jackie took the chair next to Heather.

"By continuing the good work you've already started."

"You mean that solitaire game I have going on my computer? Because let me tell you, boss, I'm inches away from completing the diamonds."

"Very funny, Agent Kowal. No, I'm talking about our burgeoning collaboration with the Tolderai, which arose from your discovery of their forests."

"Ah. That." Jackie shifted in her chair. The moment she'd seen one of those underground forests, with their magical light and spell-nurtured plants, she'd known that she would have to tell the rest of the Griffins, but she still felt bad about blowing the secret for Heather and her tribe.

"As you know, we've been looking at how best to collaborate on this," Applegate said. "The Silver Griffins can help to keep these forests safe, while the magical sensitivity of the forests themselves means that they will help provide us with early warnings of trouble. It has great potential to become, to borrow a biological metaphor, a splendid symbiosis."

He chuckled to himself, then stopped when everyone else was still staring uncomfortably at the floor.

"Well, anyway, we've been discussing this a little, but Ms. Fields here is a little perturbed at the news that I will be departing. Isn't that right?"

"I need to know who I'm working with," Heather said. "Agreements are made with people, not faceless organizations."

"I'm not sure our lawyers would agree, but I appreciate the sentiment. That's where you come in, Agent Kowal."

"Me, sir?" Jackie sat up straighter in her seat. She thought she could see where this was going, and it sounded interesting.

"Yes, indeed. I'd like you to lead this effort on our side. Look at what magic and technology we can bring to bear to support and guard these forests. Find out more about what we can learn from them and how best to share that information. You will sit at the center of this symbiosis, the permeable membrane through which we share our, um, well... It appears I've stretched this metaphor too far already, but you get the idea. You will be lead agent on the project if you feel up to it."

"I do, sir."

"Splendid. I gather that the Underfoot Brigade are already involved with these forests, so Twylan will once again be an invaluable asset, I'm sure."

"Thank you, sir." Twylan beamed with pride.

"Will there be other agents involved?" Jackie asked.

"As and when you need them, yes. I'm not giving you carte blanche, but you have a lot of leeway to use the resources you need. Run it past Sam, then if I need to see it, I will." Applegate smiled at Heather. "There, does that assuage your fears?"

"As long as Jacks isn't retiring too."

"No, only me. On that note, I'm afraid that I have many other loose ends to tidy up, so unless any of you have questions, we should wrap this up."

Once they were out of the office, Jackie took her guests through to the break room. Everything went more smoothly with the help of coffee.

"This place is strange." Heather looked around the room.

"We revamped it by committee," Jackie said. "If I'd been in charge, we would've had something much more coherent."

"Will you be in charge once Applegate leaves?"

Jackie laughed. "No risk of that. However, I'm in charge of this forest project now. Are you okay with that?"

"Yes." Heather looked from her to Twylan. "I'm working with people I trust. I feel better about this than ever."

"Thanks." Jackie smiled. "That's great to hear. Now, let's

grab these coffees and get back to my desk. I'm pretty sure Lucy left a tub of homemade cookies, and she's smart enough not to expect them to still be here when she gets back. We can relax, kick back, and plan the future of your forests while the rest of my colleagues lose their minds over who's going to be the next boss."

CHAPTER SIX

"When I meet informants, it's usually in parks or bars." Ellis bent to fit down a narrow tunnel. "Not underneath an army reserve base. Are you sure we ain't gonna wind up shot?"

"Don't be such a wet blanket." Lucy walked at a crouch, the crockery in her backpack *clinking* with each step. "If you're not used to tunnels, then you're not really an L.A. Griffin."

They did spend a lot of time in the hidden places beneath the streets, from abandoned cellars to disused storm drains to the caves dug by wild monsters. Today, though, they were heading for something particularly unusual: a Cold War missile silo. It wasn't the sort of place that they could go to directly, so they'd headed into the ground a few streets over and were working their way through the tunnels to the concrete space that Willum Grast called home.

A floating magical light lit the way as they shuffled

along a narrow tunnel. It was a relief to reach the end and emerge through a hole smashed through the end wall into something larger. A little work with a sledgehammer or a sturdy drill could open up whole new routes down here in the dark.

"I don't reckon folks were supposed to go this way," Ellis said.

"Do you stick to where you're supposed to go?"

He laughed. "Wouldn't be much of a Griffin if I did, in L.A. or elsewhere."

Lucy had expected to hear some sign of Grast by now; he wasn't a gnome to live subtly or quietly, and they were almost at his lair. She hoped that he wasn't black-out drunk, passed out next to his still again. That would make questioning awkward.

"What is it we're investigating?" Ellis asked.

Lucy hesitated. She knew that she was at risk of sounding paranoid, or at the very least flaky. But Ellis was a friend, and sooner or later she was going to have to trust others with this.

"I don't know," she admitted. "I think something bad is going on in the city."

"What makes you think that?"

"A dream I had."

"Huh." Ellis paused for a moment, halfway through a gap in the wall, looking steadily at Lucy. Then he shrugged. "If your dreams are telling you that there's a problem, then there's a problem. Even if I hadn't seen you tackle Mr. No in his realm, there ain't no one else in the Griffins with your instincts. Either it's a vision, or it's your subconscious. Either way, I trust it."

"Thanks, Ellis." Lucy stood taller and smiled at him. "I needed to hear that."

"It's like my grandma always said, there ain't nothing like a kind and honest word to give a person strength."

"I wish I'd met your grandma. She sounds like a fine lady."

"That she was."

The tunnels ended at a set of heavy steel blast doors, which had stayed wedged open long enough to accumulate decades of dirt and rust. They entered the abandoned silo, a hollow space thirty feet across and a hundred feet deep lined with bare concrete. Holes magically melted into the walls held metal girders, which in turn supported layers of platforms built from old wood and scavenged sheet metal, each with a space on at least one side for the ladders that ran up and down, connecting the improvised floors.

Lucy's and Ellis's feet clanged against the metal of the highest platform. It was a chaotic space, holding an iron bed frame with a lumpy mattress, sheets scattered across the floor, and a layer of dirty, discarded clothes beneath them. It smelled like it could have been home to a dozen over-excited teenage boys instead of the single adult gnome who lived there.

"Nice place." Ellis shook his head.

"Even by Grast's standards, this is bad." Lucy grabbed the ladder at the side of the room. "Let's get on so we can get out of here."

Her backpack *clinked* as she climbed down. She expected Grast to appear at any moment to complain about the intruders, but she and Ellis were the only ones making any sound.

"Grast?" she called. "Willum, are you about?"

Her voice echoed around the silo. There was no response. On each floor, she paused to look around but saw no sign of her informant. She tried to remember what the place had been like the last time she was here. Had the pans in the kitchen been scattered across the floor? Had those pictures on the wall been hanging out of their frames? Or had Grast been on a particularly destructive rampage this week? He did like to hear things break.

As they approached the bottom of the silo, a new set of smells rose to meet them: ethanol, stale tobacco smoke, and spent magic. This was Grast's inner sanctum and his receiving room, one floor up from the bottom of the silo. It was where he entertained his equally disreputable friends and where he kept his best friend of all, the still he used to make home-brewed hooch. Lucy suspected that Grast would have given his life to protect that network of tubes and tubs, the culmination of a lifetime's efforts in making terrible alcoholic drinks.

"I have something for you, Willum," she called as she descended from the floor above. "The new collection of Pickard china, fresh and pristine and ready for you to smash."

As she stepped off the ladder, she stared around open-mouthed. The still had been trashed, its contents running out to dribble down between the floorboards. Shattered glass and twisted copper pipes lay all across the room, and in the middle of it all lay a gnome, his eyes open and staring at the ceiling.

"Grast?" Lucy put her bag down and knelt beside him,

feeling his neck. There was a pulse there, slow but persistent. He wasn't bleeding, but there were scratches on his hands and a bruise on one side of his face.

"I'm guessing it ain't normally this bad?" Ellis looked around with his wand raised.

"The broken crockery and the torn sofa are fixtures, but the still's normally intact."

"A gnome with priorities, huh?"

"That's one way of putting it."

Lucy waved a hand in front of Grast's eyes, but there was no response. She tried shaking him and slapped his cheek, but still, he didn't react.

"Grast, I have cheap gin in my bag." She got nothing in return. "If that didn't work, nothing will."

Ellis walked slowly around the edge of the room, looking at the wreckage, assessing their surroundings. A single bare bulb hanging from the ceiling cast a stark light across the scene, creating angular shadows between twisted pipes and broken shelves.

"Hard to look for clues when the victim's home already looked like a crime scene." He lifted a sticky magazine with the tip of his wand, then let it fall back into the pool of spilled spirits. "What do you want to do now?"

"Check for magic."

Lucy closed her eyes to remove the distractions of the cluttered room, then held her hands above Grast's body. She wasn't exactly feeling for anything, but she found that the hands sometimes helped. It was a way of focusing her attention.

There was definitely magic on Willum Grast. The

magical equivalent of background radiation had soaked through his body. Lucy wasn't sure whether that came from years of abusing his magic or whether the effect of this magic was what had turned him into the wretched creature he was. For the first time, she wondered what had left him in this state, hiding from the world behind thirty feet of concrete and a constant drunken haze.

There was lingering magic in his hands too. He'd been casting before whatever happened to him. Had he used it to fight back against someone? Or had he gone nuts and used spells to trash his home? If this were anyone else, it wouldn't even have been a question, but this wasn't anyone else.

Then she noticed something else, a sliver of magic so thin it could have slipped between the pages of a book. It was constant, unchanging, and yet when she moved Grast to examine it more closely, it did shift from her point of view. It wasn't exactly filling the space where his body pressed against the floor, but it seemed related to that.

What was going on?

She opened her eyes and tried to relate that magic to what she could see, but nothing was there. Then she looked up and caught a movement beyond Ellis. A shadow was emerging from the wall, and it held a knife.

"Ellis!"

He turned. She raised her wand. The shadow lunged, slashing at Ellis with the silhouette of a blade. He staggered back, clutching his arm, blood running through his fingers.

"Refrigero!" Lucy shouted. A bolt of cold magic shot from her wand. It caused ripples in the shadow as it flew through and created a patch of ice on the wall.

"Ignis!" Ellis pointed his wand and a gout of flame shot at the shadow. The shadow flung itself aside, and the fire hit the wall, leaving soot stains on the concrete.

The shadow ran for the ladder. It was human-shaped but with something hanging over its shoulder. It seemed to have no substance at all, merely to be a flat presence that folded through the air or laid against whatever it was closest to.

"It's a Shadow Man," Lucy said. "I've fought them before."

"So how do we beat it?"

"I'm not sure. It was one short fight."

The Shadow Man scrambled up the ladder.

"Lumen," Lucy chanted, shooting a narrow beam of light at the creature. It screeched in pain as the light hit its leg, but it kept climbing fast as a squirrel and vanished through the ceiling out of sight.

"Want to go after it?" Ellis reached for the ladder. Blood was running down his arm.

Lucy shook her head. "We'll never be able to keep track of it in these tunnels. Besides, Grast needs to be taken somewhere safe, and it's going to take two of us to get him out of here."

She scooped up the gnome in her arms. Ellis's eyes went wide, and he pointed at the floor.

"Look."

Lucy stared at the ground, but all she saw were the stained boards and broken still. "I don't get it."

"Your shadow."

She looked again, focusing on that dark outline. Sure enough, her dark silhouette was there, including her outstretched arms, but it was as if they were empty. Willum Grast had no shadow.

CHAPTER SEVEN

"It's great being back at school for band practice," Dylan said, "but I'd like it more if we didn't have so many lessons."

His friends Sofia and Lance nodded at this sage observation. These were the sorts of conversations about life, the universe, and everything that had bound them together over the years. They kept them entertained at times like this as they walked Buddy along the trail in Elysian Park.

"I thought you liked lessons," Lance said. "You were totally enthusing about history with that new teacher this afternoon."

"Oh, sure, some lessons are good," Dylan agreed. "But do we need all of them? I love history, but geography seems a bit unnecessary, and I don't think I'll ever use this much math."

"You'll need it if you want to be an archaeologist," Sofia said. "Remember all those geophysics devices on the dig we helped with during the summer? Lots of math there."

"Okay, so I'll stick with all the math. Geography, that's different."

"They had to draw maps too."

"Fine, a bit of geography. There must be some things we can ditch so we could spend more time on fun stuff."

"Phys Ed?"

"Good one! Who needs sports?"

"I love sports!" Lance said.

The others looked at him like he'd broken a promise.

"Since when?" Sofia asked.

"Since always. I'm not as good at things like math and English as you guys. I like the lessons where I get to move around, to play at things. That's why I love music and drama club."

"Huh." Dylan scratched his head. It was funny how you could know someone nearly your whole life without really understanding them. "I guess we'd better keep sports in the curriculum. Isn't there anything we can ditch?"

Buddy *yapped* excitedly and tugged at his lead as he tried to get off the trail and in among some bushes.

"What do you think?" Dylan looked at his friends.

"Always follow the Buddster's lead," Lance voted. "He found us that totally awesome frog pond in the spring, remember? And that dead fox one time."

"That was gross!"

"It was kind of cool, though," Sofia said. "Lance is right. Where Buddy leads, we follow."

"Hey, he's leading us with his lead!" Lance said. "Get it? Leading with a lead. I'm saving that one for when I'm old enough to do stand-up."

They followed Buddy off the path and through a thick tangle of bushes. Something had clearly caught his attention as he was sniffing the ground, following a trail that none of the humans could see. He might not have the body of a bloodhound anymore, but he still had many of its instincts.

"When you said you wanted to do fun stuff instead of lessons," Sofia said, "you mean like band and drama club?"

There was something odd about the way she asked the question, an edge to her voice that made Dylan nervous but that he couldn't understand. He decided the only way to respond was to be honest.

"Those would be cool, but I was thinking more about magical stuff, like practicing my spells or going on patrols with the Mini Griffins. Thanks to Twylan, I can use my powers more safely than I used to, and Mia and I have been teaching each other different spells." He tugged at Buddy's lead, stopping the dog from running too far ahead. "How about you guys? What would you do if you had more time?"

He expected an enthusiastic response from them, for Sofia to talk about drawing comics, or for Lance to get into a performance from his role in the current school play. Instead, they exchanged a silent look.

Buddy was yapping again and pulling on the lead so hard that Dylan could barely hold him back. Rather than get into a tug of war, he let himself be dragged along on the dog's enthusiasm.

"Come on!" he called. "Whatever Buddy's found, we must almost be there."

They dashed between trees and bushes, their packs bouncing on their backs, shoving aside branches, and accepting the minor scratches that came with any encounter with nature. There was no point fussing about avoiding these things. If you did, you ended up missing out on the good parts.

Buddy dragged them into a small patch of open ground. In the center of a dirt circle was a flowering plant no more than a foot tall in a hundred different colors. Its petals shone brightly, and its leaves and stalks gleamed as if covered in glitter. Tiny creatures fluttered around it, like mice with butterfly wings. They squeaked as they stuck their paws and noses into the flowers to emerge holding little red berries, their fur dusted with soft yellow pollen.

"I'm no expert," Lance said, "but that looks totally magical to me."

Buddy stood by the plant, staring up at the flying mice. Their wings were thinner than tissue paper and decorated with magical runes in rainbow colors. The dog didn't try to leap up and catch them, only watched with his tongue hanging out and an expression of wide-eyed contentment. Sofia sat next to him, opened her bag, pulled out a sketch pad, and started a hasty drawing.

"Can you hold him?" Dylan handed the lead to Lance. "I should clear this away."

"What? No!" Sofia glared at him. "It's beautiful. Why would you want to get rid of it?"

"Because it's what my mom would do. It's important to keep magic hidden in case people get scared or look for ways to abuse it."

"They're only flying mice. How could anyone do harm with flying mice?"

Dylan sat beside her. "I'm sorry, but I've read about these. I don't know who put them here, but if we leave them in the wild, the mice will multiply."

"That doesn't sound so bad."

"Then they'll go into their larval stage on the bush, and when they emerge, they're these angry bear lizard things that tear down trees and attack any animal that comes near them, including people."

"Okay, that sounds less good." Sofia sighed and stared at the plant. "It's so beautiful, and I don't normally get to see magical things. Something like this would be so cool for the comic I've started making."

"I could wait, like, ten minutes while you draw it if you want?"

She smiled. "That's more like it."

Dylan and Buddy watched the mice while Sofia did her drawing and Lance tried to imitate the mice's movements.

"It's good practice for characterization," he explained.

"Don't let any of them get away," Dylan whispered to Buddy. "You can do that, right?"

Buddy wagged his tail and kept watching the amazing creatures.

Sofia sketched an outline of the bush and more detailed pictures of one of the flowers and one of the mice. There wasn't time to be thorough, but Dylan was still impressed at his friend's talent.

"You're going to be a great artist someday," he said.

"I'm already a great artist, doofus. One day I'll be a rich and famous one." She closed her sketchbook and put it away. "All right, you can take the beauty out of the world, Mister Mini Griffin."

Dylan pulled out his wand and cast a spell. A glowing net drifted from the treetops, capturing the mice as it went.

One of them flew low and out under the edge, fluttering away toward the trees on a trail of glitter.

"Buddy, fetch!" Dylan said.

Once off his leash, the dog raced after the mouse. It fluttered its wings to try to get away, but Buddy leaped and caught it between his teeth, then carried it back to Dylan, tail wagging.

"Thanks, Buddy." Dylan cupped the mouse in his hands. It was trembling with fear and a little slobbered on but otherwise unhurt. Buddy was a gentle soul.

Dylan put the mouse in with the others, then sealed the net shut around them and shrank it down until it was just large enough to hold them all. With another spell, he lifted the bush out of the ground, roots and all.

"Now what are you going to do with all this?" Lance asked.

"Um..." Dylan blushed. He hadn't thought about that part. He could call his mom, but he wanted to clear this one up for himself, to show her what he was capable of.

"I know." Sofia gathered their backpacks, then emptied hers and Dylan's, shifting the contents into Lance's bag. By the time she was done, Lance's bag bulged, and the zipper would only just shut, but everything fitted in.

"Hey!" Lance said. "How come I'm carrying all that?"

"Would you rather carry the bush?"

She stuck the plant upside down into Dylan's bag. It wouldn't all fit, but the roots sticking out of the top could have been an ordinary plant. Finally, she put the magic net full of butterfly mice into her bag.

"Why can't I carry those?" Lance asked.

"Because you're the sporty one," Sofia said. "That means you're strong enough to carry all our books."

Lance looked unsure whether to complain or take pride in that. In the end, he smiled. "I am the tough one."

They put Buddy back on the leash and headed back toward the path. The bush's roots tickled the back of Dylan's head and dropped dirt down his neck, but it was worth it.

"I can't wait to tell Mia about this," he said. "It's one of the coolest magical things we've found in L.A"

Lance snorted, and Sofia made a sound that might have been "harumph."

Dylan stopped and stared at them. "Enough of this. What's the matter with you two?"

Sofia looked at Lance. "You explain. You're good at saying words."

"You're good at picking the right ones," he replied.

"Fine." She sighed, then looked at Dylan. "You're our best friend, and we're glad that you've got all this cool magical stuff in your life, but since you started doing more Mini Griffins patrols and training, we don't get to see you much."

"It's like Mia's stolen all your time," Lance added, then made a face. "This is why Sofia picks the words."

"I still hang out with you guys." Dylan pulled his arms in at his sides, shrinking in the face of his friends' displeasure. "I'm here, aren't I?"

"Sure, but we didn't hang out together outside of school at all last week, and you even skipped a band practice."

"I had to work on a spell."

"We know, but still..." Sofia looked down at the path. "We're your friends. We miss you."

Dylan drew a deep breath.

"I'm sorry," he said. "I didn't mean to not spend time with you. I'll try to find a way to fix it."

"But you're so busy..."

"Never too busy for my best friends." He tugged at the lead, drawing Buddy away from whatever insect he'd spotted under a bush. "Come on, let's take our flying mice home. Maybe my mom will let us get them out for more drawings before she takes them away."

CHAPTER EIGHT

The Shadow Stalker slid through the gap between the wall and the sunlight falling on it. Even on an overcast afternoon, it was too bright out here in the surface world for the comfort of many of his kin. That didn't bother the Shadow Stalker.

He understood what they all should, that while the light could banish them, it could also strengthen them if they had the resilience to endure it. Those who did emerged tougher and more ready to face the world and to fight for the coming of the Shadow Time. They shouldn't be hiding in their caves, a shallow imitation of the glory to come. They should be out here, bringing forward that glory.

At least many of them would come out later when their shadows were longer and the light less bright. They had to. There was no time for idleness now. The Shadow Mage's prophecy had given them a tight timeline, days instead of centuries to prepare. That prophecy was like the light. It would harden them, force them to become tougher, or it would destroy them when they failed to fulfil its steps.

That was why the Shadow Stalker was out now, sliding unnoticed past the people in a crowded L.A. market, one more shadow on the ground. There were pieces to gather for the magic that would bring the Shadow Time and little time to wait for them.

The Shadow Stalker watched the crowd moving through the market. Most of them were humans, no more useful to him than a dog or a patch of dirt. To complete the magic, the Shadow Mage needed the shadows of magicals from as many different species as they could find. It wasn't about volume. It was about variety, which was probably why humans were of no use, with their monotonous, powerless lives. However, the people who hid among them held potential, especially those who had achieved great things. Those with wealth and influence cast a long shadow.

A few witches and wizards walked past, the humans unaware of their unusual powers. The Shadow Stalker could sense them, but he wasn't interested in making them his targets. Not today.

He stepped into the shadow of a security guard whose job involved walking endless slow loops of the market. It was a good way to ensure that the Stalker remained unnoticed, hiding within another's shadow. If the guard noticed the extra drag at his heels, he didn't say anything about it and didn't look around to see what might be causing it. He was too unobservant for that.

Together, the guard and the Shadow Stalker walked around the market. The Stalker knew the guard's route. He'd been planning this hunt for years, although he'd never expected the call for it would come. Some people found entertainment in stories or music. The Shadow Stalker found it in creeping, observing, planning for hunts that might or might not ever happen. Nothing thrilled him like preparing for his prey, anticipating the flow of blood and the moment of triumph.

Today, that planning was paying off. The Stalker followed the guard around the corner of a stall and saw her, his target. It was the right time of day and the right point in her schedule.

When she was on tour, she was absent for months at a time, a pop diva adored by millions, screamed and cheered at by fans worldwide. But when she was in L.A., the performing wigs came off, and others went on, along with dark glasses and shapeless clothes that hid who was inside. She came out to the market for her shopping once a week to remind herself that she had once been an ordinary person.

Except that she wasn't. The Shadow Stalker knew this. He could smell it on her as he detached from the guard and moved closer.

There was a reason she was so good at disguise and why none of her wigs or costume apparel let the tips of her ears show. A magical among mundanes, an elf amid the humans, a fugitive from Oriceran hiding in the bright light of Earth celebrity. Beautiful, blond, blue-eyed, with a voice so high and clear that some reviewers said it sounded supernatural. If only they knew.

The carefully disguised pop star picked out a tub of strawberries and put half a dozen oranges into a paper bag while chatting to the woman behind the stall. She always shopped like this, slow and relaxed. Did she enjoy feeling ordinary, or was it more about the thrill of a secret, the risk of discovery? The Shadow Stalker didn't know. He didn't care. He was interested in patterns, not motives. Patterns left trails in the world. Patterns made people vulnerable.

The pop star laughed at a joke from the stallholder. It didn't mean anything to the Shadow Stalker, and he wouldn't have laughed if it had. Laughter was a sign of weakness.

A knife appeared in his hand, made as much of darkness as he was, sharp enough to split a light beam in two or to shave the edge off a shadow. He slid across the ground, still unseen by the people busy looking at stalls or trying not to collide with each other, eyes only downcast when they looked at their phones. He placed the knife against the pop star's heel and sliced.

The pop star yelped and turned, one hand stretched out protectively.

"You all right there, honey?" the stallholder asked.

"I'm not sure," the pop star said. "I felt something odd, like..."

She looked down and froze.

"What the hell are you?" she whispered.

The Shadow Stalker didn't give her any more time to think or to react. He already had hold of one leg of her shadow, half severed from her body at the foot. He pulled hard on it, and the pop star lost her balance. She was still agile enough to direct her fall, and she landed on him, hands outstretched.

There was magic in one of her hands, and she grabbed a fistful of shadow. The other hand came around sparkling, but the Shadow Stalker slashed with his knife, finishing the cut at her heel, and that leg of her shadow came away. As it did so, the magic in her hand faded.

The pop star grunted in pain and tightened her grip on him. Pain ran through the Shadow Stalker as she crumpled him like a fistful of paper. He kicked, and she rolled over, dragging him with her. Her glasses and hat flew off, and her wig went askew.

Shoppers stepped back in alarm as the woman rolled across the floor, apparently grappling with nothing more than her own shadow.

"Are you all right, hon?" someone asked.

"She's having a fit," another said. "We should call an ambulance."

"Hey, isn't that..."

The Shadow Stalker swung his blade. The pop star screamed and let go of him as a deep wound opened in her arm. This was messier than the Shadow Stalker had wanted, a violation of the secrecy that kept the Shadow Men safe, but he couldn't help it. Secrecy mattered less than speed now. The Shadow Time had almost come.

He stabbed again, and the pop star fell back, clutching her side.

"Please," she said, "someone call the Griffins!"

"The who, honey?"

"Get her an ambulance."

"It is her, isn't it?"

"What's up with her ears?"

The pop star was getting weaker, and not only because of blood loss. With her shadow half detached, she was losing part of her magical strength. Power bled out through that wound, and if the Shadow Stalker could wait, she would soon be at his mercy. He couldn't stay, not with so much attention, not with so much at stake.

He reached for her other heel. She kicked, knocking him back across the ground. He got to his knees, grabbed her shadow, and hauled her to him.

"What the hell is that?" someone shouted.

"What's what?"

"That, on the ground."

"It's only shadows."

"Like hell, it's only shadows. Look!"

The pop star gave another kick, half-hearted this time. The Shadow Stalker lashed out as the foot came close to him. It was a perfect blow, slicing off her shadow at the heel. The whole shadow came away, and the pop star collapsed unconscious.

The Shadow Stalker flung the pop star's shadow over his shoulder.

"What's it doing?" someone asked. A growing number of people in the crowd were watching him in fear.

"Coming through!" someone shouted.

There was movement in the crowd, and two women approached, not only humans but witches, one with brown hair tied back, the other with a blonde bob. The brunette had her wand out, pressed against her forearm. With attention turned from him for a moment, the Shadow Stalker slid into the darkness cast by a market stall, disappearing from view.

"Is everyone all right?" the blond asked with such authority that no one thought to ask who she was. "What happened?"

"She had a fit." Someone pointed at the pop star. "Only then it looked like something was attacking her."

"Her shadow attacked her," someone else added.

"Look at her ears," a third said. "Is that a body mod? Is it an elf cosplay?"

"Isn't she—"

"Never was, never will be." The brown-haired witch raised her wand. Magic washed across the area. The faces of all the humans went slack, but the Shadow Stalker shook off the spell. He crouched in the stall's shadow, watching them.

"It is her, right, Lucy?" the blonde asked.

"Does it matter right now?"

"Seriously, does it matter if she's—"

"Jackie, is this really the time?"

"No, you're right." The blond crouched beside the pop star and felt her neck. "Still alive, but her pulse isn't strong." She shook the pop star. "Not waking up."

"A coma again." The brown-haired woman lifted the pop star a little. "And no shadow. What's going on here?"

While their backs were to him, the Shadow Stalker crept away, through the shadows and out the far side of the market. His people had the attention of the Silver Griffins now. That wasn't good, but in a few more days, weeks at most, it wouldn't matter. He adjusted the burden on his shoulder, then slid through a sewer grating into the ground and away.

CHAPTER NINE

Twylan ran her fingers through the dirt of the forest floor. As she did so, she let her magic flow, just a little of it, a trickle of power to enrich the soil. It wasn't something she'd been taught, only a trick that had come to her lately, and she was confident that the Tolderai would approve. After all, plant magic was the whole purpose of this underground forest and their tribe.

"What are you doing?" Kix asked. The gnome was wearing one of her less sparkly tops, but she still looked out of place in the underground forest. Everyone else wore their most practical, worn, down-in-the-dirt clothes, but she never went out like that. It was a matter of pride, or perhaps merely priorities.

"I'm helping the plants to grow," Twylan said. "Like fertilizer, but made of magic."

"Huh." Kix looked at the trowel she'd been using to dig holes for planting. "Do you only stick your hands in to do it, or does it take more?"

"More." Twylan looked around, then leaned in and

whispered, "Ever since I traveled through the trees with the Tolderai, it's like I have this extra connection to nature. I can feel what the plants need, what will help them to grow, what hurts them. I can use that understanding to shape my magic. I figured, if I can, I should, right?"

"Is that how they create Tolderai? They drag people through trees and make them into badass wood witches?"

Twylan laughed. "I don't think so. Nathaniel joined the tribe because he was a descendant of one. It's usually hereditary."

"Hm." Kix watched her friend uncertainly. "You said usually. Is there something you want to tell me?"

"I'm not leaving the Underfoot Brigade, don't worry. I just have some new spells in my arsenal."

"All right, but if you ever do leave, you're taking me with you. I don't want to get left behind while Leontine's grumbling about your desertion."

"Okay, I promise, no running off without you. Now, shall we plant these herbs?"

They took the small plants, with their attached balls of roots and dirt, one by one off a wooden tray and lowered them into the freshly dug holes. Soon, the plants were all around one of the trees, two rings of fragrant leaves, one in bright green, the other so pale that it was almost white.

"Does it match your vision?" Twylan asked.

"For now." Kix tipped her head to one side. "To be honest, I don't know how good this will look once it's had time to grow in, but I thought it had to be worth a go."

"This is a perfect project for you, isn't it, acting as a stylist for a whole forest?"

"I'd rather act as a stylist for the Tolderai themselves.

Carol looks okay, but the rest of them are in desperate need of a makeover. Heather never wears anything but those lumberjack shirts, like she's going to a Pearl Jam concert in 1993, and Mackam looks like the last lunatic to leave the asylum."

"Perhaps he should look that way as a fair warning to the world."

"Or maybe if he dressed better, people would treat him like a normal person, and he might start to act like one. Clothes make the man, and a tin foil undershirt makes him an idiot."

"I like your optimism."

"What can I say? I'm a shining light brightening all your lives." Kix grinned. "Ready to give this a go?"

She wiggled her fingers and chanted a spell. Small clouds appeared above the herbs, and rain fell from them, a gentle and soothing shower. While Kix kept the water flowing, Twylan reached into the soil and once again let her magic flow. It ran through the dirt, into the tangles of roots, and fed them, supercharging the plants with nutrition and magical power.

Within a minute, the plants had started to spread. New sprigs shot out at remarkable speed, leaves burst forth, and flowers unfurled. They spread and intermingled, completely covering the ground until the rings of green and off-white surrounded the tree.

"Almost done." Kix dispersed the clouds, then replaced them with brief beams of artificial sunlight, a brighter version of the magical light that filled the whole cave. As the leaves dried off, Twylan pulled her hands from the dirt and wiped them on her skirt.

Heather emerged from between the trees and looked at what they had done. She didn't tend to smile, but there was a satisfied look on her face. "Good work, both of you. Look, you've helped the tree as well."

New leaves were unfurling from the ends of branches, adding to the vibrant canopy.

Right then, voices came through the forest, two men loudly agreeing with each other.

"He won't listen," Mackam said. "It's like his ears are stuffed full with all the stupid opinions he's ever spouted."

"It wouldn't be so bad if he didn't have so much power," Leontine said. "Why does someone that stupid get to be in charge of things?"

"Ah, but that's always the way, isn't it? Power goes to the wealthy few, feeding their ignorance and idiocy. It's a conspiracy against the rest of us."

"It doesn't need to be a conspiracy. It's the broken way the world is built."

"If it looks like a scheme and it acts like a scheme, you can damn well assume that it's plotting against us. Snakes, I tell you. Snakes run this world."

"Literal snakes?"

"No, although it's lizards in England. Buckingham Palace is full of scales and flickering tongues."

The two of them walked into the clearing. Leontine's wings were spread out behind him, something he'd started doing more often recently. It seemed to Twylan that he was growing in confidence, although she wasn't sure quite why.

Maybe it was their achievements in the forest, his friendship with Mackam, or staying away from the surface, where they had to hide who they were from the crowds around them. Whatever the cause, he was happier and healthier than she'd known him for a long time.

Mackam looked at the herb beds and grinned.

"That's fine work. Who did it?"

"Who do you think?" Twylan held up her hands, dirt still under the nails.

"You two? I'd have thought this would be the work of some of ours." Mackam looked at Heather. "I'll admit it, this is going very nicely, and the new forests are growing quicker than the old ones."

"I know," she said. "At this rate, the problem will be getting new caves carved out fast enough, not filling them with life."

Twylan and Kix beamed.

"Well, we have a tribe meeting," Mackam said. "See you kids later. Remember, eyes peeled for the 5G lizard men."

He and Heather headed off, leaving the Underfoots under the tree. There was something strangely deflating about it. They all knew that they weren't part of the Tolderai tribe, but they'd been spending so much time with them lately that the exclusion felt odd.

"Things are changing, aren't they?" Leontine had a thoughtful look on his face.

It wasn't the sort of observation that Twylan would've expected from him, and she didn't want to assume that he was thinking about the same thing as her.

"How so?" she asked.

"All this time with the Tolderai, it's making us more like them. We've spent time with outsiders before, like the

Silver Griffins, but it never felt like we were in on something together. This is different."

"It's not like we're equals," Kix said. "But it's like we're connected."

"Perhaps." Twylan worried about what expectations her friends were developing and whether they matched those of the Tolderai. "The question is, what could that mean?"

"Probably nothing." Leontine folded his arms. "It's just... It's nice, you know?"

Nice wasn't a Leontine word, but it made Twylan smile.

There was a flicker.

"Did you see that?" Twylan asked. The others nodded. "Was it one of the lights?"

They walked through the trees toward the edge of the cave, then looked up its long, curving wall. Roots and branches grown into a tightly interweaving mat formed the barrier that held back the dirt above. Recessed into the wall were inverted hemispheres, again made from those roots and branches, which held magical lights that glowed like the sun.

"Is that it?" Kix pointed at one of the lowest lights a dozen feet above the ground. It flickered ever so slightly.

"It must have been more than that or we wouldn't have seen it," Twylan pointed out.

"I'll go take a look."

Leontine flapped his wings, one of them natural Arpak flesh and feathers, the other a mechanical addition to a stunted wing. He lifted into the air and up to the light, where he grabbed a branch and held on while taking a closer look.

"It's still flickering, but only slightly."

"Can you get any sense of what's happening with the magic?" Twylan asked.

Leontine let go of the wall and glided to the ground below. "I can't sense anything about magic, remember? That needs one of you."

"It's probably nothing," Kix said. "I mean, there's going to be occasional interference from the amount of magic in the city, right?"

"Maybe." These lights could be an early warning system about magical trouble, as they'd done once before, and Twylan thought the Griffins would want her to be cautious. Still, what would she say to anyone—that one light had briefly, slightly flickered? That wasn't enough to raise the alarm. "Let's keep an eye on it. If there's trouble coming, someone should know."

They walked away from the wall and back through the forest to carry on with their planting. Behind them, just for a moment, all of the lights in the lowest layer flickered, a shadow passing over their bright orbs.

CHAPTER TEN

Charlie ran into the auto shop.

"Sorry I'm late," he called, approaching the corner of the shop where Green Machine Conversions worked. Around him were the *clangs* and chatter of Gunther's regular mechanics and the tinny music from their old radio. "My other work was really busy today, made it hard to get away."

Ringo Fuller emerged from under a car, an exhaust pipe in one hand and a wrench in the other. He wasn't wearing his usual wraparound shades, and there was grease on his face as well as his fitted t-shirt.

"No problem, man." He set the wrench aside and examined the exhaust. "We've all got to fit this around our other lives, right?"

"You seem to manage." Charlie hurried to the back corner, where he'd left spare overalls for occasions like this. He started stripping off the shirt and suit pants he'd been wearing in the office in favor of something he could get dirty in.

"Advantages of the freelance life. Plus the bounties are a little thin on the ground right now."

"That's a relief. I was worried that we might not be able to keep up with the business coming in."

Charlie looked around their corner of the shop. One car was waiting for pick up, one for work to start, and between them, the one that Ringo was working on. The bounty hunter had already assembled the pieces they would add, and his wand was sitting ready to add the runes that went next to the filters. Within a few hours, they would magically remove the pollution from the car's fumes, and it would go back to one more happy, environmentally-conscious customer.

"We can't keep up," Ringo said. He pulled out his phone and showed Charlie a spreadsheet. "See these? These are the requests that came in last week. We had to schedule them for three months ahead, with hopes we might get it down to two if we work fast. People aren't going to wait forever. Our speed is reducing our impact."

Charlie finished fastening his overalls and grabbed a wrench.

"Guess I'd better get on with it then, huh?"

Gunther lumbered over. Like most of his employees, he had some trace of magical blood, in his case an element of ogre that left him towering over the rest.

"Got another one." He handed Ringo a scrap of paper with a name and number on it. The paper looked tiny in his hand. "Witch came in for an oil change, I told her about you boys, and she's in. Hey, Charlie."

"Hi, Gunther." He glanced at Ringo. "Can we really add another one to the list?"

"Who else is gonna do it?" Ringo asked. "Besides, we need to take on all the work we can if we're going to grow as a business, right?"

"Right..."

Gunther returned to work, and Charlie headed for the untouched car. It would probably be more efficient for him and Ringo to each work on a job, so they could keep them going in parallel. He'd have to keep an eye out in case parts got mixed up, or they both needed the same tool.

He got the car jacked up and crawled underneath to have a look. The exhaust and surrounding systems were more complicated than expected, as happened all too often with the cars of magicals. There was a tendency toward small changes or improvised repairs by wand. That worked fine until someone wanted to add a standardized conversion like their original engine cleaning system. Then standardization had to be thrown out the window in favor of far more work.

This was part of why the work kept piling up, although general demand played a part. It was great that so many magicals wanted cleaner vehicles. If only they had twice as many people to work on them.

More footsteps approached. From under the car, Charlie caught a glimpse of shiny shoes and tailored pants.

"Is that you, Max?" he called.

"Hi, Charlie." Max Petrie crouched and peered under the car. "How are you doing?"

"Busy."

Max chuckled. "I hear that. Some months, it seems like the law firm is drowning under clients' demands."

"Have you come with more paperwork for us?"

"Accounts."

Charlie rolled out from under the car. "Wish we could look at them, but we're already behind on work, and we've got quite a backlog."

"No problem. I'll find somewhere at the back, get my laptop set up and answer our emails. We can go over the finances when you have time."

Charlie didn't have the heart to tell him that there might not be time between fixing the car and getting home in time for his family duties. If Max had taken time away from the office to help them, it would be rude to say no. Charlie would have to make the time, which meant getting everything else done quickly. He crawled back under the car and set to work.

Two minutes later, another pair of feet appeared, this time booted and with the bottom edge of overalls.

"Sorry, Ringo," Charlie called from under the car. "Am I hogging a tool you need again?"

"No, we're good, man. I wanted to talk about something else."

"Well then, let's talk when we've finished work."

"This talk might help us get the work done."

That got Charlie's attention. He crawled back out from under the car and sat looking expectantly at Ringo. "Go on."

Ringo pointed with a spanner between the cars to where Max sat on a stool, typing awkwardly with one hand while using the other to stop a laptop sliding off his knees.

"Max is part of the business, right?" Ringo said.

"Yes, of course. He's our lawyer, accountant, and office manager all rolled into one. Not that we've got an office."

"So why don't we train him up as a mechanic too? Three sets of hands would get way more done than two."

"I don't think this is really Max's thing. He's more management than labor."

"Lots of the best managers get their hands dirty too."

"He won't have time. Look at how much trouble I have fitting this in, and I only do IT support. Max is a high-flying lawyer who does work for big investment banks and environmental charities. He's not going to have time to mess around with cars."

"Actually, I do," Max called. He looked across at them. "Sorry, couldn't help hearing."

"No problem, man," Ringo said. "Better if we're talking with you than about you."

"But surely you don't have time?" Charlie asked.

Max shut the laptop, set it aside, and came over to them. He stood with shoulders hunched, staring at his feet.

"The fact is, things have gotten a little tough for me. I'm not getting much magical legal work since the Nuada case, and magical cases had been most of my business lately. My position at the firm is looking precarious."

"Shit, man," Ringo said. "I had no idea."

"I'm so sorry," Charlie said. "Is this because of what happened with, you know..."

He let the words trail off. What was he going to say, sorry my wife's information torpedoed your career?

"It's not Lucy's fault," Charlie said. "I was on the wrong side, let myself get talked into representing a client I didn't properly know. Nuada deserved to have that evidence emerge against him. It just doesn't look good for me, you know? Between picking the wrong client and losing his case, a lot of people don't want to work with me anymore."

An awkward silence fell.

"So, are you serious?" Ringo said. "You're up for learning all this?" He pointed at the cars.

"Why not? It's my business too, and I think it's a good one. We could really make the world a better place. And right now, learning to fix things could be good for me."

Ringo raised an eyebrow at Charlie. "What do you think?"

"It's a great idea in the long term," Charlie said. "But in the short term, training anyone will slow us down, especially someone without existing mechanical skills."

"You're right. This is a dumb idea." Max shook his head. "I'll get back to the emails."

"No, wait." Charlie really didn't want to say no, for so many reasons. The trick was working out how they could say yes. "It's not a bad idea. We just need to think through how it works in practice."

"He can start by assisting us," Ringo pointed out. "Handing out tools, getting parts ready. You know the inventory, right?"

"I should," Max said. "I put in most of the orders."

"See, that might even speed the jobs up. Then when we're a bit more on top of it, and you're more familiar with what we do, we can start teaching you to do the spells, work up to the mechanical parts from there."

"My magic's not very strong. I don't know if I can provide what you're after."

"'Course you can. Right, Charlie?"

"Definitely!"

When Gunther came over half an hour later, Max was crouched between the cars, dressed in a spare set of Ringo's overalls, handing out components and tools to his business partners.

"They got you doing the crappy jobs, huh?" Gunther asked.

"It's a start," Max said. "I know I'm a bit old to start a new career, but I want to learn how this works."

"And you's learning from these two bozos?"

"Hey!" Charlie called from under the car. "These bozos know what they're doing."

"You ever trained a mechanic before?"

"No."

"Well then." Gunther scratched his head, then gave a decisive nod. "When you finish here, you come over to me. I'll set you right on the things they taught you wrong."

He stomped away, shaking his head.

"What was that about?" Ringo whispered, emerging from under his car.

"I'm not sure," Charlie said, "but I think that was Gunther's way of saying he likes having us here."

"By calling us bozos?"

"And offering to help."

"Well, this escalated fast." Max laughed. "An hour ago, I was a failing lawyer. Now I'm an apprentice mechanic. One door closes, and another opens."

"Don't be too quick to lock that old door," Charlie said. "We're still going to need our lawyer if this goes wrong."

CHAPTER ELEVEN

Lucy, Jackie, and Twylan sat at a table outside a coffee shop, enjoying the morning sunshine. It was the sort of day that hadn't accepted the arrival of fall but instead clung to the edge of summer, hoping it might not go away. People took their time as they walked past on the way to work, making the most of the weather.

"I can't wait for it to get colder," Jackie said.

"Why?" Lucy asked. "This is lovely."

"Maybe if you grew up on some fog-shrouded island of drizzle and clouds, but over here in California, you can have too much of the hot, dry, and sunny. I want to cool down for a while."

To make her point, Jackie flapped the bottom of her t-shirt as if inviting cooler air in.

"If you're too hot, why are you drinking a cappuccino?"

"Because in the great battle between the need to get cool and the need to get caffeinated, compromises sometimes have to be made."

"You could've had an iced coffee."

"I'm not even going to dignify that with a response."

"What do you think, Twylan?"

The younger witch looked at them both through her shades and shrugged. "I think I don't want to take a side between you two."

That made the others laugh.

"That's tactful," Jackie said. "But being a Silver Griffin isn't about keeping everybody happy. If you want to go down this path, you're going to end up pissing some people off."

"I know, but those are mostly the bad people, and I'm in no rush to do it."

"Sometimes it happens," Lucy said, peering into her cup of tea as if she was hoping to read a message in it.

"Kelly getting to you again?" Jackie asked.

"A bit, yes. I never wanted to hurt Max, and now she keeps hammering on about what I've done. She doesn't even have to say anything. She just gives me that glare every time we pass each other."

"You shouldn't feel guilty or like you're the problem. Max is a nice guy, but he was on the wrong side. The problem here is that his wife is a total bitch."

"Jackie, that's one of our colleagues you're talking about!"

"You're with me on this, right, kiddo?"

Twylan nodded. "I'll take a side on this one. Kelly isn't a nice person, and she shouldn't be taking her frustrations out on you."

She squeezed Lucy's arm. "Remember when you first met me and the rest of the Underfoot Brigade? You brought us food and other things we needed. Kelly wouldn't do that. She'd just barge into our home and demand that we cooperate."

"I guess." Lucy stretched, trying to expel some of her tensions. "It's exhausting to deal with."

"That's sad."

For a minute they sat in silence, drinking their coffee and watching the games store across the street.

"All right, enough of this moping," Jackie said. "We need to pay attention so we can catch our culprit and get back to some proper work instead of chasing shoplifters."

"What if our intelligence on this is wrong?" Lucy asked. "What if it's only plain old shoplifters bothering this place?"

"I talked to the store clerk and did a scan of the building. Something is definitely amiss."

"Okay, but I want to get this over with, so I can get back to working out what the big threat is that's coming."

"Maybe this is the threat: the phantom shoplifter, coming to pocket the world and carry it home without paying!" Jackie put on a dramatic voice and spread her hands wide like one of the interviewees on a TV show about alien conspiracies. "The truth is out there."

"Or maybe it's something to do with snakes," Twylan said. "Look at the gutter."

Sure enough, something was wriggling along outside the video store, unnoticed by the busy people walking by. The slender shape was dark but caught the light, glistening as if slimy or made of metal.

"Well done, kiddo." Jackie slid her wand out of her pocket and held it under the table. "What do you think, Lucy? Go grab it now or wait to see what happens?"

"Wait," Lucy said. "We don't know yet that this is what

we're after, and if it isn't, we don't want to give ourselves away."

They watched as the snake-like thing wriggled up to the door of the store and waited for a customer to open it, then followed them in.

"How did this become my life?" Jackie asked. "Watching snakes try to steal from nerds."

"You know that you're friends with plenty of nerds, right?" Lucy tapped her Wonder Woman cup. "Be careful what you say about my people."

"You don't count. You crawled out of your parents' basement and crossed a whole ocean to become this awesome crime fighter."

"The parents' basement is a tired, cruel cliché, and you're better than—look, it's coming back out!"

The door had opened again, and a slender box slid out across the pavement, the type that would hold a game or DVD. The tip of a tail was barely visible wriggling out from underneath it. Moving along at ground level, it went unobserved by the busy passers-by.

"We have our thief." Jackie got out of her seat. "Or at least we've worked out how they're doing it. Let's see where it leads us."

Jackie crossed the street and followed the game box at a discreet distance while it wriggled along the gutter. Lucy and Twylan stuck to their side until the box slid out of the gutter and down an alley behind the backs of two rows of shops.

"I know where that comes out," Twylan said. "I'll go to the far end, just in case."

She ran off down the street while Lucy crossed to join

Jackie. The two of them peered into the alley's mouth.

The game box wriggled halfway down the alley. Then someone stepped out from between two dumpsters. Despite the heat, he wore a woolen beanie hat that draped loosely down the back of his head. He bent as the game box and its snake-like bearer approached, then took the game and stuffed it into a battered backpack.

"Don't worry, I haven't forgotten you," he said.

He pulled off the hat. Where hair should have been, there was a writhing mass of tentacles.

"Atlantean," Lucy whispered.

"That explains why I sensed magic," Jackie replied, "and how they were able to do this."

The Atlantean picked up the snake-thing and pressed it against the side of his head. It latched on and joined the rest of the tentacles, becoming one more part of the squirming mass.

"Seen enough?" Lucy asked.

Jackie nodded. "Let's do this."

They checked that no one else was around, then strode down the alley, wands raised.

"Silver Griffins," Jackie said. "You're under arrest."

"It wasn't me," the Atlantean said, holding up his hands.

"Nice try, but we've caught you red-handed. Or should that be red tentacled? Either way, come quietly, and this can end with a fine and some strong words, instead of a trip to Trevilsom."

"Sure, sure."

Something about the guy's grin made Lucy nervous. Was this her paranoia playing up again? Then she saw a flicker of movement at his side.

"What's that?" she asked.

"What's what?"

"That." The tip of a tentacle disappeared into the Atlantean's pack, then the backpack shifted, and a ball fell out. It shattered as it hit the ground, exploding into a cloud of smoke.

"Later, sucker!" the Atlantean shouted as he vanished from view.

"After him!" Jackie charged into the smoke. For two seconds, Lucy heard her running. Then there was a *crash* and a groan. "Stupid dumpster."

Lucy advanced more cautiously through the smoke, wand raised, looking at where her feet went and whether there was trouble ahead. The Atlantean would probably run off, but there was a risk he might try to attack them instead, to add a couple of stolen wands to his stash.

The sound of swift footsteps told her which plan he was following. She hurried after him but couldn't see more than a foot ahead. Somehow, she lost her sense of direction and almost ran into a wall.

Then another voice muttered a spell, followed by a *crackle* of magic and a *thud*.

"Jackie, is that you?" Lucy stumbled down the alley, feeling her way along the wall to keep a sense of direction.

"That depends," Jackie called from behind her. "If they did something smart, then yes it was me."

The smoke thinned, and Lucy emerged into clearer air. Near the far end of the alley, the Atlantean lay groaning on the ground. His backpack had fallen open, spilling a stash of stolen jewelry and games. Twylan stood over him, wand raised.

"Form to contain in bonds of chain," she said.

Chains shot from her wand and wrapped around the Atlantean, pinning his arms in place.

"Good spell work," Lucy said.

"I learned from the best." Twylan smiled.

The Atlantean's hat shifted, and a pair of tentacles wormed their way out.

"Nice try, sunshine," Lucy said. "Inretio."

A net formed around the Atlantean's head, tight strands of magic holding the tentacles in.

Jackie emerged from the smoke, coughing and waving the gray haze away from her face.

"You got him?" she asked. "Good work, Lucy."

"Not me," Lucy said. "This one's on Twylan."

"Well, well, well." Jackie said. "You really are the future of magical law enforcement."

Twylan blushed. "Just helping out."

"Don't suppose you could help me out of this?" the Atlantean said. "I've got a totally sweet flatscreen I can give you, might even be able to get my hands on the new PlayStation. What do you say?"

"I say that it sounds like you're trying to bribe your way out of trouble," Twylan said. "I read the rules about this the other day, and I can confidently say that you're making things worse. We're not the police, you don't have a right to silence or anything like that, but if I were you, I'd be quiet now."

"You guys are the worst."

"We're not the ones using magic to steal from ordinary people." Jackie hauled him to his feet. "Now you won't be anymore."

CHAPTER TWELVE

With a suspect to transport and the street around them busy with morning commuters, it seemed easier to get back to Griffin HQ by magic than by car. Jackie called the transport team. A few minutes later a disk of magic appeared in the alley before opening into a portal. They stepped through, taking the Atlantean with them, and emerged into the cavernous, brick-walled space of the transport room.

The duty wizard sniffed and frowned. "Is one of you on fire?"

"Smoke bomb in a tight space," Lucy said. "Better close the portal quick before the cloud blows through."

The wizard waved his wand, and the portal slammed shut, leaving a blank wall.

"I suppose you want a holding cell for this one?" He pointed at the chained Atlantean.

"Hey man, this one has a name!" the Atlantean said.

"You can tell me what it is when we fill in the paper-work," the duty wizard said. "I'll also need your tribe, date of birth, and current or most recent address so I can log you in the system. Don't try making something up. If you have a record, we'll find it in the end, and the lies will add time to your sentence."

"This isn't fair," the Atlantean protested.

"It's perfectly fair," Jackie said. "That's why cheats like you don't like it."

The duty wizard led the Atlantean off to a cell, and the three witches headed back through the corridors toward the main office.

"Are you doing the paperwork for this one?" Lucy asked.

"I suppose so. It was my assignment." Jackie sighed and looked at Twylan. "This is why you shouldn't join the Griffins, all the bureaucracy."

"I quite like it. It's comforting to have familiar patterns," Twylan admitted.

"If it's so comforting, do you want to do the forms for me?"

"It's not that comforting."

"That's what I thought." Jackie glanced at her watch. "I have another appointment first. Why don't you go with Lucy on whatever case she's chasing today, and I'll catch up with you later?"

"I'm on night shift later, so I was going to go home now and bake snacks," Lucy said. "I'll be doing some research after that. You're welcome to come and make cakes if you like."

"Really?" Twylan's fingers twisted together. "That would be lovely, but I don't want to get in the way. I could always go back to the tunnels."

"No, come with me, it'll be fun! It might be easier to bake if someone else is entertaining Eddie."

"That's settled." Jackie waved the two of them away. "You two go make muffins or whatever it is, and I'll do some real work. But I expect baked goods tomorrow."

She hurried through the office toward reception. The stakeout at the games store had taken longer than she expected, and she'd lost track of time. For multiple reasons, she didn't want to be late, but the clock on the wall said she had about thirty seconds to avoid that happening.

She strode into reception as the outer door opened and Heather Fields arrived. She nodded at Jackie in greeting, then frowned at the receptionist.

"You're going to make a fuss again, aren't you?" she said.

"That depends," the receptionist replied. "Are you going to cooperate?"

"Heather's here as my guest," Jackie said. "Can you please give her a visitor's pass?"

"Sure, once she goes through wand recognition."

Heather slapped her wand down on the security box on the reception desk. An amber light lit up, the receptionist typed something into his computer, and an imp staggered out of the box, carrying an identity badge with Heather's photo on it.

"There's no need to go slamming things." The imp shook his head. "Some of us only want to do our jobs in peace."

"I'll bear that in mind." Heather took the badge and clipped it to her flannel shirt. "Will that do?"

"Perfectly." The receptionist offered an insincere smile. "Have a nice day."

Jackie led Heather through the office, then down the stairs. They didn't talk, but that didn't seem to be a problem. That was one of the things Jackie liked about Heather. She didn't feel a need for unnecessary words. For all that Jackie liked a good chat, there was something comfortable about the aura of peace that the Tolderai chief carried with her. It took away the pressure to come up with a joke or an insightful comment or to force small talk when there was nothing to say.

They reached the entrance to the Special Equipment and Weapons lab. Heather stared at the reinforced steel door.

"This place does not look natural," she said. "Or nurturing."

"You'd be surprised at what they can come up with," Jackie said. "Part of what we're after for your forests is protection, which they can do." She pulled out the Silver Griffin amulet from around her neck. "It might not look like much, but this weakens the impact of hostile spells, and it's probably saved my life without me even realizing."

"That's good. And silver looks good on you."

"Thanks." Jackie waved her wand, and the door opened. "Shall we?"

In the short corridor behind the door, magical traps had caught a collection of creatures. There was an imp stuck to the wall with glowing twine, a green rat in a magic jar, and a pigeon frantically flapping its wings as it tried to escape a net on the ceiling.

"See, security," Jackie said. "Nothing gets in or out of here without Jenkins' approval."

"I like that. Can we have these nets in human size?"

"Maybe, but I expect he'll have something new for you."

They emerged into the testing range as a gout of flames burst from a tub in the middle of the floor. It shot into the air, spread across the ceiling, then turned from fire into ice, which fell across the room in a drift of snowflakes.

Toliver Jenkins and his assistant Nigel emerged from behind a protective screen.

"What do you think, Nigel?" Jenkins asked. "Eight-point-two, eight-point-three?"

"I'd say eight-point-five." Nigel's pencil hovered over a clipboard. Then he looked up and smiled uncertainly. "Um, I think we have guests."

Jenkins wheeled, his lab coat flapping behind him.

"Agent Kowal! And you must be Ms. Fields. Please, come this way. Everything is ready."

He strode through the melting snowdrifts to the far end of the lab, and the others followed.

"Did you get the, um, the information I found for you?" Nigel asked.

"Oh, yes, thanks." Jackie gave him a quick nod. " I'm not here for that today, though. Jenkins, what have you got for us?"

With a big grin on his face, Jenkins picked up a small, shiny black box with magically infused wires hanging off the sides.

"This is the latest magical sensor out of you know where." He tapped the side of his nose.

"No, I don't," Heather said. "Where is it from?"

"From, you know, where the tech comes from..."

"From this lab?"

"No, I mean, um..."

"It comes from Mana Valley," Jackie said.

"Oh, sure, say it out loud." Jenkins flung his hands up but thankfully held onto the device. "If this place gets infested with gremlins, I'm charging you for the damages."

Heather frowned. "What is he talking about?"

"I'll explain later." Jackie pointed at Jenkins. "You explain now, what is this thing?"

"It's a magical detection sensor." He held it out in cupped hands. "Extremely sensitive. Agent Kowal said that your lights have been responding to magical interference, so set these next to the lights. They'll pick up on the readings and give you much more detail on what's happening. That will help you identify the source early on and determine whether to take ameliorative or preventative measures.

"It has a magically boosted Internet signal, so you should have no trouble making a connection, but I'll need to set up the associated software on your computer."

"I don't have a computer," Heather said.

"You don't have a..." Jenkins rubbed his forehead. "I'm sorry, are you some sort of time traveler from the Stone Age, and Agent Kowal failed to inform me?"

"Not everything is about machines," Heather growled. "In fact, this place has too many of them."

She turned to go, but Jackie grabbed her arm.

"Wait. This really could help. Jenkins doesn't mean to be rude. He just doesn't know any better, right Toliver?"

"Oh, yes." Jenkins shook his head. "People are messy and complicated. It's so hard to get things right."

"This is true." Heather faced him again, arms folded and

scowling, but at least she was listening. "What else do you have?"

"Shielding spells." Jenkins handed her a printed book. On the cover was a photo of him and Nigel, waving at the camera. "We developed them ourselves. You can use them to reduce the impact of interference on your forests and anyone in them. Chapter four includes some nifty enchantments to minimize the odds of people stumbling across your groves by accident."

"That's good. We need to keep people away."

"We used one of those online book printing places to get bound copies for ease of reference. Looks rather professional, don't you think?"

Jackie stared at the stack of books on the table with their photo of the grinning researchers, their names and title in big red letters underneath. She'd seen more professional productions come out of kindergarten classes equipped with wax crayons and glitter.

"Anything else?" she asked.

"I've saved something special for last." Together, Jenkins and Nigel ducked under the table, then carefully lifted out a cylinder. It was the size of a slender tree trunk but perfectly smooth. They laid it down, one end on the stack of books, and Jenkins touched his wand to it. The whole cylinder glowed with a light that made Jackie instantly feel peaceful and calm.

"This came out of the Nuada Industries mess," Jenkins said. "It absorbs background radiation, both magical and mundane, and turns it into a special sort of light. Think of it as sunlight plus. It will encourage faster growth of plants and greater wellbeing for the people working with them.

Early tests indicate that it's good for both mental and physical healing.

"We'll have to calibrate it carefully to ensure that it doesn't mess with the spells you've already cast. We might even connect it up to those sensors for a fully integrated system. In time, we could put a string of these in every cave, an extra boost for these wonderful forests you're growing."

"I'm surprised you like what we do." Heather raised an eyebrow. "It's about nature, not technology."

"I like clever solutions. Using underground forests to make the city's air cleaner is ingenious, as is what I've heard about how you've executed it. If it's all right with you, I'd like to be the one to install and calibrate these light pillars once we're past the initial test phase. I would love to see what you've done."

"I will consider it."

"Thank you. Well, that's it for today." Jenkins took a step back from the table. "By all means, take copies of the book. Nigel can liaise with Agent Kowal to arrange for the rest of the equipment to be delivered, can't you, Nigel?"

"Yes, boss." Nigel smiled at Jackie. "Maybe we can—"

"Send me an email with the information you need," Jackie said. "Best way to avoid a mix-up. Thanks for this, Jenkins. You've been a real help."

She led Heather out of the test lab and back along the corridors toward the main office. As they went, Heather leafed through the garish book of spells.

"Is he always like that?" Heather asked.

"Pretty much, yes."

"Strange little man."

"He's mostly harmless."

"I like harmless. And his skin?"

"He stays underground and lives off pizza and soda."

Heather shook her head. "Not a good sign. Can I trust him in our forests?"

"Do you trust my judgment on that?"

"Yes."

"Then yes, I'd say let him come along to set up his tech. But keep an eye on him. He won't mean to do any harm, but he gets carried away."

"Will I have to get a computer to use these sensors?"

"You can come 'round and use mine if you want."

"I would like that." Heather held up the book. "First though, I need to cover this with paper. Jenkins may be mostly harmless, but I don't want him grinning down at me from my bookshelf every day."

CHAPTER THIRTEEN

"Come on in." Lucy walked through the front door and set her backpack down next to the hallway table. Buddy trotted out of the living room, tail wagging and tongue hanging out. "Hey boy, how are you doing today?"

Buddy gave a pleased *yap* and leaned his head forward for her to pat him. Then he spotted Twylan walking in behind Lucy and trotted over to get her attention. Why be treated like a good boy by one person when you could have two?

"Are you guys home?" Lucy called.

"In here," came the reply from the living room.

Lucy walked through to find Eddie sitting in the middle of the floor, assorted building blocks and boxes scattered all around, with Emily Sanders sitting next to him.

The gray-haired witch smiled at Lucy. "As you can see, we've been building a city."

"Gosh, that is impressive." Lucy crouched next to them and ran a hand through Eddie's disheveled hair. His look of serious concentration broke, and he grinned at her.

"Mommy!"

He flung his arms out, and Lucy swept him up in a hug.

"Hello, my little builder. Is there a house for me in your city?"

"Silly Mommy. You're too big."

Emily got to her feet with a helping hand from Twylan.

"I should get going," Emily said. "I have book club this evening, and I need to tidy the house."

"Thanks so much for babysitting," Lucy said. "He wasn't any trouble, was he?"

"As if this one could ever be trouble!"

"There was the gibbon incident..."

"I suppose there was. No, he's been good as gold today." Emily lowered her voice to a stage whisper. "Probably saving the trouble for you."

With that, she headed out.

"Would you like to do some baking?" Lucy asked.

"Yay!" Eddie flung his arms in the air. "Bake cheese!"

"I was thinking more like chocolate peanut butter Cheerios cups. How does that sound?"

"Yay, chocolate!"

"Well, someone's full of beans. Now, do you remember Twylan?"

"Wylan!" Eddie wrapped his arms around Twylan's leg in something that enthusiastically approximated a hug.

"Hi, Eddie." She ruffled his hair.

"Eddie, I need you to tidy this up before baking," Lucy said. "Can you do that?"

Eddie frowned. "Wanna chocolate butter cups."

"We'll make them. In fact, I'll go get the ingredients out now. But I need these toys back in the boxes."

"Okay." Eddie gave a dramatic sigh and slowly started picking up blocks.

"Maybe I could help?" Twylan asked. "I mean, if that's okay?"

"That sounds good." Lucy lowered her voice. "The important thing is that he does some tidying, not that it all ends up in the right place."

She disappeared into the kitchen, leaving them to clear away.

"Where do these go?" Twylan picked up some of the plastic robots that had inhabited the town.

"There." Eddie pointed to a plastic crate. "All there."

Together, they started filling the crate with robots, dinosaurs, and building blocks. It was soon so full that Twylan suspected some of these toys belonged elsewhere, but she remembered what Lucy had said: this wasn't about getting things exactly right. It was about Eddie doing his part.

"Is there somewhere for the cardboard boxes?" she asked.

Eddie looked thoughtful.

"Flat," he said.

"You mean we fold them flat first?"

"Flat!" The air around him shimmered, and Eddie turned into a large, round piglet. He trotted up to the nearest box and rolled over onto it, crushing it into an approximation of flatness. It had certainly done the job, but Twylan feared that it would be hard to get the box back into shape if he wanted it again.

"How about if we try something else?" she asked.

She pulled out her wand and tried a spell that Kix had

taught her. On tendrils of magic, the boxes lifted into the air. Their flaps pulled out, and they folded flat before stacking themselves neatly in the corner of the room.

Eddie the pig used his teeth to pick up the box he had squashed, carried it over, and dropped it on the top of the pile. Buddy, who had watched the flying boxes with his tail wagging excitedly, leaped onto the heap and settled down, apparently ready for a nap.

"Now for some baking?" Twylan asked.

The piglet led her into the kitchen, where Lucy was setting up a small portable table. She'd already lined up boxes and jars on the counter, and there was a step by the sink.

"What a splendid pig," Lucy said. "But you'll need to wash your human hands if you want to play with chocolate."

Instantly, the air shimmered, and the little boy reappeared. He hurried over to the sink and washed his hands, then went to stand at the foldaway table.

"First things first." Lucy put out a cupcake tray. "Can you set this up, please?"

Eddie took a stack of cupcake papers and started carefully placing them in the tray, one at a time, lining the holes.

"That should keep him busy for a few minutes," Lucy said. "Would you like a cuppa?"

"Yes, please."

"Coffee?"

"If you're having tea, I'll try that."

"Adventurous." Lucy smiled. "At least someone in this country understands a good hot drink."

By the time Eddie finished, they were both sipping from steaming mugs.

"Now chocolate?" he asked.

"Now chocolate." Lucy put a large ceramic bowl in front of him and a bar of cooking chocolate. "Break that up into there."

Eddie dutifully did as he was told, turning into a small gorilla at one point to give him extra strength, then back to a boy so he could tell them when he finished.

"Do you guys cook like this a lot?" Twylan asked.

"Oh yes," Lucy said. "I've done it with all the kids. It's a lovely way of spending time together."

"Cool." An unexpected sensation rose in Twylan's heart. It would have been easy to be jealous of this, the family bonding that she didn't get to have. Instead, it was comforting. Lucy made her feel included, let her into that family feeling for a few minutes at a time. It was a wonderful thing.

Lucy put a jar of coconut oil and one of peanut butter next to the bowl, with a clean spoon next to each.

"This many spoonfuls." She held up a hand. "Got it?"

Eddie nodded and started scooping peanut butter out of the jar.

"I'm trying different ways of communicating," Lucy explained. "Seeing whether he responds better to visual cues or things I say. It'll be useful to know what sort of learner he is before he gets to school."

"Wow, that's planning."

"I've learned from the other two that it's good to think ahead, and from the PTA that teachers are usually busy and stressed, so anything you can do to help is a good thing."

"All done." Eddie held up the peanut butter spoon, about to lick it, then looked at Twylan. "You want?"

He held the spoon out. His fingers were almost as covered in peanut butter as the spoon was.

"That's very kind of you," Twylan said, "but you're the one doing the hard work. You should have it."

While Eddie gave the spoon a thorough cleaning with his tongue, Lucy added brown rice syrup to the bowl.

"Now the fun part," she said. "But this involves the stove, so we need to be careful, okay?"

Eddie nodded seriously. "Not get burned."

"Exactly."

Eddie brought the step from the sink to a position in front of the stove. A pan of water was on the heat, steaming just below a boil. Lucy set the bowl on top so it rested on the edges of the pan, with a lot of the bowl in the hot water.

With a wooden spoon, Eddie started stirring the contents of the bowl. He watched with rapt attention as the chunks of chocolate melted and the ingredients mixed, turning into a rich brown goop. The kitchen filled with the sweet smell of chocolate.

"Here." Lucy handed Twylan a cookie. "To see you through."

Once everything was thoroughly melted, Lucy carefully lifted the bowl off the pan and set it back down on Eddie's table. Then she handed him a bowl of dry Cheerios.

"Last part of the mix."

Eddie tipped the cereal in and gave it a thorough stir. When he was satisfied that he'd mixed everything, he started spooning out dollops into the paper cupcake liners.

The blobs were unevenly shaped and varied in size with how much he got on the spoon, but neither witch tried to help. If the results were good enough for Eddie, they were good enough for them.

"Just a moment," Lucy said once he'd filled half of the liners. She grabbed a pack of gummy worms from the cupboard and trailed one over the edge of each remaining paper. "This way it'll look like the worms are crawling out from underneath."

"Ick!" Twylan said.

"Cool!" Eddie said.

Once all liners were full, Lucy fetched another packet from the cupboard. She took out a handful of Oreos, put them in a plastic sandwich bag, and smashed them up with a rolling pin. "One final touch. Let's all join in this time."

Together, they sprinkled crushed Oreos over the top of each cupcake.

"Next," Eddie said.

"That's it."

He shook his head. "More."

"We don't need anymore."

"More sweeties! More chocolate! Cakes with everything!"

"But if we put everything in, we'll be stuck here forever, making this one lot of cakes. If we stop instead, we might have time to make more cakes later."

That was logic Eddie couldn't argue with. "More cakes?"

"More cakes."

"Okay."

Lucy took the tray and put it in the fridge.

"Now we wait for them to cool," she said.

"Not eat?" Eddie pulled a sad face.

"You know full well, Eddie Heron, that you have to wait for cakes. But there are leftover Oreo crumbs and a mixing spoon to lick."

Eddie held up the chocolaty spoon. To Twylan's surprise, he once again offered it to her.

"Don't you want that?" she asked. "It looks delicious."

There was something in Eddie's expression she couldn't quite read, not exactly scheming, but a hidden thought.

Lucy laughed. "He thinks that if he gives you the spoon, I'll let him lick the bowl."

"In that case, it would be rude not to." Twylan took the spoon and gave it a lick. Maybe it was her comfortable surroundings or Eddie's satisfied smile, but she couldn't remember tasting anything more delicious.

"Bowl?" Eddie reached for it with sticky hands.

"For such a good little cook?" Lucy asked. "Of course."

CHAPTER FOURTEEN

Ellis and Sarah strolled hand-in hand-through Silver Lake Meadows. Other people were rushing past, hurrying to get somewhere now that lunchtime was nearly over, but neither of them wanted to get where they were going. Time together was a thing to be treasured and lingered over.

"I almost feel guilty, dragging you away from the office," she said. "What happens if there's a magical crisis and you're not around to fix it?"

"That's okay, they never schedule them when I'm not in," he replied. "Evil overlords, eldritch monstrosities, rogue magicals from the nether realms, they all know better than to try and take over the world between twelve and two on a Tuesday."

"That's very thoughtful of them."

"Good villains are like that. After all, what's the point of monologuing if the hero ain't around to hear it?"

"You think you're the hero of the story for the Silver Griffins?"

"You think I'm not? I'm insulted."

"I'm just saying there are other options. Lucy gets involved in almost everything. She could be the hero."

"I guess that's plausible..."

"Ooh, or Jackie! She's got that feisty heroine thing going on. And her love life's so unstable that she could end up with the eye candy at the end of each adventure, like James Bond."

"I didn't realize that being an emotional disaster zone was a qualification for heroism."

"Emotional disaster zone?" Her tone became indignant. "What are you saying about my friend?"

"But you said that—"

"I'm teasing." She squeezed his hand. "It's not the romances that make Jackie a hero. It's everything else she does."

"If we're stuck in a TV show, or a movie maybe, that doesn't bode well for old Applegate."

"It doesn't?"

"Think about it. He's the experienced mentor, days away from retirement. If that guy doesn't turn up dead, I'll eat my wand."

"Oh no! Well then, it's a good thing this is real life."

"Still, I should head back soon." Ellis pulled his phone out to check the time. "Supervillains might not be on the schedule yet, but I've got a meeting. You working this afternoon?"

"Not at the hospital, but I have my surgery."

Sarah's home surgery was a critical feature of the local community. She provided care to sick and injured magicals from all over L.A., people who couldn't go to a regular doctor without raising serious questions. In her way, she was as vital to maintaining the secrecy of their lives as the Silver Griffins were.

"You know, you might be the best, kindest woman I've ever met." Ellis pulled her to him.

"Does that make me the hero?"

"Reckon so."

"I guess that makes you the eye candy." She kissed him, lingering over the moment, feeling his body pressed against hers. "Now I really do have to go. You still coming over for dinner this evening?"

"Wouldn't miss it for the world."

"I'll see you then."

Ellis headed for the nearest Starbucks and the subway to Griffins HQ while Sarah walked up the streets overlooking Silver Lake Reservoir, back to her house. When she got there, a car was waiting outside. At the wheel was a nervous-looking Arpak, his wings hidden by a coat that was too warm for the weather. Sweat dripped from under his baseball cap down his face, and he clutched the steering wheel tight.

"Are you here for the surgery?" Sarah asked.

"Uh-huh." The Arpak looked at her intently. "You Dr. Smith?"

"That's me. Come on in."

"Uh..." The Arpak glanced up and down the street. "It ain't for me, and the person it's for, she can't exactly move herself."

"Can you carry her in?"

"Yeah, but..." He gestured at the surrounding houses. "What if someone sees? Won't it look suspicious?"

"Don't worry. I established alibis with my neighbors years ago."

Sarah opened a side gate into the yard and from there the door to her house. The Arpak opened the back door of his car and lifted out someone draped from head to toe in sheets. With his bulging muscles, he had no trouble carrying them, and he did so with a surprising delicacy as if he was afraid that something might break if he moved too fast.

Sarah led him through the kitchen and into the surgery at the back of her house. The room was painted white, the floor tiled, and there was a hospital bed in the center. Along the walls were monitors, instruments, and cupboards full of tools and drugs.

The Arpak laid his burden down on the bed, then pulled back the sheet, revealing a female Arpak. She was also well-muscled, her sleeveless t-shirt cut to let not only her arms but also her wings emerge. Her eyes were open, staring blankly into the middle distance, and her whole body was limp.

Sarah felt for a pulse, then took out a stethoscope and listened to the heartbeat. Both were steady but faint, weak enough to cause worry.

"What's your name?" she asked the male Arpak.

"Caldwin." He paced.

"And hers?"

"Seraphiel. She's a leader in our community."

"What happened to Seraphiel, Caldwin?"

"I don't know!" He thrust his hands through his hair. "We were talking last night, a bunch of us. Nothing special. No serious meeting, or stress, or anything like that.

Suddenly, in the middle of it all, she jerked and looked behind her. Then she keeled over, and she never woke up."

Sarah removed most of Seraphiel's clothes and examined her body, looking for any sign of trauma. This made Caldwin even more uncomfortable, and he hovered in the doorway, unable to look at what was happening but unable to look away.

"What's happened to her?" he asked.

"I don't know. She's comatose, but I can't see any cause. Perhaps something happened in her brain." Sarah waved a flashlight in front of the patient's eyes. There was no response.

There was a knock, then a scrabbling of claws across the kitchen floor, and half a dozen Willen burst into the room. They were carrying another Willen between them, his rat-like face staring blankly at the ceiling.

"Sorry to run in on you like this," said Tibtib, a Willen who Sarah had met at her surgery before. "We can't exactly hang around out there."

"No problem." Sarah pulled down another bed attached to the wall, and the Willens laid their patient on it.

He was older than most of them, his fur starting to go gray at the tips, but he still seemed in good shape, with all his teeth and no bald patches. Just like Seraphiel, he was limp, eyes unresponsive, breath and pulse steady but not strong.

"This is Old Rambler, right?" Sarah asked. She'd met the Willen elder once, a respected member of his community, as well-liked as a Willen could be. She had no idea what his real name was, but an hour of his stories had told her where the nickname came from.

"He just fell over." Tibtib clutched his paws together. "Is it a heart attack? Or a stroke? Or one of those things in your brain, where the blood vessel pops?"

"An aneurysm?" Sarah studied Old Rambler. "I'm not discounting it yet, but this doesn't seem quite right." She gestured at the two patients. "Did these two know each other?"

"Don't think so."

"Not that I know of."

"Hm."

Something wasn't right. It was niggling at the edge of her mind, but she couldn't work it out. She sat Old Rambler up so she could examine his spine. Then, as the shadow of her hand passed across his fur, she finally worked it out.

He was casting no shadow.

She laid him back down, then went to Seraphiel and lifted her arm. Sure enough, no shadow was cast across the bed or the floor, no matter how Sarah angled the lamp above the bed.

"This isn't only medical," she said. "It's something magical."

She pulled out her wand and ran it across both bodies, looking for any sign of a spell or a curse. When that didn't work, she took out chalk and candles and started on a diagnostic ritual.

"Is this..." Caldwin the Arpak stared, wide-eyed. He was younger than she'd realized when she first met him and less used to facing disaster than the Willens. "Is this bad?"

"Of course it's bad," Tibtib snapped. "Look at them!"

"I don't know what it is yet," Sarah said. "I need space to

work. Can you all please go through to the living room and wait?"

Once she was alone, she sketched out runes on the floor, then lit the candles and started to chant. Her magic was interrupted by a knock on the door.

She went out through the kitchen and opened the door to a pair of gnomes.

"Our friend," one of them said. "He just fell over..."

By the end of the afternoon, Sarah had half a dozen assorted comatose magicals filling her home and no more idea of what was going on than she'd had at the start. If there was a pattern, she couldn't see it.

They were all different species, from different backgrounds and parts of L.A. There were no spells on them and little trace of any sort of magic, although something had used it because none had a shadow. She tried dozens of different diagnostic devices and spells without any luck.

As evening approached, she sat exhausted on a stool in the kitchen. She picked up her phone and dialed Ellis' number.

"Hey, honey," he said. "Am I running late?"

"No, no. In fact, I wondered if we could eat at your place tonight. Mine is full of patients."

"Sure, of course. Why don't you stay over, get away from work?"

"That would be great. See you soon."

She hung up, then walked wearily into the living room, where friends and relatives of the sick magicals waited. "I've done all I can for now. I can't keep my home full of you. If you want to make a rota and take it in turns to watch the patients through the night, that would be great."

"What's going to happen to them?" Caldwin asked. Next to him, the Willens looked nervous now.

"Honestly, I don't know." Sarah was too tired to find a softer way to say it. "I promise, I'll do my absolute best."

CHAPTER FIFTEEN

Lucy sat in the subway car from the Silver Griffins' HQ to her local Starbucks, her backpack in her lap. She wasn't a fan of the night shift, which meant missing family dinner and time with the kids, but she didn't complain. After all, everybody had to pull their weight.

Kelly, on the other hand, loved to moan when she got this shift and was doing exactly that. Since she still refused to talk to Lucy, Kelly had found one of the admin gnomes instead and was venting at him. He shifted uncomfortably in his seat, like a teenager cornered by a crazy uncle at a family dinner.

"It doesn't make any sense," Kelly said. "I mean, there are plenty of Griffins who don't have children to look after. They should work the night shifts."

"So all the single people would be stuck working nights?"

"And couples without children, or older ones where the kids have left home. That should be enough people so they can all have some day shifts too."

"Isn't that a little unfair, making people work nights because they don't want children? What if they can't have them, and every round of the rota reminds them that—"

"So my actual children don't get to see me because of other people's non-existent children?"

"That's not what I—"

"You're an idiot; you know that?" Kelly crossed her arms and turned away from the gnome. "You've reminded me why I don't talk to admins."

The gnome blinked, clearly taken aback by the verbal attack, then shrugged and got back to reading his book. It seemed that he could live pretty well without Kelly's particular brand of conversation.

The subway carriage reached its stop, and the doors *hissed* open. Lucy waited until Kelly got out before she stood. The more distance she could put between the two of them, the better. It wasn't like she had a suspect to chase down yet, so she could afford to take her time.

As she ambled up the staircase, the admin gnome passed her.

"Sorry about my colleague," Lucy said. "She can be a bit of a—"

"Don't worry about it," the gnome said. "I'd rather be the one stuck listening to her on the train than the one who has to work with her."

He had a good point, but sadly Lucy couldn't get away from working with and around Kelly. At least not without quitting her job, and she loved being a Silver Griffin far too much for that.

She emerged through the magical doorway at the top of the stairs, into the back of another Starbucks. Tuesday night after dark wasn't prime time for coffee since the place was almost empty. She walked through, past a barista mopping the floor, and out into the parking lot.

Kelly was standing beside Lucy's SUV, and there was a whiff of magic in the air.

"What are you doing?" Lucy strode over.

"Nothing." Kelly shifted her arms, not quite quick enough to hide the wand disappearing into her bag.

"Bollocks, it was nothing. You were casting something."

She didn't have the patience to dance around the subject, like when Kelly had cast a stink spell on her brownies at the PTA bake sale. That had been petty malice, but the past couple of days had been a steady stream of bad attitude, and Lucy didn't trust Kelly not to cross a line.

"Why would I cast anything? I'm only walking to my car."

Kelly spun on her heel and strode away.

Lucy glared after her, but there wasn't much else she could do. Nothing was obviously wrong, and if Kelly had done something, she was a smart enough witch to cover her tracks. Lucy would have to take her time to check the Rivian over thoroughly before she went anywhere.

A pigeon fluttered out of the sky and landed on the roof of the vehicle.

"What do you want?" Lucy asked.

"Coo, coo." The pigeon held out its leg, showing her the slip of paper tied there. Lucy unfastened it and read the message.

Flying carpet over Echo Park. Get it down before mundanes spot it.

So much for taking her time to check out the car.

The paper turned into a handful of worms, and Lucy flung them away. The pigeon fluttered down to gobble them up off the pavement while she leaped into her Rivian.

"Over Echo Park" wasn't exactly a precise location for her to navigate by, but a flying carpet should be obvious to anyone looking for it. She brought up an app on her phone, one displaying spell results that Ellis had shown her, then fixed the phone into its holder on the dash.

Next, she waved her wand at the roof of the SUV and through it the sky above, casting a detection spell. Sure enough, a bright spot appeared on the ceiling, indicating the direction of the flying carpet. She shifted the magic into the phone app, and an arrow appeared on the screen, showing her which way she needed to go to catch the carpet.

Lucy rolled out of the parking lot, her car's electric engine letting out a gentle purr, and headed through the evening traffic. It was a good thing the streets were relatively empty, as the app only showed Lucy a general direction to drive in. Although she knew the local roads well, swerves of the arrow forced her to make sudden and unexpected turns.

The carpet rider wasn't going anywhere in particular as they veered back and forth across the sky. Every time Lucy thought she was getting close, they changed direction, and she had to double back.

By the third U-turn, she was almost cursing under her breath, but she was at least getting close. A dot on her screen showed her that the carpet was nearly overhead, and when she looked up through the panoramic roof, she spotted a hazy outline of a rectangle, marked out in a magical glow.

During the day, an incident like this would've been a disaster. The Griffins would've had to use the "never was" spell on half the inhabitants of Echo Park to stop word of the carpet getting out. At night, though, it should be easy to cover up. She only had to bring the carpet down somewhere safe and deal with its driver.

"Almost got you." She pulled out her wand and wound the driver's side window down. They were heading for Elysian Park, the perfect place for her to force a landing.

Then her SUV started to slow down. She frowned and pressed her foot against the gas. For a few seconds, nothing happened, then the vehicle suddenly accelerated, and she had to swerve to avoid hitting a van in front of her. She hit the brakes, and again the response was delayed.

"What the..."

The wheel turned itself under her hands, turning the car toward the wrong road. Lucy yanked hard, and it turned the right way, but she felt something straining against her. Then the lights started to flash on and off.

This was getting far too dangerous. She hit the brakes and pulled into the side of Academy Road just by the Elysian Park Trail. Something squealed in frustration.

Lucy waved her wand and chanted. "Revelare!"

Sparks of magic danced across the dashboard. A cluster of small creatures appeared, none more than six inches tall, all with mottled, warty skin. They stood on two legs and were grasping parts of Lucy's car with their webbed fingers. Two were clinging to the steering wheel, three were messing with the pedals, and one had opened the casing of the dash. It grinned as it reached inside and grabbed a fistful of wires.

"Gremlins." Lucy glared at them. "I should've known." She pointed her wand at the one messing with her wiring. "Stupefacio."

Caught by surprise, the gremlin had no chance to respond to the spell. His eyes rolled back in his head, and he slumped, stunned, to the floor.

She lowered her wand, aiming it at the gremlins on the wheel. One of them squeaked and jumped clear, but the other caught the full blast of her freeze spell.

The gremlins in the footwell scrambled up the door, making a bid for the open window. Lucy caught two of them in a net spell and flung them, entangled, into the back seat. The third jumped clear and dashed out across the road.

"Oh no, you don't!" Lucy leaped out after him and raised her wand. "Dormio."

The spell caught the gremlin as it reached the curb. It collapsed to the ground and started snoring, fast asleep.

Lucy hurried across the road and scooped up the gremlin before some passing motorist could see it.

She spun. One last gremlin was still hanging onto the steering wheel. It waved at her and grinned with malice, then reached for the door. But the stretch was too much. Though it strained, it couldn't pull the door shut before making its getaway.

"Gotcha, sunshine." Lucy wrenched the last Gremlin off the wheel and hit it with a stun spell. Then she summoned a magical cage in the passenger seat and shoved them all inside: netted, stunned, frozen, sleeping, the troublesome creatures all went in together, and the cage slammed shut.

With a sigh, Lucy sank into the driver's seat. She looked at her phone, expecting to see an arrow toward the flying carpet, but one of the gremlins had got to the phone. The screen was nothing but gray fuzz, and when she looked up at the sky, she couldn't see any sign of the telltale magic.

"You're Kelly's doing, aren't you?" She glared at the gremlins. Of course, she couldn't prove it, and Kelly would deny everything if this went to Applegate. She would probably say that Lucy was making excuses for her failure to catch the flying carpet. Lucy knew the truth as sure as she knew that the creatures had ruined her phone. Kelly's meddling had caused the gremlins, and it had let the carpet rider get away.

In the past, Lucy had let a lot of these things slide. If Kelly gossiped about her or made snide comments or cast a malicious spell, it was usually best to rise above it. This time, she'd gone too far. Lucy was going to have her revenge.

CHAPTER SIXTEEN

Gruffbar rode his Harley into the parking lot, turned off the engine, and hopped down off the bike. He looked at the building the lot was attached to, a concrete block with no plants in sight. Its only decoration was a Nuada Industries sign lying on the ground outside, where someone had removed it from the wall. This didn't seem like the right spot to meet with a tribe of forest witches and wizards.

He pulled out his phone and double-checked the message from Heather Fields. This was it. Either she'd mistyped or he was in the right place.

He secured his bike and walked up to a side door of the building. When he knocked, a twenty-something wizard with a blond ponytail and a thin goatee appeared.

"Hey, man," the wizard said.

"Where do I know you from?" Gruffbar looked up at him.

"I made a deal with Zero," the wizard said. "To help find my tribe. You were his courier."

"That rings a bell." Gruffbar stroked his beard. Even trimmed to disguise his dwarf nature, it was a lot more impressive than the wizard's thin chin growth. "Your name's Maplecloak, right?"

"Oakmantle. Nathanial Oakmantle."

"Near enough. If you're here, I guess you found them."

"You found them too."

"True, but this is less a homecoming, more of a business transaction. Speaking of which, are we going in, or do we do this in the doorway?"

Nathaniel made space for Gruffbar to pass, then closed the door behind them. They walked through a small, flimsily built office and into the main working floor of the factory. It was like stepping inside an Apple device, the walls and ceiling painted bright white so any spec of dirt would show.

Assembly lines ran down the middle of the room, conveyor belts with robot assembly arms hovering around them frozen in mid-operation. Against one wall were hoppers full of materials, pallets of supplies, and rows of tools. The place would have been gloriously industrial if someone hadn't brought in a row of potted plants and set them up against the back wall, basking in the light that came through clear panels in the ceiling.

At one side of the factory floor was a meeting area. There, a dozen witches and wizards had gathered around a table. Heather Fields sat at the head, arms folded. She didn't stand as Gruffbar approached but nodded at him in greeting.

"Good to see you, Gruffbar," she said.

"And you, Ms. Fields."

Someone had raised one of the chairs and added extra cushions, making it easier for Gruffbar to reach the table and make eye contact with the others. That wasn't the sort of consideration he got from every client. It turned out that working for the good guys had some advantages beyond the pay check. He climbed up into the seat, put his backpack on the table, and pulled out his laptop.

"This isn't what I expected from the Tolderai." He gestured around him. "Given your reputation, I thought we'd be meeting in some wooded glade or secret forest."

"What do you know about secret forests?" A crazed-looking wizard with beads in his gray beard glared down the table at Gruffbar.

"About as much as you know about mining machinery, I expect. That it's probably out there somewhere and I'm glad I don't need to know about it."

"Hm." The wizard sat back, folding his arms, and something made a crinkling sound.

"Don't worry about Mackam," Heather said. "It's his job to be wary of outsiders."

"I thought you were all wary?"

"Warier."

"Well, my people like living in holes hidden underground, so I can't criticize anyone else for paranoia."

"You're mocking me." Mackam leaned forward again, and one of his hands slid to a knife sheath on his belt.

"I'm mocking myself, but if I hit the wrong mark, I apologize. I'm a lawyer, not a comedian. Sometimes the jokes fall flat." Gruffbar brought his attention back to Heather. "What's the deal with this place?"

"A new acquisition," she said. "An investment."

"Good to see that you're making good use of your earnings from your ancestors' art. These Nuada facilities have bad associations right now, but the quality of their tech is inarguable. Whatever you paid for this when they dismantled the company, you should be able to flip it for twice that in six months."

"That is not the plan. We want this to be the beginning of a business of our own."

Gruffbar looked around the table at the collection of hippies and hedge wizards. One of them was wearing a stained apron with an artist's brushes poking out of her pocket. Nathaniel Oakmantle still looked like he should've been on a college campus, staring at screens in a basement lab and playing hacky sack on his lunch breaks. Mackam looked like his idea of customer service would be shanking anyone who made a complaint. This was not the stuff that made corporate empires.

"When you say you want to set up a business." Gruffbar felt his way tentatively into the conversation. "You mean like one of those shops where you can sell your arts and crafts? Because a place like this, it's not commercial real estate."

"We mean a real business," Heather said. "Not some outlet for hobbyists and bored housewives. It's our job to protect nature and the world around us. To do that, we need power and influence, and real power now lies with corporations. That is what we will become."

"Okay..."

Gruffbar used powering up his laptop as an excuse not to look her in the eye. A successful corporation needed many things, a range of skills from people management to technical knowledge to accounting. It required discipline and focus and a willingness to present yourself in a way that would appeal to investors. That wasn't what he saw here.

"I see that look," Heather said. "You don't think we can do this because we don't have suits and MBAs."

"I didn't say that."

"Your face did."

Gruffbar drew a deep breath. "Look, you're the client. As long as you're paying for my time, I'll do whatever you need from a legal point of view: incorporation, contracts, governance rules, the works. By my beard, I've been around enough companies that I can even advise you on writing your business procedures. But you people as a corporate power? I wouldn't be doing my job as your lawyer if I didn't say that I have doubts."

"I understand." Heather leaned forward, hands spread on the table. "For centuries, the Tolderai have lived in the shadows, seeking to protect what matters to us through magic, secrecy, and connivance.

"In this world, it's harder to stay hidden. Sooner or later, someone will reveal anything we make. By moving into the open, by adopting the tools of the corporate hegemony, we intend to strengthen ourselves, protect ourselves, and raise a barrier around that which is most precious to us."

"You want to turn the system against itself?"

"And bring it down from within!" Mackam slammed his fist down on the table. There was a gleam of excitement in his eyes.

"And turn something ugly into something beautiful," said the artist.

"We don't know exactly where we're taking this is," Heather said. "That's the nature of journeys."

"You understand what a business is, right? What's involved in running one?"

"We are not children. We're ready to adapt, to adopt the roles that suit us. Tell me, are the most successful businesses the ones that cling closely to what they and others did before?"

Gruffbar thought about the most successful businesses in the human world. Rollerblading mavericks who let their staff work on whatever they wanted one day a week built Google. Amazon had turned selling books into the biggest marketplace in the world. Even in Mana Valley, the standout businesses were the ones that did something different, that approached magic from a fresh angle.

Maybe the Tolderai could do something like that. They certainly weren't going to be among the standard players, the second-tier successes that kept going through momentum and conventional work.

"All right, you've got me," he said. "So what is your business going to do?"

"We don't know yet." Heather's look defied him to tell her how stupid that sounded. "Anything that helps protect nature and the planet. That starts with solar panels."

"It's a good start and a potentially profitable one." Gruffbar opened a document he used for new client meetings and started making notes. "If you're going to make this work, you'll need people to fill a few key roles. Chief executive officer, obviously, and I assume that will be you, Heather."

"I am already chief of the tribe."

"I'll take that as a yes. You'll need someone who's good with money as chief financial officer, someone who understands tech as chief technology officer, heads of functions like sales, facilities, and HR. Will you be appointing from among yourselves or recruiting externally?"

"No outsiders!" Mackam slammed his fist on the table again. "We can't have them poking around in our secrets. The man already watches us with his spy satellites and his secret radio signals. We can't have him sneaking agents into our midst."

"Interesting perspective," Gruffbar said, because saying "you're a whack job and you should shut up now" seemed like a sure way to lose this job. "Heather, your thoughts?"

"Mackam is right, in his way," she said. "We need to appoint from within. This is our business and should only include people we trust."

"Great. So, which of you is the accountant?"

They looked at each other. There was an awkward silence.

"Then who's going to learn accountancy?"

Again, an awkward silence. Some of them looked expectantly at Nathaniel, who shook his head.

"My Ph.D.'s in reforesting," he said. "The only financials I know are macroeconomic incentive mechanisms for sustainable investment."

Gruffbar sat back and gave them a minute to contemplate their situation.

"I don't want to be the rockfall in your mine," he said.

"This is an admirable dream you've got. But even running this one factory will take a lot of people with a wide range of skills. If all you know is forests and magic, you won't get very far. So the question is, how are you going to fill your personnel gaps?"

CHAPTER SEVENTEEN

"What do you think old Applegate's going to do now he's retiring?" Jackie asked from the passenger seat of the Rivian.

"I don't know." Lucy was only half paying attention to the conversation as she navigated the streets of Echo Park. "Go on a cruise, maybe? Or go read in the park? I don't know what he does with his spare time."

"That's exactly my point." Jackie grinned. "Guy like that, dressed up so smart, keeping his home life quiet, he's got to have some dark secrets he's hiding."

"I thought you knew about his home life. You're the one who speaks to his wife."

"Oh, sure, I've met her a few times, but that'll only tell you so much. They seem so conventional. I hope they have some really crazy plans now. A big gambling spree in Vegas. A year out overthrowing corrupt governments in eastern Europe. Seven nights a week in one of those clubs where everybody wears a lot of leather."

"Jackie! I did not want to picture our boss that way."

Jackie laughed. "Sorry, couldn't resist putting that image in your head."

"I don't think I have any mind bleach handy, but I'm definitely going to need a cuppa to wash that thought away."

"We were already going to your place for a coffee."

"Now it's medicinal."

They pulled into the driveway of Lucy's home and climbed out of the SUV.

"What's this?" Jackie pointed at a paint stain on the pavement.

"Remnants from before Charlie found a new base for his business. I thought he was going to clean it off." Lucy checked that no one was looking, then pulled out her wand and magicked the stain away. "There, all gone."

Buddy met them at the front door, his tail wagging and tongue hanging out. He was so excited to see them that he ran around their ankles in circles until he got dizzy and had to sit in a corner.

"Silly creature." Lucy smiled fondly. "I thought Dylan was home with you?"

There was no sign of any of the kids. The house was peaceful and serene. Lucy put the kettle on. Jackie pulled out her phone and stared intently at it.

"What are you doing?" Lucy asked.

"You know how this works. Whenever we think it's gone quiet in a workday and go to get a coffee, an urgent case comes in. So now, I'm making sure to expect an urgent case. I figure that the harder I expect it, the less likely it is to turn up."

Lucy laughed. "That's an Eddie level of logic.

"Small children are a great source of wisdom."

"You're mixing up wisdom and mud stains."

"Whatever, Supermom, just make me my coffee. Please."

Lucy poured a cup for Jackie and made tea for herself. As she was fetching the milk from the fridge, an unexpected movement caught her attention. Two mugs lifted off a shelf and floated through the air across the kitchen.

"What the..." Lucy caught one of the mugs and examined it more closely. There were no strange creatures on it, no sprites or magical insects lending it their wings. If there was a ghost or a spirit, it kept quiet in every other way, which was rare for a haunting. A magical field hung around the mug, but it was subtle more than strong, perfectly designed to do the job of levitating the mug and no more.

"Why don't we follow and find out?" Jackie pointed at the other mug, which was floating toward an open window.

They set their cups down and headed out the back door after the free-flying crockery. It floated along the back of the house, through a thick stand of bushes, and down the side. As she led Jackie through the undergrowth, Lucy had a good idea where the mug was going, and sure enough, it descended through an open hatch hidden at the side of the house into the tunnel lair her kids had built.

Lucy and Jackie climbed down the ladder into the headquarters of the Heron children and their Mini Griffins group. The mug led them down a corridor and through the first room, a reception area with beanbags and whiteboards, then down another couple of tunnels and into the training room.

Dylan stood in the middle of the area, his eyes closed and his hand outstretched. Off to one side, Twylan was watching. Like Dylan, she had her wand in her hand. Hers hung by her side while his was up with magic swirling around the tip. The mug floated to his empty hand, and he caught it by the handle, then opened his eyes.

"What do you think, Mom?" He grinned.

Lucy and Jackie both burst into applause.

"That must have taken so much concentration," Lucy said. "Not only moving the mug so far, but doing it without disturbing anything else, and keeping track of it along the way, even when it was out of sight. I'm very proud of you."

She hugged her son, who blushed. That didn't stop him from hugging her back.

"Dylan wanted a chance to show you how much progress he's been making," Twylan said. "The control he has now is amazing. Right, Dylan?"

Dylan shrugged and looked down at his feet. "It's pretty good."

"This from the kid who wrecked the school playground with his accidental rainforest?" Jackie said.

Now Dylan looked really embarrassed, his hand pressed against the back of his neck.

"That was, um..."

"Why don't you show us what else you can do, sweetheart?" Lucy asked.

"Sure."

Dylan stepped away from them all, muttered the words of a spell, and waved his wand. Specs of dust drifted from the floor and slowly spiraled in the air in front of him.

"Name someone," he said.

"Roger Applegate," Jackie said.

"You remember Mr. Applegate, right, Dylan?" Lucy asked, carefully not catching Jackie's eye, in case they both cracked up at the memory of their previous conversation.

"I think so." Dylan's wand shifted slightly, and his lips twitched as he whispered the words to reform the spell. The dust gently swirled, moving into lighter and denser patches, forming a shape in the air. Each mote shone like a tiny star in the glow from the overhead lights as they formed a body and a head that, after a few more moments, resolved into the ghostly but unmistakable image of Roger Applegate.

"That's amazing," Lucy said.

"It really is." Jackie walked slowly around the dust Applegate. "I couldn't do this now. I really couldn't have done it when I was your age." She grinned at Lucy. "Careful, this one's going to take over the world."

"How did you learn so much?" Lucy asked. "I knew you had the power, but it's not that long since it was getting wildly out of control."

"The things you taught me helped," Dylan said. "But it was mostly Twylan. She's been teaching me tricks to direct my magic, how to use a part of my power while containing the rest, giving me spells that are good for growing those talents."

"That's brilliant. Thank you, Twylan."

"I don't deserve the credit," Twylan said. "This is down to Dylan's hard work."

"Dylan's always worked hard, but he couldn't do this before."

"I suppose I've taught him some useful tricks. A lifetime

of struggling to hide my power has made me good at controlling it."

The magic in her eyes flared, a reminder of the one mark of magic she could never shake off, the reason why she could never simply relax and fit in among mundane humans, unlike her fellow witches.

"Show us another one," Jackie said.

Lucy smiled in gratitude for her friend's enthusiasm. She wanted to see more of what Dylan could do, but she was worried that, as his mom, a request from her might put him under pressure. Being asked to show off by Jackie was precisely that: a chance to show off.

Dylan waved his wand, and the dust Applegate disappeared. Then he pulled a seed out of his pocket and placed it in the center of the floor.

"Remember the schoolyard jungle?" he asked.

"Yes..." Wariness grabbed Lucy by the guts.

"It's okay, Mom. You don't need to worry about that ever again."

Dylan waved his wand. The seed sprouted into a tree, roots spreading across the floor, trunk soaring toward the ceiling, branches shooting out in every direction. Leaves and blossoms burst into the air. Then Dylan waved his wand again, and the whole thing froze. He lowered the wand, and the tree started to shrink, raised it, and the tree grew again.

When he waved in one direction, the tree grew that way. At another signal, it pulled back in, branches tightening, then became covered in blossoms, flowers crowded in so close together that they knocked each other and petals fell to the floor.

With one final flick of the wand, all the leaves and petals fell, and the tree retreated inside the seed. If not for the brown leaves lying all around, it would have been as if the plant had never been there.

The three witches stared, amazed at the power and control on display.

Then Lucy's phone rang. It was Sarah.

"What's up?" Lucy asked, still staring at the seed.

"I've found something," Sarah said. "Something that I think the Silver Griffins need to see."

"Can you bring it into the office?"

"Not without a fleet of ambulances."

That got Lucy's full attention. "Ambulances?"

"Can you come around and see?" Sarah's voice sounded strained. "And bring Jackie, if she's with you."

"Of course."

Lucy put the phone away and turned to Jackie.

"We're needed."

"What did I tell you? The minute you relax and forget about work, duty calls."

"Sweetheart, this is amazing," Lucy said to Dylan. "I really want to see more, but it'll have to wait."

She and Jackie headed back out along the tunnel and up to the sunlit world above.

"Your kid's amazing," Jackie said.

"So is Twylan, to have achieved so much with him."

"We have to find a way to make more use of that girl."

"I agree. For now, we've got to get over to Sarah. It sounds like something very bad is going on."

CHAPTER EIGHTEEN

Lucy and Jackie got into the car and headed out from Elysian Heights, over the Glendale Freeway, to Silver Lake. It wasn't far to Sarah's house, and if it had only been a social call, they would have walked, but this was a workday, and they needed to be ready to chase off at any moment.

After a few minutes, they pulled up outside Sarah's home.

"Is it me, or is there something in the air?" Jackie asked as she climbed out of the car.

Lucy closed her eyes for a moment and stood with her hand on the car's roof. "You're right. There's magic at play, or more like a remnant of it..."

"I meant the talking."

Lucy took a moment to listen. Sure enough, there was a susurration of voices, the whispers drifting out to them from somewhere nearby. The two witches looked at each other. Strange events weren't always bad, but they seldom got called in for the good ones.

Through the side gate, they found a small crowd of

magicals hiding out in Sarah's back yard: Willens, Arpaks, gnomes, even a few creatures that Lucy didn't recognize. Her hand went to her wand pocket, but none of them seemed hostile, though they stared at her with an intensity that was far from happiness.

Jackie opened the back door, and they walked into the kitchen.

"Sarah?" she shouted. "We're here!"

Sarah emerged from the clinic. She was wearing hospital scrubs and a face mask, with surgical gloves on her hands. When she tugged the mask down, the anxiety on her face was clear.

"Thank goodness you're here," she said. "I probably should have called you in sooner, but I was trying to deal with this as a medical issue. Then I was struggling just to deal with it all."

"All of what?"

"Let me show you."

Sarah led them into her living room. She'd pushed the furniture aside and rolled the rugs back to make space for plastic matting and narrow portable cots. Every one had an unconscious magical occupying it. Sheets draped their bodies, and intravenous drips fed into their arms. They stared blankly at the ceiling.

"They're all in comas," Sarah said. "They weren't taking in any food or water, so I've hooked them up to keep them hydrated and provide nutrients. Fortunately, nobody's shown any issues with their respiratory system yet, but if that happens..." She shook her head. "Well, hopefully with you guys on board, we can avoid that."

"What's causing this?" Lucy asked. She crouched next to the nearest of the patients, a Willen with graying fur.

"That's what I was hoping you could work out. I've not found any toxin common to all of them, or any sign of a virus. Some of them had sustained physical injuries, but there's no consistent pattern. Possibly they had been attacked, and some of them had more chance to fight back than others, but that's pure speculation. There is one thing they have in common..." Sarah picked up the Willen's arm and pointed underneath. "What do you notice?"

Together, Jackie and Lucy stared at the cot. If they hadn't seen it before, it might have taken all day to notice what was wrong, but instead, it was a matter of seconds.

"No shadow," Lucy said quietly.

"No shadow." Sarah laid the arm gently down at her patient's side. "I don't know if it's a cause or an effect of the other symptoms or if there's a third factor binding them all together, but the correlation is unmistakable. Every single one of these patients is missing their shadow, and I've not seen anyone yet without a shadow who wasn't in a coma."

"We've seen a couple of other cases, with the coma and the shadow. A gnome and an elf."

"A gnome?" Sarah's expression grew thoughtful. "That's the first case in a while to surprise me."

"Why is that a surprise?"

"Look around. What do you notice?"

They scanned the room, assessing each patient in turn. A Willen, an Arpak, a Kilomea, an Atlantean, a nymph, a shifter...

"They're all different species," Lucy said.

"That's right. Except..." Sarah pointed to a small bed in

the corner, where a gnome lay under a quilted blanket. "With your patient, that makes two gnomes."

Jackie wove her way between the beds, then crouched beside the gnome. She pulled the sheet down a little, then tipped the gnome's head from side to side. "He's a very different lineage from Grast."

"That's a thing?" Lucy asked.

"I grew up around a lot of powerful magicals and their gnome servants. It's a thing. Subtle, but identifiable."

"Are they different enough to count as separate species?"

"Definitely not, but..." Jackie looked around, and her expression mingled suspicion with anger. "Imagine you're some kind of collector, looking to steal shadows from a variety of magicals. Maybe you're building a collection. You start with different species, but after a while, those begin to run short.

"You're hooked on the thrill of collecting, so you need some way to continue. Subsets of species are the next logical option." She looked at Lucy. "It's only a theory, of course. What do you think?"

Lucy tilted her head and considered what Jackie was saying. "It's got potential. And we've seen collectors before."

"It would explain that business in the market as well, if the collector is trying to keep the thrill alive, so he's making things more difficult for himself."

"Market?" Sarah asked.

"The elf we have sustained an attack in the middle of the day in a crowded place. We nearly had a major incident on our hands, with witnesses around and her being a celebrity. What people saw there fits with your observation about something attacking them."

"That's useful to know. Who was the attacker?"

"I think it was a Shadow Man."

Lucy explained the strange creatures living in the darkness under the city and the brief encounters she'd had with them, most recently in Willum Grast's home.

"If they're made of shadows, that would explain them having power over shadows," Jackie said.

"It probably means that's the cause," Sarah said. "They're stealing shadows, which is putting people into comas because it's separating them from a magical part of themselves. Your collector theory works."

"Woohoo," Jackie said without enthusiasm. "I'm right."

"What if it's something else?" Lucy asked. "Shadow men spend their lives in the gloom. Shadows surround them. Collecting shadows for the sake of collecting seems like a strange choice for them. It has no novelty, no curiosity to it."

"So they're collecting with a purpose?"

"Maybe. Or maybe they have something against these people."

Jackie sighed. "I sense desk work coming."

"Why's that?" Sarah asked.

"We'll interview the relatives, of course, but these days, ninety percent of the work looking for connections between people involves going online. Checking webpages, social media profiles, memberships of organizations, participation in forums, past employers, on and on and on. Trying to find how this lot is connected, we'll be staring at screens for weeks."

"If they even are connected."

"Thanks for that note of optimism."

"Sorry, I'm tired. This has been a lot of work."

"We can help with that." Lucy took out her phone. "There's space in the infirmary at HQ, and we have the capacity to expand it magically if we need to. I'll contact the transport team and ask them to send someone over to work out the safest way of shifting so many patients."

"Thank you. It'll be great to have some help and to get my home back."

Lucy stepped out into the kitchen to make the call, leaving Jackie and Sarah with the comatose magicals.

"Why did you come to us?" Jackie asked.

"Who else would I turn to if not the Silver Griffins?"

"That's not what I mean, and you know it. Won't Ellis' feelings be hurt that you came to us first instead of him?"

"Oh gosh." Sarah shook her head. "I hadn't even thought of that. Partly, it was habit to think of calling you. I also think it was partly not wanting to cross the streams. I love Ellis, and things are going really well with him, but he's my safe space, away from all of this. I don't want work complicating that."

"You know it's going to happen eventually, right? You two are both in the equivalent of emergency services. Sooner or later, your working lives are going to cross."

"What if that goes wrong? What if we don't work well together, or we do, but that turns into the only thing we talk about? What about if it takes over and ruins our relationship?"

Sarah chewed on her lip, eyes shifting back and forth as

she surveyed a range of unpleasant futures. Jackie laid a hand on her shoulder and waited for her to look up.

"Stop creating worries out of nothing," Jackie said. "If there are problems in the future, you can face them together, but that's a big if. You guys fit together well. You're going to be all right."

"What if—"

"Stop! I've spent a lot of time being single recently, and I'm okay with that, but one of the reasons why I'm okay is because I get to live romance vicariously through you and your ridiculous boyfriend. He might talk like a redneck and dress like a clown, but he's not going to let work ruin things any more than you are. If you throw away a perfectly good thing by getting weird about this, when I don't have anything going on at all, I'm going to kick your bony ass into Silver Lake Reservoir. Understood?"

Sarah laughed. "Okay, Jackie."

Lucy came back in.

"Transport is sending someone over." She looked across the patients again. "You want us to stick around until then?"

"No, I've got this." Sarah ushered them toward the door. "You go do your desk work."

"How could you mention the D-word?" Jackie groaned. "I thought we were friends."

CHAPTER NINETEEN

Ashley sat at the edge of the playground, wearing an earpiece with a tablet in her lap. She watched as other kids dashed back and forth, scrambling up the climbing frame, shooting down the slide, chasing each other around. They laughed and screeched and made over-excited noises. To her, it was all a bit strange.

It wasn't that she couldn't understand at all. She'd seen how much fun Eddie had, and she even played herself occasionally, though that was mostly playing with devices she'd created. Still, the idea that you would regularly choose to spend your time like this, when you could be doing anything at all in the world, from an engineering project to a YouTube channel to reading about something new? That didn't make sense to her emotionally. That was why most other eight-year-olds also didn't make sense.

Two kids around her age ran up, holding a skipping rope between them.

"Do you want to play?" one of them asked.

"No, thank you."

"We're skipping. It's fun!"

"I'm sure it is, but I'm here on a mission."

"Like a spy?"

Ashley considered that one. There definitely was an element of the secret agent to how she and the Mini Griffins worked.

"Yes, like a spy."

"We could be spies too," the other girl said.

"Ooh, we could spy on Johnny!"

The two of them giggled and ran off, trailing the skipping rope.

"Have fun," Ashley called after them, then got back to her work.

Her string robots were widely spread around the park, their miniature cameras sending her views from different perspectives. Together, they gave her a good overview of what was happening. Right now, that didn't seem to be much of anything. If her intelligence-gathering was anything to go by, that wouldn't last.

Tommy strolled over and sat next to her. "I'm bored."

"Then you should go back to patrolling the perimeter. That'll keep you entertained, and the exercise will be good for you."

"I get plenty of exercise."

"That won't stop it being good."

"But it's boring now."

"Well, this can't be all excitement all the time."

"Why not?"

"Because life's not like that."

"Well, it should be." He patted his pocket, where he'd hidden his wand. "Can't we cast a spell to make these trolls come out? If they're living under the playground, we could levitate them or something."

"Then we wouldn't know for sure that they were bad trolls causing trouble. They could be innocent trolls who live near where strange things are happening."

Tommy sighed. "But I'm boooooored."

"Here." Ashley handed him the tablet. "Why don't you try controlling the robots?"

She always enjoyed working with the robots, so she figured it should be entertaining for anyone, even Tommy and his low boredom threshold. More than that, she'd noticed the power that novelty had over other people.

If you gave them something new, especially a piece of technology, they would throw themselves into using it, to the exclusion of whatever they'd been thinking about at the time. It was wasteful of sometimes perfectly good thoughts, but it was also good for getting out of moments like this.

Sure enough, Tommy seized the tablet and started playing with the controls, adjusting the robots' views, making them slither through the long grass and the dirt, hidden from the mundane kids and the parents watching over them.

"This is so cool," he said. "What are we looking for?"

Ashley took another set of string robots from her bag, set them on the ground, and took out another tablet to control them. "Anything that could be a troll. Small bodies. White fur. Brightly colored hair. Or signs that they're moving things, like rocks leaping around or playground equipment shaking."

"Like over there?" Tommy looked up from his tablet and pointed across the playground.

The slide was swaying from side to side, despite legs that were normally firmly anchored in the ground. Kids jumped off the steps rather than risk the movement flinging them off. At the top, a girl shrieked before sliding down, arms waving as the whole thing threatened to collapse under her.

Parents ran up and ushered their children away from the slide. Others grabbed their kids off the climbing frame as it started to imitate the slide's unexpected movements. People called out about earthquakes and subsidence and sewer collapse, but none realized what was going on. They did know that they wanted to get away, and most importantly to get their precious children away. Soon, the only ones left were Ashley and Tommy.

"Yes," she said at last. "I think that might be them."

Fingers darting across the tablets, the two of them directed their robots toward the play equipment. As they got closer, figures appeared on camera. They were only a few inches tall and had neon pink hair: a gang of trolls.

Hidden hatches in the ground around the playground equipment showed how they'd appeared and how they had shaken the slide and climbing frame so badly. From under the ground, they could grab hold of the foundations of the equipment and shake it back and forth.

"What do we do now?" Tommy asked.

"Weren't you listening to the mission briefing?"

"I was reading a comic."

Ashley sighed wearily. "Use the electric prods and herd them across the playground."

"Toward us, so we can catch them?"

"No." The thought of her and Tommy trying to catch a band of agitated trolls sounded like absolute madness to Ashley. "That way."

She pointed across the park to a stand of trees. Based on local social media posts, with their talk about disturbing noises and rustling in the night, she suspected that those trees provided the trolls' other main hiding place and source of entertainment. It shouldn't be hard to steer them that way. Then the trap could be sprung.

"How do I operate the electric prods?" Tommy asked.

Ashley showed him the control he needed.

"Cool." Tommy pressed the button. There was an electric crackle, and he grinned as one of the trolls leaped into the air. "Let's do this."

Their screens showed flashes and sparks from the electric prods. Ashley made a note to move the cameras next time so the electricity wouldn't mess with her view. Some of the trolls tried to fight back, punching and kicking the strange silver snakes that had appeared on their home turf. However, kicking something electrically charged was merely a way to get electrocuted again, turning their hair even wilder. There was a jabbered conversation among the trolls, the words impossible for Ashley to decipher, and they started backing away.

"That's it." She steered her robots forward. "Into the woods."

The trolls' slow retreat soon turned into full-on

running away. They dashed into the woods, leaping and howling as they went, and the robots followed them.

"Stop there," Ashley ordered Tommy as the robots reached the edge of the trees.

"But we've got them on the run."

"Now we need them to stop running."

In the woods, the trolls stopped and looked back. The silver snakes had stopped but seemed to be staring at them, those vicious electric prods and their cold electronic eyes pointing into the woods.

The trolls had options. They could stop here and rest. They could keep running and find a new home. They could expand in size, now that the humans were gone, and fight back against the robots. First, they had to argue among themselves about how to do it.

To one side of the trolls, Dylan rose from his hiding place in a bush. On the other side, Mia lowered the invisibility spell she'd been hiding behind. They stretched out their arms.

One of the trolls looked up and spotted them. He glanced back and forth, confused, trying to understand what this was and how it related to the strange silver snakes.

"Stupefacio turba," Dylan and Mia said in unison, holding out their hands.

Magic flowed, beams streaming in curves from each of their hands. The rays met in the middle, forming a pair of arcs that fenced the trolls in on both sides. The creatures stared at them for a long moment and jabbered at each other as they tried to work out how to respond. One of them started growing.

Dylan and Mia twisted their wrists. The magic flowed inward, rushing across the trolls. There was a flash, and all of the creatures fell to the ground, knocked out cold.

"It worked!" Dylan exclaimed as they let the magic go.

"Of course it did," Mia said. "You're a brilliant wizard."

"This was you too. It wouldn't have worked if it was only me."

They pulled a sack from behind one of the trees and started filling it with trolls. Ashley and Tommy came over, the string robots swarming around them, and used the machines to help with the lifting effort. The robots could combine into thicker, stronger strands, which easily lifted even the troll who had grown to three feet tall.

"It's so cool how much we can do when we work together," Dylan said.

"I know." Mia tied up the top of the sack. "We should work on some more combined spells. Maybe a really big illusion, or something for detection."

"Could you work together on transporting these away?" Ashley asked, prodding the sack. "We need to get them locked up before they wake up."

"Sorry, I can't teleport," Mia said.

"I'm not allowed even to try," Dylan said. "Mom says that it's too dangerous to try unsupervised, even with all the practice I've been getting."

"Then how are we going to take our perps home?" Tommy asked.

"We're not." Dylan took out a phone.

"No, you can't get the grownups in now!" Tommy protested.

"We've done all the hard work and proved what we can do. Do you really want to spend ages clearing up the mess?"

"When you put it like that..."

"Hi, Mom?" Dylan's voice changed as Lucy picked up his call. "I'm calling on behalf of the Mini Griffins. We have a present for you..."

CHAPTER TWENTY

"A whole sack full of trolls?" Charlie asked, his mouth hanging open, spaghetti dangling forgotten from his fork.

"Not a small sack, either." Lucy spread her arms wide, then pulled them back in as she almost hit a passing waiter. The Italian restaurant was lovely, but it wasn't huge, and there wasn't space for her to get too carried away.

"How did they do that?"

"Dylan, of course. Well, Dylan and Mia. They've been working on casting spells together, and they're achieving amazing things for such young people."

"Remember when we first tried casting magic together?" Charlie waggled his eyebrows.

Lucy laughed and blushed. Those were some fond memories and not ones she'd thought about in quite some time. Raising a family had taken a lot of the time that they would once have spent on each other, whether to experiment with shared spell casting, go out to a gallery, or just to lie around in bed doing not very much. She wouldn't have given up the life they had for anything, but it was good to remember the one they'd had before and to snatch back moments of it, like these date nights.

"Wait." Charlie raised an eyebrow. "If they're casting magic together, does that mean that they're..."

"No, she's not his girlfriend." Lucy hesitated. "At least, I don't think so. Dylan's only twelve. He hasn't shown any interest in that sort of thing yet. Has he?"

"Not that I know of, but he would hardly tell his dad."

"More likely than his mum."

"Should I talk with him?"

Lucy considered that for a moment while she ate a little of her spinach and mozzarella ravioli. It seemed a shame to let thought get in the way of good food.

"No, I don't think that's needed. He has a new friend, one who's also a magical and can help him grow as a magic user. We don't want to turn that into something awkward."

"Okay, but if you change your mind, let me know."

"Oh, I will. You'll definitely be the one talking to him about relationships."

"That seems unfair. I thought we shared duties equally where the kids are concerned."

"That's why I'll talk with Ashley when the time comes."

"Ashley, who approaches everything with pure logic and calm scientific method? That sounds like the easy option to me."

"Really, you think applying science to relationships is going to go well?"

They both laughed at that.

"At least we have a few years before we have to think about it." Charlie sipped his wine. "How's your food?"

"Delicious. And yours?"

"Great. I like the atmosphere here too. Not that I dislike the experimental places, but it's nice to try something more traditional."

Lucy looked around. Traditional was exactly the right word for La Pergoletta, with its wooden fixtures and furniture, red and white checked tablecloths, and candles burning in the middle of the tables. If not for the occasional customer pulling out a cell phone, the place could have been exactly the same at any time in the past eighty years.

"This should be Dylan's sort of place when he does start dating," she said. "Somewhere with a sense of history."

"Let's not think about what's going to happen next with the kids. They're already growing so fast. I want to enjoy them being young while it lasts."

"You won't say that next time Eddie rampages through the house in ostrich form. Then you'll want him to grow up."

"Like Eddie is ever going to grow up. That kid will be playing around until he's a hundred and racing nurses through the care home in his wheelchair."

"I thought you didn't want to think about them getting older?"

"Guess I forgot already." Charlie yawned wide enough to show off his tonsils. "Sorry, blame it all on the tiredness. I've been working so hard lately that I don't have much energy left for thinking straight."

Lucy skewered a piece of ravioli on her fork, then pointed at him with it.

"You, young man, need to get to bed at a decent time." She waggled her eyebrows. "For many reasons."

Charlie grinned. "I'm trying, but work's been busy."

"Work work, or the car work?"

"Cars, vans, bikes, the whole lot. We've had a couple of campaigning organizations ask us about fixing up buses so they can do less harm while they're on the road. Max is in negotiations with some magitech company about working on their fleet of vehicles. If we get that, we could make a huge difference."

"Do you have time to make that difference?"

"I'd like to. It has the potential to lead to even bigger things. If that company likes what we do in L.A., they might ask us to do work for them in Mana Valley, which would let us set up a branch there."

Having mentioned the Valley, Charlie waved his fingers under the table, making a quick magical ward against gremlins. Sometimes, it was easiest to name the place, but you could never be too careful with that naming.

Lucy reached across the table and took her husband's hand.

"Charlie, you don't even have a proper branch in L.A., you can't go set one up you-know-where. Besides, who would run it? You and Max both have families here."

"Ringo then, I guess."

"That doesn't address my first point. How can you talk about setting up a second branch when you don't even have your own premises here?"

"I'm not sure we need them." Charlie swirled his spaghetti thoughtfully around his plate. "Working around Gunther and his crew has been really useful, not only for finding work but for tapping into their mechanical skills and experience. If we did set up a workshop, I'd want to keep working with them somehow."

"Is setting up a workshop something you're looking at?"

"Max has been running the numbers and looking at properties. He's got a lot more time on his hands these days, so even with learning how to do the cars, he's fit that in."

Lucy looked down at her plate with a frown. Talk about Max and his lack of legal work made her feel guilty. She hadn't meant to damage his career, but the universe seemed set on reminding her that she'd done it.

"Does Max really need the work?" she asked.

"It's certainly not doing him any harm." Charlie squeezed her hand. "I'm sure his legal work will pick up soon enough, but in the meantime, this is keeping his spirits up."

"How about you? You've never needed the work, but are you enjoying it more than the day job?"

"Heck yes. There's the same problem solving, but I get to work with my hands, and I'm making a real difference in protecting the environment. What's not to prefer about that?"

Lucy hesitated. Charlie's job brought stability and security, something that was invaluable for the family. But his lack of time and energy was starting to affect all of them, and if he had to choose between the two jobs, it was clear which he would enjoy more. Of course, as a responsible and caring husband and father, he wouldn't think to choose it, which was why she needed to make the suggestion.

"You have enough work now to keep you busy full time. Why don't you give up the day job and focus on the cars?"

Charlie drew a sharp breath as if about to say something, but the words got stuck. He set his fork down and leaned forward.

"Are you sure?" he asked quietly. "This is a really big decision, and it doesn't feel like the responsible one."

"It's the most responsible one." Lucy took both his hands in hers. "This was always a dream job, and now that dream could be a reality. Showing our kids that they can chase their dreams, that they're allowed to make themselves happy, is one of the most responsible things we can do for them because it opens up the path to future happiness. So, do you want to do this?"

"I..." Charlie laughed. "It's harder to say, now that it's a reality, but yes, I really do."

"All right, then. Tomorrow, you go hand in your notice and book whatever spare leave you have left. The sooner you can focus on the work you love and on us in your spare time, the better for everyone."

"I am so lucky I found you." He leaned across the table and kissed her. "You are the best person in the world."

"You're not too bad yourself, sweetheart."

"I guess I'd better make the most of this meal. We'll need to tighten our belts if we're taking this risk."

"Nonsense." Lucy extricated one of her hands from his and waved a waiter over. "A bottle of champagne, please. We're celebrating my husband's new job."

"Congratulations, sir," the waiter said. "I'll just be a moment."

He hurried off.

"Lucy, what are you doing?" Charlie asked. "Think about the money."

"I am thinking about it. We still have my job, and with Max hustling like mad for clients, you'll soon be earning more than you ever did fixing corporate computers. You've earned this champagne, and we're going to enjoy it."

The waiter reappeared with two champagne flutes and a bottle. There was a *pop* as the cork flew out, and he poured them each a glass before setting the bottle down on the table.

"I'll leave you to it," he said. "Congratulations again."

Lucy raised her glass. "To old things ending and new ones beginning."

"And to some things staying the same," Charlie replied, looking into her eyes. They *clinked* glasses, and each took a sip. "I suppose we are entitled to treats on date night."

"Of course we are. But this change doesn't get you out of your other duties."

"My other duties?"

"Even once you're running a green tech empire, you'll still be the one talking to Dylan about his love life."

"That's fine. Teenage boys are always calm, stable, and reasonable. I'm going to have no problems at all, right?"

"Nothing that a sack full of trolls can't fix."

CHAPTER TWENTY-ONE

Lucy stepped off the subway car and into the immaculately kept station beneath Silver Griffins HQ. It was early, with no other Griffins on the platform yet, and that suited her. She needed an early start with no one around for what she had in mind today, less a piece of work than a private passion project. If ever there was a day for her to beat the rush, this was it.

As she hurried past the station master's kiosk, Normandy popped up from behind the desk.

"Good morning, Agent Heron," he said.

"Good morning, Normandy," she said. "Would you like a chocolate peanut butter Cheerios cup?"

She took a box out of her backpack, took off the lid, and held it out.

"Thank you, Agent Heron, that's very kind of you." Normandy reached out to take one of the cakes, but instead of eating it, he set it down on the counter. His brow was wrinkled, and he was wringing his hands. "While you're here, um, I was wondering, is it true about Muddlesom Varley?"

It took Lucy a moment to remember what that name meant. Then she got a flashback to the comatose magicals lying in the Griffins' infirmary and the gnome in one of the beds, a handmade quilted blanket spread lovingly over him.

"You mean his sickness?" she asked.

Normandy nodded. "The other gnomes are terribly worried, and a lot of them know that I work here, so they asked if I could find out more about what's happened to him. I mean, if it's all right for me to know. I wouldn't want to break the rules, you understand, I just... well, he..." His voice trailed off, and his fingers fumbled with the gleaming buttons of his beloved uniform jacket. "Never mind. I shouldn't have asked. It's probably an abuse of my position, isn't it?"

"Normandy, who is Muddlesom Varley?"

"Who is..." He looked at her in bafflement. "You don't know who that is you have up there?" He pointed at the ceiling, above which rested the Griffins' L.A. HQ and, farther above, the Griffith Observatory.

"As far as I can see, he's a slightly elderly gnome."

"Varley is one of the greats, Agent Heron. He helped to make the gnome community in L.A. what it is today. He united us, strengthened us, guided us. He provided us with a voice, though of course, it remained a quiet and respectful one. Why, it was Varley who recommended me for this job here."

"So he's a powerful gnome?"

Normandy scratched his head. "That's not how we would talk about it or think about it, but if you need to fit it into a human framework, then yes, you could call him powerful. Or perhaps influential would be a better word."

"What about Willum Grast? How do other gnomes view him?"

"Grast is a scoundrel." Normandy scowled. "A bad gnome who gives other gnomes bad ideas."

"But he's influential among those bad idea gnomes?"

"Far too influential, if you ask me."

Two influential gnomes and an elf pop star. These were important, powerful magicals, in their way. Thinking back, Lucy remembered the small crowd of magicals waiting for news about the other patients at Sarah's place. She had assumed they were concerned families, but what if there was more to it than that? Were they waiting to hear news about people who mattered to them, leaders or celebrities within their communities?

There was a pattern here. Perhaps she could use that.

"Varley is still in his coma," she said. Normandy and his people deserved to know. "We have some ideas about what's causing this, but we haven't found a cure yet. I'll let you know if there's any news, shall I?"

"That would be wonderful. Thank you, Agent Heron." Normandy managed a small smile. "And thank you for the cake."

Lucy carried on down the corridor and up the stairs. That had been a valuable conversation, and she was glad that she could offer Normandy some comfort, but it had taken up precious time, and she didn't know how much of that she had. A lot depended upon when Kelly came in.

The door into the Observatory swung open at a touch of her wand, and she hurried through the empty building to the next door, into the Griffins' reception. At this time of day, she had half-expected the reception desk to be unoccupied, but the receptionist was there, eating a Danish pastry and drinking a cup of coffee.

"Good morning," he said. "Wand, please."

Lucy tapped her wand to the security scanner, and the light went green.

"Would you like some dessert to go with your Danish?" She offered him the open cake box.

"Oh, thank you." He took one and laughed as he saw the gummy worm hanging down its side. "That's certainly novel."

"Practicing for Halloween." Lucy put the box back into her bag and carried on through.

The office was quiet, only the occasional administrative gnome passing. Lucy set her bag down beside her desk, took a screwdriver and a jar out of her bag, and checked that no one else was around. Then she hurried over to Kelly's desk.

She crouched beside the desk and carefully unscrewed the casing of Kelly's computer, then took the lid off her jar. A gremlin stared up at her from inside, its warty face crumpled in annoyance. It made an angry chittering sound.

"Don't worry," Lucy whispered. "I have somewhere far better for you to go."

She set the jar against the side of the computer and tipped it. This would serve Kelly right for what she'd done to Lucy's car. Turn her gremlins against her and see how she felt about it. Sooner or later, Kelly had to learn that Lucy wouldn't take this sort of treatment lying down.

Except that the gremlin wasn't accepting its treatment either. It spread its arms and legs wide, bracing itself against the sides of the jar, and refused to come out.

"Come on," Lucy whispered, shaking the jar. "There's a lovely tasty motherboard out here and all sorts of peripherals for you to mess with."

The gremlin stuck out its tongue. Lucy banged the side of the jar, trying to dislodge it.

Footsteps approached. Lucy scrambled into the space under Kelly's desk and out of sight. She watched as Roger Applegate's impeccably polished shoes went past, followed by Sam's black Doc Martens. A door opened at the far end of the office, and more people came in, chatting to each other. After a minute, another door opened, and the voices disappeared, but more footsteps were approaching up a corridor.

It was no good. People were arriving for work, and Lucy couldn't let people find her down here. If the gremlin didn't want to cooperate, she would have to finish the job later, maybe stay after her shift or come in early again tomorrow. She screwed the lid back onto her jar, hastily fixed the side of the computer back into place, looked around to make sure no one was coming and hurried over to her desk.

She was just in time. Two seconds after she put the jar back into her bag, Kelly came into the office. She glared at Lucy, who forced a sweet smile back at her, then took her seat.

"Howdy." Ellis took his seat next to Lucy. "How's it going?"

"Oh, not bad." Lucy looked around for something that she could pretend she had been working on. "Just thinking about this business with the Shadow Men."

"It ain't getting any better." Ellis shook his head. "Sarah's struggling with it all. She came in with me this morning so she can go check on the patients, but I'll tell you this, she ain't sleeping well."

"It must be really difficult for her, poor lass. She's used to being able to treat illnesses, but for this, we've got nothing that works."

"Not yet, but she's trying everything she can think of. Those patients are lucky to have her."

"They certainly are."

Sam walked over. "Lucy, Mr. Applegate would like to see you in his office."

"Sounds serious." Lucy took a cake out of her box. "You two help yourselves to those but don't eat them all. Jackie will be mad if she misses out."

Lucy walked into Applegate's office and set the cake down on his desk.

"A little treat, sir, to help you through the morning."

"Oh, thank you, Lucy."

He smiled, but only briefly. Then Kelly walked in and closed the door behind her. The tension in the room was so strong it could have bench pressed a Honda Civic.

"Take a seat, both or you," Applegate said, pushing the cake aside and putting on a stern expression. "I need to have a word."

The two witches sat stiffly, looking at their boss and waiting for whatever bad news was coming their way.

"Lucy, what were you doing under Kelly's desk this morning?" Applegate asked.

"Nothing," Lucy said, doing her best to sound innocent. It was even true, sort of. She hadn't managed to do anything in the end, though she had tried.

"And Kelly, what were you doing to Lucy's chair after she left the office last night?"

"Nothing."

"I see. So it's only a coincidence that when I asked Jenkins to have a look, he found a spell attached that would've released a cloud of stink gas when someone sat on it?"

Kelly clenched her hand in her lap but didn't say a word. Lucy squirmed in her seat. Learning that Kelly had tried to get at her again made her want to lash out, to release a whole plague of gremlins on the other witch. Being called into Applegate's office made her aware of how irresponsible and childish all of this was.

"I know that you two haven't always been on the best of terms," Applegate said. "But this is going too far. You don't need to like each other, but you can't be calling down clouds of locusts in the office or unleashing gremlins into our computer network. Am I clear?"

"Yes, sir," they both mumbled.

"I'm sorry, I barely heard that." Applegate cupped his hand around his ear. "Repeat, please, as if you mean it."

"Yes, sir," they both said firmly.

"Thank you. Now get back to work, and let's hear no more of this."

Lucy and Kelly walked out. As the office door swung shut behind them, Lucy turned to Kelly. This was their chance to clear the air and find a new beginning, to put the past few days' unpleasantness behind them.

"Truce, then?" she asked sheepishly.

"Oh, no." Kelly shook her head. "If you think you're off the hook because one old man has started paying attention, you've got another think coming."

CHAPTER TWENTY-TWO

"I assume your doctorate's not in medicine, Dr. Jenkins?" Sarah asked as she watched the wizard set up a new monitoring device at the side of the infirmary.

"No, neither of them is." Jenkins switched some wire around, then nodded at his assistant Nigel, who switched the power on at the wall. Crystals on the top of the box started to glow. "Why do you ask?"

"Because you seem to be interfering in medical treatment."

"I wouldn't say interfering, more trying to increase our understanding."

"You're attaching electrodes to one of the patients."

"Purely for observational purposes."

"And that cable seems to be sending pulses of magical power into them."

"Yes, it's sort of like radar, but in a less mundane way."

"Dr. Jenkins?"

"Yes, Dr. Smith?"

"I need you to switch that thing off."

Jenkins stood blinking at her in confusion. "Why?"

"Because those magical pulses could affect the patients' condition. We can't do something like that without considering the medical risks and getting the consent of their relatives."

Jenkins looked at the cables in his hand, at the elf they had been attaching wires to, at his assistant, at the machine, and finally back at Sarah. Finally, his expression changed, some realization spreading across his face.

"Ah, there seems to be a misunderstanding here," he said. "Perhaps because of all the beds and stethoscopes, you've fallen into thinking of this as a hospital, but this is a Silver Griffins facility, and our priority is finding the cause of this problem. It's my workplace, not yours, Dr. Smith, and trust me. I know what I'm doing."

Sarah walked over to Jenkins and stood face-to-face with him. They were around the same height. When she grabbed the cables out of his hand, he looked surprised, but he didn't protest.

"Dr. Jenkins, I have been left in charge here while the regular witch physician takes a much-needed rest. I am responsible for the care of these patients, and I am making the same decisions that your colleague would make if she were here. I know you mean well, and I don't mean to undermine your authority, but if you touch my patients again, I will stick this machine so far up inside you that they'll have to call a bowel surgeon."

It wasn't the sort of thing that she would normally say, and she felt guilty even as the words came out, but she was tired and stressed and had no patience left for people who weren't contributing to making her patients safer. She expected Jenkins to react with shock or outrage, but instead, he shrugged, quite used to this sort of response.

"Very well, Dr. Smith. Could we have a conversation about those medical risks you mentioned and about getting the relatives' consent? I think this device really could help."

Sarah relaxed as much as she could with so much at stake. "Yes, we can talk about it, but first I need to finish checking on the patients."

"Can we help?"

"Yes please, that would be lovely. Bring that cart along, and hand me things when I ask for them."

They made their way around the room, examining each of the coma patients in turn. Sarah took temperatures and pulses, tested reflexes and pupil reactions, examined the frayed ends where shadows had been cut off, and scanned for any new signs of magic in their bodies. As well as checking and recording the patients' condition, she took the time to make them comfortable. She adjusted pillows, pulled up sheets, replaced drip-feeds that were running low.

She had expected Jenkins to interfere as he followed her around, to make suggestions or tell her things he thought she was doing wrong. Instead, he observed, asked questions, and made occasional notes on his phone. It took her a little while to realize that he was studying the situation, gathering data on her, the patients, the treatment regime, even the way she collected data. Faced with the fascinating challenge of these magically sick people and the added challenge of justifying the use of his machine, he was learning first and acting later. He was following the science.

"If you want, you can take one of the empty IV bags," she said. "seeing what's in those fluids might tell you more about how I'm keeping them alive."

"What a splendid idea!" Jenkins took two of the bags out of a bin and handed them to Nigel. "Thank you, Dr. Smith."

"You can call me Sarah."

"Then thank you, Sarah."

The last patient they came to was the first one she'd seen, Seraphiel, the Arpak chief. Her wings hung limply off either side of the bed, and loose feathers had fallen on the floor. They lay there, dark streaks against the white tiles, symptoms of something terrible now or omens of worse to come.

Seraphiel was currently the only patient with a visitor in attendance. Despite their best efforts, none of the Silver Griffins had persuaded Caldwin, the younger Arpak, to leave his leader's side. He sat by the bed day and night, watching her, waiting for anything to improve. His eyes were bloodshot, his expression gaunt, and at times he twitched as if on the verge of sleep, but still he remained.

"How has she been?" Sarah softly asked as she started examining Seraphiel.

Caldwin blinked and shook his head. It took a moment for him even to realize that someone had spoken, never mind that they'd directed the words at him.

"Nothing has changed," he said.

"So you've seen this before?" Sarah held up a few of the fallen feathers.

Caldwin stared, then touched one of the fathers with a trembling hand, running his fingers across it.

"Molting," he said. "And they're dried out. This is very bad."

"Dr. Smith?" Jenkins said.

"Not now, Toliver," Sarah replied. "Caldwin, could you tell me more about when Arpak feathers fall out?"

"Really, Sarah," Jenkins said, his tone rising. "You really need to look."

Sarah turned. Seraphiel's hand was twitching. Her eyes rolled back in her head, and her whole body started to shake. Feathers were falling all around.

Sarah felt for the pulse in Seraphiel's neck. It was fast but erratic. Her body was struggling against something. She started to flail, arms and legs flying back and forth.

"Hold her still," Sarah said. Caldwin and Nigel rushed to do as she'd said, but Jenkins stood watching. "Dammit, Dr. Jenkins, I said hold her still!"

"You said not to touch—"

"Just do it!"

Seraphiel's head started banging against the wall. Jenkins thrust his hands in and grabbed hold, putting himself between her head and the hard surface. He winced and tightened his grip, trying to keep her still.

Sarah grabbed a sedative off the cart and injected it. The twitching slowed but didn't stop. She reached for a second dose, then thought better and grabbed her wand. Stupefacio wasn't only a spell for fighting with, and if they couldn't get her settled any other way, it might stop Seraphiel from hurting herself.

Before she could cast it, Seraphiel went rigid and

stopped moving. They stared at her. Several seconds passed, then she gasped and fell limp.

Sarah felt for a pulse again. Nothing. She climbed onto the cot, straddled Seraphiel, and started pressing on her chest, performing CPR.

"Toliver, get the defibrillator," she shouted. "Nigel, adrenaline off the cart."

Even before they fetched those things, she could tell that it would be too late. She fought on, desperately trying to keep Seraphiel alive, while Caldwin wailed and the others did everything she told them to, but it was no use. Magic was killing Seraphiel, and without an answer to that magic, they couldn't keep her alive.

Sarah had lost track of time before she climbed off the patient, and in a voice dulled by grief, announced the time of death. Feathers covered the floor. She looked around at the other patients. This was coming for them, wasn't it?

Caldwin sat with his back against the wall, tears streaming down his face. Jenkins and Nigel stood stunned. She should help them all through this. That was part of her job, not only healing the body but tending to the injured heart. She couldn't. She was too tired and drained and beaten. Instead, she stumbled out into the corridor.

She slumped against the wall and pressed her hands against her face, struggling to hold back a great wail of frustration. Footsteps passed, then another set, as she stood there, drawing deep breaths, trying to slow her racing heart.

Then came a third set of footsteps, which stopped in front of her. She peeked down from behind her hands and saw a pair of red sneakers.

"Ellis," she whispered.

"Hey there, honey." He pulled her away from the wall and wrapped her in his arms. "Someone said they'd seen you here."

"I can't cure them," she mumbled into his shoulder. "I can see the problem, and I can see it killing my patients, but there's nothing I can do about it."

"It's okay." He stroked her hair.

"No, it isn't!" She pulled back so that she could look him in the eyes. "These are my patients. They're counting on me."

"Could you save every patient before?" he asked quietly.

"No, but..."

"There ain't a 'but' to this. It's one more sickness that you're doing your best to help people through, but if there's no cure, then there's no cure."

"There might be a cure, and if there is, I have to find it."

"No, you don't. There are other folks here for that too. You're part of the process."

"I'm failing."

"Are you kidding? You're the one who spotted this was going on, who kept these folks alive when they slipped into comas, who brought them to the Griffins. Without you, this would all be a dang sight worse."

She drew a deep breath and steadied her shaking body.

"Seraphiel died," she said. "I don't think she's going to be the only one. Unless we can find a way to fix this magic, to remove this curse and get their shadows back, then sooner or later, they're all going to pass away."

"Sooner or later is a long time. Until then, with you around, these folks are in the best of all possible hands."

She smiled and shook her head. "How do you always know how to say the right thing?"

"Guess I'm just great like that." He took her hand. "Come on, let's go get you a coffee."

"No, I need to get back in there, sort the others out, make plans for the body. And I want to find out if Jenkins' contraption can help us spot this point coming."

"Good for you. If you need me, call."

"I will."

She opened the infirmary door and went back to work.

CHAPTER TWENTY-THREE

Ellis strode up to Lucy's desk, his face like thunder.

"You've been investigating these Shadow Men," he said. "How do we catch one?"

"Catch one?" Lucy looked up at him.

"So Sarah and the medics can question him about this darned magic they're using."

"Oh. Well, I'm all in favor of catching as many as we can, but I don't have any great leads."

"Then tell me your not-so-great leads."

"Well, something struck me this morning. The people we've seen so far, they're usually powerful or influential in some way. It wasn't obvious at first because what makes someone significant can vary with their species and how they relate to the human world, but I think there's something there. We've had an elf pop star, elders from the gnome and Arpak communities, people like that."

"They're after the shadows of powerful people."

"Maybe. It's a theory, at least."

"Knowing that, can we work out who they'll target next?"

"Sorry, but this is L.A., it's full of powerful and influential people, from politicians to business leaders to Hollywood stars, not to mention people who are important because of something they do within their community. Figuring out who they'll come after is like looking for a needle in a haystack."

"Dagnabbit. I really need to find something. This business is driving Sarah nuts."

"I really want to help, but with such a wide range of targets—"

"That's it!" Ellis grabbed a notebook off his desk and started flicking through, looking for something he'd thought of before. "They're getting folks from different species, right?"

"And groups within those species, yes."

"So they probably won't go for another Willen, or an Arpak, or one of those musical elves, whichever type that is."

"Sure, makes sense."

"Who ain't they gone after yet?"

"Dwarves, some of the other elves, witches, and wizards..." Lucy slapped her forehead. "Of course. Witches and wizards are crucial to L.A.'s community. They'll have to go after them. Probably more than one. Based on what we've seen so far, they could potentially go for anyone who's powerful within their community."

"That's what I like to hear. It only leaves one question: who's the most influential witch or wizard who might let us use them as bait?"

"This is absurd," Heather said as she ambled down the alleyway. "I don't walk like this."

"Don't worry about that," Lucy answered. She was sitting in a car around the corner, on the other end of a phone line. Ellis was in the passenger seat beside her, wand in his lap and ready to spring into action. "We don't need you to look normal, only like a tempting target. After the market incident, we know they're not cautious, so they'll risk a suspicious situation if it looks like an opportunity."

"I'm a good opportunity?"

"The leader of a feared and powerful tribe, CEO of a newly emerging business empire, well connected with the Silver Griffins? I think you'll appeal."

"Thanks. Maybe." Heather kept walking while the others waited and listened. "Was Jacks too busy to help you today?"

"She wasn't in the office when we thought of this. You think she might have had a better idea?"

"Maybe. I'd certainly feel better as bait with her as backup."

"I'll pass on the compliment."

"No, I...yeah, sure, do that."

"Are you all right still?" Lucy asked. Heather sounded distracted.

"Something's moving between the dumpsters up ahead. I can only see a shadow at the moment."

"That could be it. Don't look at it. Just keep moving, and if anything happens, call for us."

The Shadow Steward waited and watched as his target approached. The Tolderai chief, the infamous Heather Fields, was out here on here own. It was almost too good to be true, and the Shadow Sentry had warned him that there was danger here. Fields was independent, the sort of witch to wander on her own, but she was also cunning and connected to powerful people. He shouldn't underestimate her.

Then again, if she weren't cunning and influential, she wouldn't be worth pursuing, would she? Her strength meant that her shadow would contribute powerfully to the spell and help to bring about the Shadow Time. She would be a great mark in the Steward's dark ledger, the accounting of all that the Shadow Men had reaped for their magic.

Catching her shadow would stop the Shadow Stalker from looking at him with that smug superiority, the certainty that he, the Stalker, was the superior Shadow Man, the only one aside from the Shadow Mage who mattered. Today, the Steward would become more than their accountant. Today, he would make a difference.

As the woman approached, he drew his knife. It was long and slender, a sliver of darkness so sharp that it could cut through brick. He could kill her with it in a moment if he needed to,, but he wouldn't need to. He would simply wait for his chance, then cut her shadow away and let her fall where she was.

She walked up to the place where he was hiding amid the refuse humanity abandoned. The Shadow Steward stood perfectly still. Then she was past him, still walking, strolling at this lethargic pace that would have maddened him with its wastefulness if it didn't give him the opportunity he needed.

He emerged and crept after her, caught an edge of her shadow in his hand, raised the knife, and...

The ghost of a spear slammed into the ground in front of him, blocking his arm. It was the memory of a weapon, a thing made of magic rather than wood or metal, and the witch was holding it.

"I see you," she growled. "Lu, we've got a live one."

The Shadow Steward slashed with his knife. Against any mortal weapon, it would have cut straight through, but it caught against the shaft of that spear. Sparks of magic flew as the shadow weapon ground against the ghostly one.

Heather gripped her spear and gave the end a twitch. The movement flung her attacker back, and he sprawled on the ground. It was strange to see a creature like this, only a shadow, but Heather was used to dealing with strangeness. She slammed the butt of the spear down, meaning to pin him to the ground.

The Shadow Steward rolled clear before the spear could hit him. He reached the side of the alley and leaped to his feet, his knife outstretched. As the witch turned, he lunged. Now the tactics had changed. No more subtlety. He would kill her and steal her shadow. All that mattered was getting the job done.

She backed away, spear shifting from side to side, parrying his blows. He had her on the defensive. All he had to do was keep this up, and sooner or later he would get a lucky hit. All it took was one.

A bolt of magic hit him from behind. He staggered but kept on his feet. The wards the Shadow Mage had cast on him provided protection. He could shrug off all but the most powerful spells.

Heather lunged with her spear. It caught the Shadow Steward in the chest. The tip went right through and pinned him to the wall. He struggled and strained but couldn't break free, trapped by her ancestral weapon.

Lucy and Ellis ran up, wands at the ready.

"Well I'll be..." Ellis said, staring at the shadow. "He don't look like much, does he?"

"Stay back," Heather said. "That blade is deadly."

The Shadow Man watched them. The blow Heather had struck him with, driving the spear through his chest, would have killed most mortal creatures in an instant. It was killing him now, the damage too great to survive without the Shadow Mage's attention. He could feel himself unraveling, streamers of shadow peeling away around his edges, floating away to be obliterated by the sunlight.

"You'll never stop us," he hissed. "The Shadow Time is coming."

"The Shadow Time," Lucy repeated. "What is that?"

"The coming of darkness. The purging of the light from this world so we can walk freely upon it. The Shadow Mage has foreseen it. He has said that the end will come soon. We feed its power, and it will become unstoppable."

"That's what the shadows are for, some magic to bring about the end of the world?"

"To bring about its true beginning. To rescue us from the light." The Shadow Steward groaned. His whole body was unraveling now, strands falling away in every direction.

"You won't get away with this. The Silver Griffins will stop you."

"I've seen the ledger. I've kept its tally. I know how much power we have gathered and how little is still needed. There's no stopping the shadows now. A new world is coming."

With those words, the last scraps of the Shadow Man fell away from the wall. Caught on a magical current, they drifted across the alley into the sunlight and vanished.

Heather shifted her hands, and the ghost spear vanished. "Was that what you needed to hear?"

"It was a beginning," Lucy said.

"They ain't just collecting," Ellis said. "They're planning some big magic, using these stolen shadows to power it."

"We've got to stop them."

"We sure do, but first we should head back to headquarters. Anything we can tell Sarah might help her save those lives, or at least help her feel like she's got some control."

"Then we need to research where these Shadow Men live. It sounds like they're all set on bringing about the apocalypse, and I quite like the world as it is. I wouldn't want to lose sunlight or donuts or moving in three dimensions." Lucy turned to Heather. "Do you want to come back to headquarters with us? We could fill you in on this some more in case the Shadow Men come after you again. You never know. Jackie might be there."

She grinned and waited to see how Heather would react to that last comment.

"Thank you." Heather pulled out her phone and looked

at the time. "I would like to go there, but I have another appointment. All this slow walking has wasted a lot of my day."

"If you change your mind, you know where to find us."

"Sitting at our desks, trying to work out how to stop the apocalypse," Ellis added. "It sure is one heck of a life."

CHAPTER TWENTY-FOUR

While Ellis and Lucy got into their car and drove away, Heather went in search of the nearest tree. It was usually fairly easy for her to find one, even here in the city, now that she'd gotten used to the urban environment. The trees called to her, and she heard them. It was disentangling that from the background noise that gave her trouble.

She walked a couple of streets to a small public park. There were people around, walking their dogs or enjoying the fresh air and sunshine, so she had to wait a few minutes standing under a tree until no one was passing by. Then she pressed her hands against the bark, and the tree opened. She stepped into it, and the magic whisked her away.

She hurtled through the greenwood—the Earth's heart, the kingdom of the wild, a magical space with as many names as there were cultures in the world, and through which all trees connected. She felt at peace as she rocketed forward, surrounded by nature in all its glory. Then the wood in front of her burst open and she stepped out of a tree into one of the Tolderai's underground forests.

Mackam stood nearby, arms folded, watching as Toliver Jenkins strapped a sensor onto the wall. A light was blinking on the side of the black box and wires dangled from its sides. Where they touched the wall, the Tolderai magic that had grown the cave interacted with the technological magic on which Jenkins relied, and there was a shimmer in the air.

"It's hurting the roots," Mackam said. "I can see it."

"It's not hurting them," Jenkins said. "It's testing, taking readings."

"Next, you're going to tell me the lie that testing never hurt anyone?"

"I wasn't planning to—"

"Tell it to all the people the government has experimented on, or the lab animals in their cages with the electric shocks to make them move. Testing is a dangerous thing, science man, and if I think you're endangering our work here, I'll gut you."

"Oh, absolutely, science can be dangerous. So can a lot of things. That's why we need these tests." Jenkins noticed Heather and looked at her with relief. "Good to see you, Ms. Fields. Could you convince your colleague that I'm not a threat, and he can put his knife away?"

"Come on, Mackam." Heather gestured into the woods. "We have a meeting."

"You're leaving this one alone?" Mackam narrowed his eyes. "How do you know we can trust him?"

"Because if he does anything wrong, I'll set you on him."

They walked between the trees to the clearing in the center of the forest. Water rose in a steady fountain from a central pool. The magic of this place was strong, even by the cave's standards. It was the heart of it all, the point where the magic flowed from. That made it the perfect place to gather.

A dozen Tolderai stood around the clearing, the leading members of the tribe. They looked a lot more relaxed than they had around the factory conference table a few days before. Most of them had their shoes off so they could feel the moss and grass against their feet.

The Underfoot Brigade was with the Tolderai, as they often were now. The teenagers had been helping with the forest again that morning, while Heather was too busy to teach them. They probably learned as much this way as they did in the classroom, taking lessons from the Tolderai as they worked, picking up knowledge about plants and magic. It sometimes seemed to her that the Tolderai were also learning, given the eclectic knowledge of the Under-foots, with their diverse backgrounds and interests.

"Let's begin," she said. "We've seen magical interference again?"

"A flickering of the lights," Carol Winters said. "Like last time."

"We should get out there and deal with it." Mackam had his hand on his knife and a grin on his face. "Like last time."

"Responding without thought last time almost brought a world of trouble down on our heads," Heather said. "You will not repeat that, Mackam, and neither will anybody else. We will take the time to examine the situation and to work with our friends and allies on a solution."

"The Tolderai should be able to stand alone," Mackam growled.

"But you don't have to anymore."

Twylan stepped forward. She smiled, and the magic sparkled in her eyes. It was a perfect gesture to placate Mackam, friendly but showing strength. Heather wondered if the girl knew what she was doing or if it was instinct.

"We're here to help you," Twylan continued. "We know more about what lives in these tunnels, about the city above, even about bits of technology that you've been doing without. We've spent years scavenging and repairing to keep our home running. We can help you, and we want to."

"The lights that had trouble were along the north and east walls," Heather said, "where Jenkins is putting up the sensors now. Go over there, all of you. Look at the walls. Look at the lights. Look at the plants. Use whatever skills and abilities you have, and talk to each other about what you find. We need to work out what above us is causing harm."

They followed her back through the forest. Twylan and Leontine, leading the Underfoot Brigade, looked around as they walked.

"This still amazes me every time," Twylan said. "That we're making something so beautiful."

"It's nothing I ever expected," Leontine said, "but it seems right."

"I've been counting the trees," Siltor the elf said from behind them. "There are over seven hundred in this cave alone."

"You counted the trees?" Leontine looked back across his wings, incredulous.

Siltor shrugged. "I like numbers and distances and things I can count. Getting them right is useful for perfecting illusions." He waved, and an image of a spider appeared there. "See, eight legs, not six or ten. Numbers matter."

"Why don't you become an accountant?"

"Ms. Fields found me some books on more advanced math and finances. It's more interesting than I expected."

Twylan laughed. "A world of magic and mystery, and we're growing an accountant. Good for you, Siltor, breaking out of expectations."

"Not just me. Look at you. The teenage runaway turned Silver Griffin."

"I'm not a Griffin."

"Not yet, but give it time. We all know it's a sure thing."

They reached the edge of the cave and stood staring up at the wall of intertwined roots and branches. Farther along, Heather was talking with Mackam and Jenkins while they set up a light pillar close to one of the sensors. In between, other Tolderai and Underfoots were examining the wall and the lights fixed into it.

"So how do we do this?" Leontine asked, and to Twylan's surprise, he pulled a notebook from his pocket. "By we, I mean you. I have all the magical talent of a brick, so all I can do is take notes."

"I suppose we start by feeling our way through the background magic." Twylan sat cross-legged and began to focus herself. "What do you think, Siltor?"

"I'm going to set up a thin illusion and see what happens to it." The elf was twisting his fingers through the air, spinning filaments of magic. "Maybe nothing, but if there is disruption, it could tell me something."

Illusions weren't Twylan's specialty, so she closed her eyes, let her thoughts drift away, and focused on the magic already in the world around her.

The magic was strong down here, a force of nature carefully shaped by the work of the Tolderai, holding the place together. It was nurturing and reinforcing, and when she paid attention to it, she felt as though it was holding her up.

Around her, there was the power of her fellow magicals, from the ephemeral sparks of Siltor's illusions to the bright weave of Kix's crafting skill to the raw power of the Tolderai, nature in all its strength.

Then there was the magic from the city above. It was fainter, the magical equivalent of noise pollution drifting down through the streets and the dirt, but it was unmistakably present. They were sharper, darker, more uncomfortable threads of power than the rest. She focused on those strands, looking for any sign that they were harming the nature magic or that they had the strength to disrupt it, but they all seemed too faint.

"Guys, have you seen this?" Siltor asked.

Twylan tried to ignore him, to focus on her inner landscape and the magic it revealed.

"The lights," Siltor said. "They're flickering. That's what happened before, right?"

Twylan opened her eyes to look up. Sure enough, the

lights were flickering. Along the cave wall, other magicals had spotted the same phenomenon. Some climbed up to look at the lights more closely. Others conjured spells to examine them. Siltor appeared to be counting.

"You've noticed something, haven't you?" Twylan asked.

"Maybe..." Siltor held up a hand. "Give me a minute." He stood silent, staring at one of the lights, then moved his attention to one further down the wall. "Leontine, write down thirteen, and..." There was a long pause. "Sixteen." He moved his attention to one in the lowest layer of lights, right in front of their faces. His lips twitched as he counted. "And twenty-one."

The three of them gathered around Leontine's notebook, looking at the numbers.

"What is this?" Twylan asked.

"How often they flicker in a minute. The lower lights are flickering more often." Siltor tapped the twenty-one. "That means they're more affected by whatever's interfering."

"That doesn't make any sense. Magic from the city above should affect the higher lights more because it's not been through so much of the Tolderai's magical field, so there's more of it left. Unless..."

She closed her eyes and let her mind open to the magic again. There was the forest's magical field, and her friends' powers, and the faint drift of magic from above, all the things she expected to see. There was also something else, something she hadn't seen because she wasn't looking for it, just like nobody else was.

She opened her eyes and rushed off around the edge of the cave, past the gathered magicals, her way lit by the flickering lights. Heather turned from talking to Jenkins as Twylan approached.

"What is it?" the Tolderai chief asked, seeing the look on Twylan's face.

"The interference," Twylan said. "It's not coming from the city above. It's from down below."

CHAPTER TWENTY-FIVE

Charlie sat in the corner of the IT team's office, behind the row of monitors connected to his computer. Two screens showed parts of his job, including windows for job tickets and for a computer he controlled remotely, as he tried to fix a problem someone in finance had created on their machine. The third window showed the software he ran in the background to monitor events on the magical web, looking for any problems that Lucy should be aware of.

Soon, he would have to find another way to run that program. He could hardly run it on the office machines if he wasn't here. Maybe he should set up a rig at home especially for that purpose, and get it to monitor commercial opportunities for Green Machine Conversions too. Or perhaps he could suggest that the Silver Griffins install it on their network if they didn't have something like that already.

That wasn't Charlie's biggest worry about leaving this place though. His biggest worry was how the rest of the team would manage without him. High turnover meant that none of them had been there more than three years, and between their ages and personalities, they didn't exactly have the stuff needed to manage the awkward gap between what management requested and what was possible. What would happen to them without Charlie as a buffer?

"If you could be the hero of any movie, which one would it be?" Steve leaned back in his seat on the far side of the room. It was a quiet afternoon, the sort when they not only had time for idle chatter but needed it to keep them sane. These were the moments when Charlie appreciated having Steve on the team.

"Depends." Keiran, the youngest of the IT team, looked up from the monitor he'd been huddling close to. "Do I become the existing protagonist, so now I'm living as Luke Skywalker or Moana? Or is it a situation where I, myself, take their place and have to survive the film with the skills I have?"

"Ooh, good counter-question." Steve leaned forward. "Let's go with option two. That's way harsher."

"You think harsh is a good thing?" Charlie asked.

"In real life? No. In creating awkward hypotheticals for us to answer? Definitely."

"I'd pick a computer film," Keiran said. "Something like *Hackers* or *Sneakers*, where I could use my existing strengths."

"Good call, but you're thinking too small." Steve spread his arms wide. "Why not *The Matrix*? You could give yourself whatever skills you need, thanks to your elite programming abilities, then kick Agent Smith's ass."

"Too much responsibility. I don't want the whole of humanity depending on me."

"It's a film, man. You've got to lean into the stakes."

"I don't have to do anything. You wanted my answer, and that's it. *Sneakers*."

"Fine. What about you, Charlie? What film do you want to be in?"

Charlie pushed his keyboard aside and tried to ignore the other things on his mind. This seemed like as good a distraction as any. "Probably something early Linklater, like *Before Sunrise*."

"What is that, a *Twilight* knockoff?" Steve asked.

Charlie laughed. "It's about as far from *Twilight* as you can get. No vampires, no werewolves, just a couple falling in love over one night in Vienna, then deciding whether they'll ever see each other again."

"Romantic angst? Sounds a lot like a *Twilight* film to me."

"Well, it's a film with no danger and where the fate of the world isn't in my hands. If I'm stuck in a movie, that's the sort I want. Although I'd want Lucy there with me, in the female lead."

"Wait." Keiran held up a hand. The other was darting over his keyboard, looking up facts about the film. "You could be hooking up with a young Julie Delpy, the actual female lead of this film, and you're writing her out?"

"I don't want to hook up with Julie Delpy. I want a chance to fall in love with Lucy all over again."

Steve picked up his waste paper bin and made ostentatious barfing noises into it.

"I think it's cute." Keiran shrugged.

"Am I being patronized by you two?" Charlie asked. "Do I have to remind you who's the oldest one here?"

"With a film choice like that?" Steve asked. "No, you don't."

The door handle rattled. *Thumping* followed it.

"Did you idiots lock me out again?" Gail called through the door.

"Got to maintain security." Steve grinned. "Can't have outsiders wandering in here without permission."

"Or managers," Keiran added.

"Well, I'm not an outsider, so let me in," Gail retorted.

"Not until you tell me the password." Steve was really grinning now.

"What password?"

"The security password to get through the door. Don't you remember it?"

"No, I don't remember any damn password! This is me, let me in."

"Sorry, but no password, no entry."

"Fine. The password is 'Steve is an asshole, and he's going to get his ass kicked if he doesn't open this door right now.' Does that work for you?"

"Sorry, too long. Please try again."

Charlie sighed. "Keiran, go let her in."

"No, Keiran." Steve shook his head.

"Yes, Steve." Keiran made for the door. "You're not the boss."

Keiran unbolted the door and turned the handle. Gail burst in, fury in her eyes.

"I am going to get you back for that, jackass," she said, hurling a soda can at Steve.

"Totally worth it," he replied.

While Keiran was sliding the bolts back into place on the door, Gail walked over to Charlie's desk. He hastily switched off the magical monitoring screen and looked up at her. She raised an eyebrow.

"I just had a very interesting conversation with HR," she said.

"Really?" Charlie asked. "Have they asked you again to stop shouting at the junior accountants for using unauthorized macros?"

"No. Well, yes, but that wasn't this conversation. This one was about whether I'd like to lead this team."

"Ah." Charlie looked around the room. They all stared at him, Steve and Keiran dumbstruck, Gail enjoying her moment of power. "Look, I was going to talk to you all today, but we were busy this morning, then Gail wasn't here, so..."

HR was moving fast. He'd only just handed in his notice, and already they were seeking a replacement. He'd thought that he would have more time to deal with it all, but then he'd asked to leave as soon as possible, so what did he expect?

"You're leaving us?" Keiran looked crestfallen. "Why?"

"No way, man," Steve said. "Is this about Keiran annoying you because we can get rid of Keiran."

"Yes, we can get rid of me. No, wait..."

"It's not about any of you." Charlie stood and walked around to the front of his desk so they could all see him clearly. Gail stepped back, and the three of them formed a row, watching him expectantly.

"Look, I've been working on something else for a while,

a business with some friends of mine. It's starting to make money, we're getting more customers, and I'm proud of what we're achieving. If I want it to work, I need to commit myself to it full-time, so I'm leaving here."

"Wow." Steve nodded. "I mean, that is kind of cool. Are you gonna be the next Bill Gates, creating your own company from nothing?"

"That's unlikely."

"If it happens, you'll invite us to your celebrity parties, right?"

"Sure. If that happens."

"What sort of software are you making?" Keiran asked.

"I'm not. We work on cars."

"No programming?"

"Nope."

"But you love programming."

"I love this work too."

"Why would anyone give up on programming?" Keiran looked genuinely baffled. He was a young man who spent both his work and his leisure time in front of the computer and would have slept that way if he could. Nothing else fitted his worldview.

"What are you doing with cars?" Steve asked. "Speed boosters? Drag racing? Stereo systems?"

"I'm making them more environmentally friendly."

"How?"

Charlie hesitated. He couldn't tell them the truth, that it was mostly about magic, but he needed to tell them something, and he didn't want to get caught up in an awkward lie.

"That's proprietary information," he said with an

embarrassed smile. "You know how it is, got to protect the tech from competitors."

"Damn straight." Steve grinned. "You don't want Gail stealing all your ideas."

Gail rolled her eyes.

"I still enjoy what we do here, but I need a change." Charlie went back around his desk and rummaged for something he'd left there. "I'll miss you guys, though, and we'll have to meet up for drinks once I settle into my new routine. In the meantime, I brought you this..."

He pulled out a box and set it down on Keiran's desk. The others gathered around as Keiran opened the lid.

"Korean soft drinks," the junior programmer whispered in awe. "Some of these are so full of caffeine they're almost illegal."

"Japanese candy bars." Steve pulled out something with a bright pink wrapper. "Nice."

"What they mean to say is thank you," Gail said.

"Oh, yeah, thanks," Steve said around a mouthful of candy.

"Yes, thank you." Keiran opened a bottle and sniffed its contents. "Mm, glorious sugar and chemicals."

"Well, those should help us through the rest of the working day." Charlie smiled to see the others happy again. "Any more questions?"

There didn't seem to be. Both Steve and Keiran were distracted by their treats, and Gail looked through the basket to see what might suit her.

Charlie got back to work. After a few minutes, Gail came over and leaned against his desk, toying with a black-wrapped candy.

"Congratulations," she said quietly. "Good luck. I think you're making the right choice."

"Thanks." Charlie also kept his voice low so the others wouldn't hear. "Are you going to take the job? Somebody's going to have to lead this team once I'm gone, and I don't see either of them in charge."

Gail chuckled and shook her head.

"Not a chance. I handed in my notice today as well."

"Really?"

"Yep. Got headhunted by a Silicon Valley startup. I'm off to do some real programming."

"When are you going to tell the others?"

"Never. I'm going to vanish like a ninja into the night." She winked. "Leaving drinks are three weeks on Friday. You should bring Lucy."

Charlie looked back at his screen, with a list of support requests once again piling up. He didn't know how the place would get by without him or Gail. Chaos might be coming for his employers if they didn't recruit quality new staff fast. Fortunately, that wasn't his problem anymore.

CHAPTER TWENTY-SIX

There was a knock on the door of Gruffbar's office. He took his feet off the desk, brushed away the mud where they'd been, and shuffled a pile of papers into position, making the place look as professional as he could.

"Come in," he called.

The door opened, and two more dwarves walked in, followed by the mechanical noises of the auto shop floor. The dwarves were similar in appearance, with long dark beards and square features, probably part of the same clan rather than close relatives. The older one wearing traditional robes and with his beard flecked with gray led the way. It was the younger one wearing a suit who closed the door behind them, then pulled a seat into position for his elder.

"Chief Engineer Daffydson." Gruffbar bowed his head respectfully to the elder dwarf. "It is my honor to host you."

It usually paid to lean into traditional with people like Daffydson, who spent their lives deep down the tunnels and whose minds were fixed deep in the past. They expected respect, protocol, and familiar gestures, and took their absence as a sign of poor character.

"Gruffbar Steelstrike." Daffydson nodded back. "It is a good place you have here, setting up office alongside real workers."

Gruffbar ignored the "real" with all its implications about his work. He could afford to let a comment like that slide when there was so much else at stake. What was pride next to a contract working with one of the largest cross-world mining consortiums? Not only a mining consortium but a dwarf mining consortium, the gathering of many clans with all their skills and experience for the sole purpose of digging up minerals and making money off them. This single meeting, if it went well, could double Gruffbar's profits for the year and set him up for even more in the future. Oh yes, he could accept the implied insult, accept it with a smile.

"Would you care for refreshments?" Gruffbar asked. "Mead, perhaps? Or tobacco for your pipe? I have coffee, of course, but..."

"Erdric will have coffee." Daffydson gestured at his assistant. "I see that you have cigars..."

"Of course." Gruffbar opened the tactically positioned box of Cubans and pushed it toward Daffydson. Let the older dwarf think that Gruffbar meant to keep those to himself, that Daffydson had got one up on him, not that they were bought specially for the occasion. From what Gruffbar knew of the other dwarf, such a win would put him in a good mood.

He went to the machine in the corner and made two coffees. The assistant Erdric accepted one with a grateful nod. Gruffbar returned to his seat and lit a cigar for himself.

"Nice." Daffydson nodded at Gruffbar's solid lighter, with its cogwheel skull insignia. "A dwarf should own tools worth taking pride in."

"Thank you, Chief Engineer." Gruffbar sat back and blew out a cloud of smoke. This was how everyone should negotiate deals. "Now, what can I do for you?"

"I'm seeking new legal representation for our consortium after our previous lawyers failed us in a particularly crucial deal." Daffydson waved his cigar in the air. "Before deciding who to hire, we're bringing small pieces of work to a variety of firms to test their capabilities. I'm aware that you work alone, so you don't have the resources of some of your competitors, but you come highly recommended. And, of course, you have the advantage of being a dwarf."

"I'm honored that you would consider me at all." Honored and relieved. It would have been frustrating for them to exclude him after all the time and money Gruffbar had thrown into getting the consortium's attention. "What work have you brought me?"

Daffydson gestured at Erdric, who opened a briefcase and rustled through the papers inside.

Another movement caught Gruffbar's attention. A shadow shifted as if something were sliding under the door. It stopped when Gruffbar looked at it directly, but something about the shadows in that part of the room seemed off. Did they normally make those shapes?

Gruffbar looked at the nearby furniture, trying to see what he was missing.

Erdric held out a large envelope. "Here we have—"

"Wait." Gruffbar held up a hand. "Did you bring anyone else with you? Perhaps some sort of spirit guardian or a hidden bodyguard?"

"Certainly not." Daffydson's tone was indignant. "I would never bring deception into such a serious negotiation, and if that is the way you view my clan, perhaps you are not the lawyer for us."

Gruffbar reached under his desk and put his hand around the grip of his shotgun. "In that case, we have a spy in our midst."

He pulled out the shotgun as the shadow leaped at him. It was human-shaped, with a knife in each hand, and seemed detached from anything that might cast it.

A Shadow Man.

Gruffbar pulled the trigger. The shotgun roared. The Shadow Man jerked back as the shot tore his hand to shreds, smashing one of his knives on its way to blow a hole in the wall.

"Get back!" Gruffbar shouted at his guests as he pumped the shotgun to load a new round. The ax blade attached to the barrel glinted as he shifted his aim.

Daffydson scrambled from his seat and backed into the corner of the room. He pulled an ancient ax, more ceremonial than practical, from his robes and held it in trembling hands. Erdric stood between him and the shadow, briefcase held out like a talisman, one hand reaching inside his jacket.

Gruffbar half-expected the Shadow Man to go for

them. After all, Daffydson was an important man, the sort who accumulated enemies and drew the attention of assassins. Apparently, Gruffbar could collect enemies too because the Shadow Man lunged at him, the remaining knife stretched out.

Gruffbar pulled the trigger again, but at that moment the Shadow Man twisted so he was shooting at a shadow sideways on. The blast hit the filing cabinet instead, riddling it with holes and filling the room with an almighty *clang*.

Before Gruffbar could aim again, the Shadow Man was on him. It struck him across the face with the stump of its damaged hand, and the blow had incredible strength for a creature with so little substance. It knocked Gruffbar to the floor and set his head spinning. He tried to raise the shotgun, to at least use the ax to fend the creature off, but his fingers wouldn't do what he wanted. The Shadow Man crouched by Gruffbar's feet and raised its knife.

Two shots rang out in swift succession. The bullets hit the Shadow Man, knocking him back against the wall.

Erdric was in the middle of the room, a Desert Eagle pistol in his hand. He stood braced like a professional, the gun steady, his gaze holding steel that hadn't been there moments before.

"Hold right there," Erdric said. "One more move and I will end you."

"You?" the Shadow Man's laugh was rasping and hollow. "End me? With your pathetic, mundane toy?"

As the Shadow Man peeled itself away from the wall, Erdric fired again. Two shots punched through the Shadow Man's shoulder, and for a moment the creature faltered. Two dots of light showed against the wall where the bullets had punctured the shadow. With terrible speed, they closed up, leaving the creature intact. Then it was moving again, flinging itself at Erdric.

The gun fired, but the Shadow Man had twisted, and the bullets missed. Darkness fell on Erdric, his head jerked back, and the shadow knife slashed. His beard fell as his throat was sliced open by a blade sharper than any razor. With a *thud*, he hit the floor.

The room spun around Gruffbar as he forced himself upright. He tried to aim the shotgun, but everything kept shifting, and it was hard to keep his hands steady.

"Monster." Daffydson waved his ax. Magical runes glowed along the blade. "That was my cousin's eldest you killed there. I'll rip you open from top to tail for that."

The dwarf swung his ax. The Shadow Man caught the blow on its knife, then raised its other hand. Whatever damage Gruffbar had done, it had grown back, and the silhouette of a new knife darted through the air. Daffydson tried to dodge clear, but he was no warrior. The blow went straight into his chest. He gurgled and fell.

Gruffbar braced himself against the desk, trying to get the shotgun steady. The Shadow Man would be coming for him next, and if he were going down, he would go down fighting.

Except the Shadow Man didn't move toward Gruffbar. Instead, it crouched over Daffydson.

"You will do, Chief Engineer," it said in a voice like dead leaves. It slashed its blade across the floor by Daffydson's feet, then peeled his shadow away.

Footsteps approached cautiously on the stairs outside.

"Gruffbar?" Gunther shouted through the door. "You all right in there?"

"Does it sound like I'm all right?" Gruffbar's shout echoed off the blood-slicked floor and bullet-riddled walls.

The Shadow Man looked up.

The door burst open, and Gunther strode in with his largest wrench in his hand. Behind him came Charlie and Ringo, Charlie holding a wand, Ringo a Glock handgun. They stood uncertain, trying to make sense of what they were seeing.

In their moment of confusion, the Shadow Man took his opportunity. He dived between Gunther's legs and rolled out onto the stairs, then dashed down them two at a time, Daffydson's shadow hanging over his shoulder.

"Holy cow, man, what the hell was that?" Ringo pointed his gun after the fleeing shadow. "Should I shoot it?"

"Too late." Gruffbar set his shotgun down on the desk and walked over to the dead dwarves. His head was clearing, but it was too late for that too. Too late for anything, as far as Chief Engineer Daffydson and his bodyguard assistant were concerned. "Sorry about the mess. I'll pay for the repairs."

He stared down at Daffydson. What a terrible lost opportunity, a chance for profit torn away. Strangely, that wasn't the part that bothered him. It was the senseless waste of two lives, the sight of Erdric dead far too young.

Dammit, he really had been hanging around with the good guys too much when that was how he thought.

"What was this?" Gunther asked.

"A Shadow Man," Gruffbar said. "I used to deal with

them on behalf of Zero. I wonder if that's why they know me."

"Lucy said that they're up to something." Charlie knelt by the bodies and shook his head. "This is awful."

"I know these fuckers. I'm going to make sure it gets a whole lot worse for them," Gruffbar said with grim resolve.

CHAPTER TWENTY-SEVEN

Lucy took the chocolate peanut butter Cheerios cups out of the fridge and put them on a tray, along with cupcakes, donuts, and bowls of chips. Buddy looked up at her and *yapped* excitedly.

"Sorry, lad, but these wouldn't be very good for you. I'll get you a treat of your own later, okay?"

It was hard to tell whether or not Buddy had got the message, but he followed her either way, out of the house, around the side, through the bushes, to the trapdoor that led into the Mini Griffins' underground lair.

"I haven't thought this through, have I?" Lucy looked down the ladder. "How can I carry a loaded tray down there?"

Buddy barked.

"Yes, you want down as well," Lucy said. "I suppose I could carry you, but..." She pulled out her wand and waved it over the dog. "Subvolo."

Buddy lifted a few inches above the ground. He kicked his feet, made an excited noise, and rolled over in the air.

With a gesture of her wand, Lucy directed him down the tunnel until he landed at the bottom and she let the spell go.

"Now for you." She pointed at the tray. "Subvolo."

Levitating the snack tray above her, Lucy climbed down the ladder. At the bottom, the tray settled onto her outstretched hands, every snack still in place.

The tunnel lair was the liveliest she'd seen it in a long time. Two dozen kids, the whole host of the Mini Griffins, were there. Some of them sat on beanbags, playing board games or building Legos. Others stood in small groups, talking and practicing spells. In one corner, Ashley was showing off her string robots to the more science-minded kids.

Lucy made her way through the crowd to the refreshments table and set the snacks down next to bottles of soda, a jug of lemonade, and a stack of party cups.

"Who wants cake?" she called.

Immediately, a swarm of children descended. Aside from Eddie, the youngest of them were Ashley's age, while the oldest were peers of Dylan. Despite the gap in age and maturity, they all seemed to be getting along fine. Lucy wondered if that could last once the older ones hit their teens, but that was a worry for the future. For now, it was nice to see them all having fun together.

"Cakes!" Eddie said excitedly, taking a chocolate peanut butter Cheerios cup. A jelly worm dangled from underneath, and he swung it about so that the worm seemed to wriggle.

"Cakes you helped me to make," Lucy said. "Aren't you the crafty little baker?"

Eddie beamed, then tugged on one of the other kids' shirts.

"I made this." He held up the cake.

"Cool." The Mini Griffin smiled at Eddie. "Thank you."

There was a general sense of bustle and business as the kids collected their snacks, then a period of calm as they settled down to eat them. Conversations continued, but with pauses to consume the treats.

On the wall was a banner proclaiming "CONGRATU-LATIONS MINI GRIFFINS!" Dylan and Mia stood underneath it, talking spells and eating chips.

"Are the congratulations for anything in particular?" Lucy asked them.

"Nothing specific," Dylan said. "But we've had a lot of successes recently, and it seemed like a fun idea to celebrate."

"Plus we don't get to meet up much," Mia said. "Our conversations are usually over the Internet, or through the headsets Ashley made for us, so it's nice to meet in person."

"I didn't realize there were so many of you." Lucy looked around the room. She had seen some of these kids on Ashley's screen, but others were completely new to her. "It feels like Ashley's recruiting every young witch and wizard in L.A"

"Don't give her ideas," Dylan said. "She's already well on the road to world domination."

Lucy left Dylan and Mia to their conversation and went to see how Ashley was getting on. She wasn't the most enthusiastic of the kids where parties were concerned, but she seemed to be enjoying this one. With one hand she was holding a cupcake, and with the other she was tapping at the screen of a tablet, giving directions to a collection of her string robots. Half a dozen kids watched in excitement as the robots combined in different shapes, sliding over each other to form a pyramid, then a tube, then a cube.

"Usually, I use them to make more specific shapes for what we're doing," Ashley said. "But it's important to understand the fundamentals."

"Can you send them anywhere?" one of the kids asked.

"Anywhere they'll fit, yes, although they're slow to get there."

"Can you make any shape?"

"Almost. But the shapes aren't always as strong as I would like. I need to find a way to reinforce the robots for weight-bearing structures and heavy lifting."

"Can I have another go with them?" Tommy asked eagerly.

"Yes, but be careful." Ashley handed him the tablet and started eating her cake while she watched his efforts. The shapes he made were wobbly, but he was getting the hang of the new technology.

"What happened to your old robot?" one of the kids asked. "The one with all the sensors that you used to use to collect information?"

"Octo?" Ashley blinked. "He's still around somewhere. I haven't needed him since I've had the string robots."

She took another tablet off the shelf behind her. Like all of Ashley's electronics, she'd customized it to suit her needs, although Lucy barely understood what those needs were, never mind how she achieved them. Ashley tapped a button on the bright blue casing, the screen lit up, and she entered some more instructions.

There was a whirring sound from down the room. A shape rose out of a pile of beanbags and walked over to them, a large metal box with eight mechanical legs, a pair of grabbers, and an array of sensors and antennae. Lucy was sure it had been simpler at some point but had no idea how long ago that point had been.

Octo came to a standstill in front of Ashley. She stuck the tip of her finger in her mouth and sucked on it while she contemplated the machine.

"It's all right, sweetheart." Lucy crouched to talk on a level with her daughter. "I'm sure Octo doesn't mind that you've been leaving him alone all this time."

Ashley shook her head. "Of course he doesn't, Mom. He's a robot. But it seems like a waste not to use him."

She tapped her tablet screen, and the robot settled down in front of her, its legs retracting until its body was on the floor. Ashley drew a screwdriver from her pocket and started unfastening the side of the robot.

"Don't you want to play with your friends?" Lucy asked. "The party's now. You can rebuild your robot later."

The minute she said it, she realized that it was a stupid thing to say. The other kids were already crowding around, wanting to see inside what Ashley had created. More were coming from different parts of the room to see what the fuss was about.

Lucy stepped aside. She wasn't going to get in her daughter's way. Besides, Eddie was gobbling down his fourth or fifth chocolate peanut butter Cheerios cup, and she really shouldn't let him have any more sugar if she didn't want a very grumpy three-year-old when the rush wore off.

"Why don't you have a glass of milk to wash those down?" she asked, then whisked the plate out of sight while he was busy with his cup.

Of course, stopping him from consuming more sugar didn't eliminate what was already in him.

"I'm a monster!" he announced loudly. "Roar!"

The air around him shimmered, and he turned into a four-foot lizard, its tail swishing back and forth, teeth gnashing up and down. Lucy could hardly complain about him transforming at a party for magicals in their secret lair, so instead, she took a step back, pulled out her phone, and took a photo as other kids crowded around to see what Eddie had become. It was good to keep a reminder of these moments.

With so much attention, Eddie couldn't resist a chance to show off. The lizard became a gorilla, became a lion, became an eagle, all in quick succession. Then the eagle flew onto the table, strutted back and forth in an over-sugared way, slipped on a cupcake, and fell squawking on the floor.

"Ow!" Eddie wailed as he turned back into a little boy.

"It's okay." Lucy picked him up, dusted him off, and distracted him from whatever hurt. "You were a fantastic eagle. Everyone was very impressed."

"Best eagle?"

"Best eagle in the world."

As the afternoon wore on, the cakes and chips vanished. Eventually, the kids packed away the games, and the Mini Griffins started setting out rows of chairs and beanbags. At the front of the room, Dylan and Mia set up a whiteboard and markers.

"What's all this?" Lucy asked Ashley.

"Our meeting," Ashley replied.

"But the party..."

"That was lovely, Mom, but it's not the main reason we got together. We have to hear reports, assess our performance so far this year, and make plans for the next three months."

"This is all for a quarterly meeting?"

"What did you think it was for?"

Lucy shook her head. The ways of the Mini Griffins were a mystery to her, too serious for children and yet somehow not the same as the adult world.

"I worked out what to do with Octo," Ashley added.

"What's that, sweetheart?"

Ashley typed something into her tablet. With a whir of tiny motors, Octo walked over. String robots lay across its back and around its neck. Others clung to the arms and legs.

"Octo can act as a delivery system to get the string robots to places more quickly," Ashley said. "And as a core for some of the more difficult structures I want them to make."

"So he'll help them out?"

"It's a symbiotic relationship, both helping each other. They can get into spaces he can't reach and can act as an extended sensor array. Together, they're better than on their own."

"Sounds like a review of the Mini Griffins."

Ashley looked thoughtful for a minute, then nodded.

"You're right. Now please leave, Mom. Only Mini Griffins allowed from now on."

CHAPTER TWENTY-EIGHT

Twylan walked into the coffee shop and looked around. After the bright light outside, everything was a little harder to make out in here with her sunglasses on, but she could hardly take them off and let her magic show. Sometimes it was the little things that reminded her that she didn't fit in.

On the other hand, some moments made her feel like she was important, like she had a critical role to play in the part of the world that belonged to her. Today, that moment had been receiving a call from Heather asking her to meet. Twylan didn't know what it was about or why the woman had singled her out, but if the chief of the Tolderai could come to her with something important, that was surely a good sign.

From a table in the corner of the coffee shop, Heather waved. Twylan walked over and took the seat across from her.

"What would you like?" Heather asked by way of greeting.

"Hot chocolate, please," Twylan said.

Heather went to the counter. She returned a few minutes later with a tray holding two mugs and two plates of cake.

"I don't know what cake you like," Heather said. "There's apple or caramel. You choose."

Twylan took her mug and one of the plates, then tucked straight into the caramel cake. The Underfoot Brigade found enough food to get by, but there wasn't usually much spare for snacking, and good cake was a rarity. She devoured the first few mouthfuls eagerly, then paused, forcing herself to savor the rest.

"You have both." Heather slid the second plate across the table to Twylan. "You're hungrier than me."

"I can't." Twylan shook her head.

"You can and you will. You kids are poor. Thanks to our ancestors' art, the Tolderai are better off than we've been in years. If I want cake, I'll buy more later."

It was strange to hear an adult being so direct about matters of wealth and finance. Usually, they trod carefully around such subjects, especially when there was a big difference, which left many people feeling awkward. Twylan felt both unsettled by and appreciative of Heather's approach. It was unfamiliar but easier to deal with.

"Do you want my help with something?" Twylan asked.

"I want you to follow me," Heather said.

"Like, as a bodyguard? I think Leontine would be better for that. Or if it's to record what you're doing for social media, then you should get Kix and Siltor. They're both good at making people look better."

"It's not for those things."

Twylan tried to think of why else someone would want

another person to follow them, but she struggled to come up with any ideas. "Then what is it?"

"I think someone else might be following me. Someone who means me harm. If you follow from a longer distance, you might spot them, see what they do, learn more about them."

"I've never done anything like that before."

"You're a smart kid, observant, thoughtful. You know how to avoid attention. You've got the magical skills to spot strange things. You can do this."

"Why not ask one of the Tolderai? Mackam usually does investigation for you, doesn't he?"

"Mackam is..." Heather paused, frowned, and sipped her coffee. "If Mackam sees what's after me, I think he'll want to attack it. I don't want that. I want to learn how it works, how it behaves, what it can do. I don't want to capture it or kill it or chase it away. At least, not yet."

"That makes sense. Information is very useful."

"I said you were smart."

"Do you know who it is that's following you?"

"You've heard of the Shadow Men?"

"They attacked our home once. Now they're causing trouble all over the city." Twylan stabbed her second slice of cake with a fork. "Yes, I've heard of them."

Heather frowned. "Are you sure you can follow without getting carried away?"

"It's all right. I'm not Mackam. I don't want to get into a fight with one of them. Especially not on my own."

"Okay." Heather looked around. "It's hard to tell, but I think he was stalking me earlier, looking for a chance to catch me on my own. I killed one of them the other day, and this one is more cautious, biding his time."

"Give me three minutes. Then we can go." Twylan tapped her mug. "I don't want this going to waste."

"You're getting more assertive. That's good. Take your time. There's no rush."

In the end, it was ten minutes before Heather left the coffee shop. In that time, they worked out a route for her to follow. They chose one that would create opportunities to bring the Shadow Man into the open, for Twylan to spot him and watch what he did in different circumstances. Working out the route also meant she didn't have to stay in sight of Heather to follow her. If she had to fall back, she could pick up the trail again without trouble.

Heather stepped out of the building and headed up the street. As she went, a shadow peeled away from under a table outside the coffee shop and followed her.

A moment later, Twylan emerged. She looked along the street in the direction that Heather had gone. Sure enough, there was a shadow that wasn't quite right, something else moving in the shade cast by a builder on his way back to work. Twylan sensed the magic radiating from it. She waited a moment longer to make sure the shadow wasn't paying attention to her, then she followed.

They made their way through the streets of Los Angeles, along sidewalks that were active but not busy. There were never so few people that the Shadow Man could have attacked Heather without drawing attention from others, but seldom so many that other people's shadows completely obscured him. Twylan kept her distance, with

Heather sometimes in sight and sometimes hidden around a corner.

Watching the Shadow Man at work, Twylan almost admired his ability to stay hidden. It was a gift that the Underfoot Brigade had to use to survive from day to day, and she had plenty of experience in hiding her reality from the world, especially the magical side of herself.

This guy was a master of the art, sliding from shadow to shadow, using a mixture of magic and cunning to avoid drawing anyone's attention. From time to time, he had to risk emerging into the open as the person whose shadow he was hiding in headed in the wrong direction, and he latched onto someone else.

There was an extra jolt of magic any time he did that somewhere brightly lit. He could pass through bright spaces, but it was draining, dangerous perhaps, and he was throwing up defenses to make it possible.

Heather's path eventually took her off the streets and through a park. This was the riskiest part of the route and the one with the most potential. If there were fewer people around, the Shadow Man might try to attack Heather in another effort to steal her shadow. Conversely, if there were fewer shadows around, he might have to expose himself to keep her in sight, revealing more about his powers and his limits.

The Shadow Man stopped at the edge of the park. The person whose shadow he'd hidden in was walking past, so instead he attached himself to the shadow of a tree, staying mostly out of sight. Twylan watched from across the street as Heather walked farther and farther away and the

Shadow Man waited for someone he could follow. No one was going in the right direction.

If she'd wanted to trap the Shadow Man, Twylan could've stepped forward then, made hers the useful body to follow, and drawn him off to somewhere out of sight where she could apply her magic. She remembered the conversation with Heather, though. This was about learning. Fighting back could come later. Besides, someone so skilled at sneaking was likely to be a deadly fighter too, and Twylan wasn't confident she could take him on.

The Shadow Man grew impatient, swaying toward anyone who passed, hoping to hide in their shadow. When no one headed across the park, he broke away from the tree and started walking that way by himself. It was a sign of how far the Shadow Men were willing to push themselves.

The bright light meant that he might draw the attention of mundane people. It also meant that he was using a lot of magical power to protect himself. It was the magical equivalent of a flare lighting up in front of Twylan's eyes, something bright and sudden and dramatic.

It also wasn't enough. Whether running out of magic or deciding that it was better to be cautious, the Shadow Man retreated to his tree.

Heather disappeared from view.

The Shadow Man waited a few minutes longer, then attached himself to the heels of a man in a suit heading up the street. Twylan followed again. This wasn't the route that she and Heather had agreed, but the whole point was to watch the Shadow Man, and that was what she was doing. She saw him switch from one person to another, steadily working his way across the district until he reached the mouth of an alley.

It was quiet here, with very few people anywhere nearby and none in the alley. The Shadow Man gave up on concealment and skulked down the passage, a dark figure in the daylight. Then it slid down the gap around a utility hole cover and disappeared.

Twylan waited a few minutes to ensure he was gone, then walked over to the metal cover. She ran her fingers along the edge, felt the residual magic there. The Shadow Man left a distinctive trace, and though it was hard to be certain, Twylan felt like he had been here before, and the trail wasn't entirely fresh.

She pulled out her phone and called Heather.

"Where are you?" Heather asked. "I reached the end of the route, but you never turned up."

"I think I found one of their routes into the city," Twylan said. "I've learned a little about their tricks. Meet back at the coffee shop to talk about it?"

"Good idea. This time, I'm having cake too."

CHAPTER TWENTY-NINE

Jackie lurked outside the restaurant's doors, her phone in her hand. She knew she was a little early, unfashionably so, but she hadn't wanted to be late. Normally, the disapproval of stern people was something she could live with, even relish. She took it as a reflection on them rather than her. Still, she didn't want to disappoint Heather.

Sure enough, at only a couple of minutes past the hour, Heather arrived. "Sorry I'm late."

"Two minutes doesn't count as late, at least not by my standards."

"I should've been here, but I was working on something with Twylan."

"So that's why I haven't seen my sidekick all afternoon."

"Sorry, did you need her?" Heather frowned.

"No, no, I'm just getting used to her being there." Jackie pushed her hair back behind one ear. "I guess she has responsibilities to your forest too, now."

"It wasn't that." Heather shook her head. "Life is

becoming complicated. Hopefully, dinner will make it easier to deal with."

"Let's get some food then and maybe a couple of drinks to help the business talk go down easier."

"That would be good."

Jackie opened the restaurant door and ushered the Tolderai chief in. Heather was wearing her usual jeans and flannel shirt, but the shirt was better fitted than usual, and there were no mud stains on the jeans. Was it Jackie's imagination, or had Heather made an effort tonight?

She hoped it wasn't only her imagination. Then she got cross at herself for thinking like that. They were here to talk about the Tolderai forest. If she wanted anything else, she should be direct about it, not get into some schoolgirl nonsense.

The waiter led them to a table and handed over a couple of menus.

"Can I get you a drink while you're choosing your food?" he asked.

"Margarita, please," Jackie said.

Heather hesitated, then nodded. "I'll try that too."

"Very good." The waiter headed off.

"I don't drink a lot of cocktails," Heather said like it was a confession.

"Well, you can't go wrong with something tequila-based in a Mexican place." Jackie scanned the menu. Lots of food she was likely to make a mess with. Just great. On the other hand, it all looked pretty delicious.

Heather nodded and set down her menu, apparently having decided already. Jackie allowed herself a couple more seconds to decide, then did the same. Part of

Heather's appeal was her decisive, no-nonsense approach, so she might as well imitate it.

"We should talk about the forest," Jackie said. "How the Griffins can help you protect it, and how we can get early warnings from it about danger."

"Your Jenkins has helped with that already," Heather said. "One of the Underfoot children noticed a pattern in the magical interference on the walls. Jenkins' sensors let us measure the pattern more precisely. There is some interference from below. I don't know what it means yet, but Jenkins seems insistent that the precision will help."

"Jenkins always thinks his devices are going to help. Sometimes he's even right. Have you tried reading that book of spells he gave you?"

"The cover put me off. I've put it away for now."

"Same here. It's hard to concentrate when you know that Jenkins and Nigel are on the other side of the page, grinning like idiots."

The waiter returned with their drinks, took their food orders, and hurried away again. Heather sipped her cocktail, looked at Jackie, and even managed a little smile. "That's good."

"One of my favorites."

"That's good to know."

A comfortable silence fell as they both sipped their drinks. In the background, a mariachi band played over the restaurant's speaker system.

"How are the tribe getting on with Jenkins and his forest visits?" Jackie asked.

"Fine. He's helpful, in his way."

"In his way?"

"He's odd but no odder than Mackam."

"I've met Mackam, and that's the faintest praise I've ever heard anyone damned with."

"Fair. But it's true. There are certainly worse people you could've sent, so thank you."

"Happy to help." Jackie hesitated, her fingers around the stem of her cocktail glass, slowly rotating it on the table. The alcohol was starting to relax her, but there was a lot of tension to fight against. "Would he be suitable for a liaison between the Griffins and yourselves?"

"A liaison?" Heather looked up from her glass.

"Someone needs to coordinate between the two groups. If you get on with Jenkins, he might be a good choice on our side."

"I get on with you. Can't you carry on being my contact point?"

"Is that what you want?"

"Yes."

Jackie smiled. "All right then, I'll do it. You said 'my contact point,' so I presume you'll still be the representative of the Tolderai?"

"If that works for you."

"Yes, definitely."

"Good."

"Then here's to a successful liaison." Jackie raised her glass. "So to speak."

"So to speak." Heather raised her drink, and they *clinked* glasses, then drank. That little almost smile was back, and it made Jackie want to grin too. It was hard to remain professional when you had cocktails. She didn't know yet whether that was a good or a bad thing.

The waiter appeared with a laden tray.

"Ladies, your meals." He set each dish down in front of them. "And some jalapeno poppers to share, on the house." That plate went in the middle of the table. "You two have a great night now."

He winked ostentatiously and hurried away.

"What was that about?" Heather asked.

"I think...." Jackie drew a deep breath. "I think that he thinks we're on a date."

"Oh."

Silence fell. To Jackie, it didn't seem half as comfortable as it had before.

"The thing is—" she started to say.

"I thought that—" Heather began in the same instant.

They both stopped, laughed awkwardly, and looked at each other, waiting for the other to speak.

"You go first," Jackie said.

Now it was Heather's turn to draw a deep breath.

"I was thinking that I wouldn't have minded it being a date," she said.

Jackie grinned. "The thing is, I was thinking that too."

"Really?"

"Really. I mean, we were meeting for dinner outside of work, and I know we don't technically work at the same place, but still, going for dinner feels different from talking over coffee in the staff room."

"I agree."

"So I wasn't sure what you were expecting, and I was half-hoping you might also see it as a date."

"I wasn't sure either." Heather downed the last of her

margarita, then waved the glass at the waiter. "I was also hoping... I don't know what, but I was hoping."

"It's not very professional of us, is it, mixing work and pleasure like this?"

"I'm the chief of my tribe. I don't have that boundary."

"Nice excuse. Wish I had one like it."

"Borrow mine. I'm happy to share."

Heather laid her hand down on the table next to the sharing plate. Jackie did the same. The tips of their fingers touched.

"Another margarita," the waiter said, setting the drink down in front of Heather. "Would you like one too?"

"Yes, please," Jackie said.

"Good, because I made you one." The waiter set a margarita down in front of her, whisked away the empty glasses, and vanished from view.

"Shall we..." Heather gestured at the poppers.

"Good idea." Jackie grabbed one of the spicy stuffed peppers. "I need to get some food inside me before this next drink, and I do want this next one."

A quiet fell between them again as they ate. With some of her other friends, Jackie would have found it uncomfortable. With most of them, someone would have spoken to fill the silence. With Heather, it seemed easy. There wasn't a need to make lots of noise and fuss. She wasn't like anyone else Jackie knew, and in this case, that was a good thing.

"We should probably talk about the forest," Jackie said as she neared the end of her quesadilla. "After all, that's why we came here."

"Is it?" Heather raised an eyebrow.

Jackie laughed. "The answer to that is both yes and no, but let's have the conversation anyway. That way, I'll have something to report to my inquiring colleagues tomorrow."

They talked for a while about the practicalities of what they were planning. What they could learn from the underground forests, what the Griffins could supply for their defenses, and how they would coordinate their efforts. Jackie made notes on her phone so she could write it up the next day.

There would be procedures and protocols to craft and lots of details to iron out, including ones around costs and people's time. However, she felt more confident now, and not only because of the margaritas. This was going to work.

They finished their meal, and a third round of cocktails, before leaving a big tip for their waiter and heading out onto Sunset Boulevard. It had gotten dark outside while they were talking, and there was the very first hint of a fall chill on the breeze. Neither witch asked where they were going. They simply started strolling down the sidewalk together, arms so close that Jackie could feel Heather's presence as a tingle of excitement across her skin.

"You should probably come into the office soon," Jackie said. "To approve the procedures and set a seal on the work part of this evening."

"What about the part that isn't work?"

They turned to face each other. Jackie wasn't sure who took hold of whose hand, but their fingers interlaced, Heather's thumb brushing Jackie's skin with a softness that was teasingly different from the Tolderai's usual gruff manner.

"We can set the seal on that now," Jackie said.

They kissed, and for a long moment, the city faded away. All Jackie noticed was the softness of Heather's lips, the warmth of her body, and a firm hand running up her back.

A car roared past, the engine making an unhealthily loud noise.

"Hell yes, ladies!" someone yelled from the car window.

"The sweet serenade of an L.A. night." Jackie laughed. "That's about as romantic as this city gets."

Heather pulled her close again. "This is as romantic as I will ever need."

CHAPTER THIRTY

Lucy crept along the back of a row of stores, her wand in her hand. Although most of the stores were retailers, their trash full of innocent packaging, a couple of them sold food, with the inevitable smell of rotting remains from one of the dumpsters. She waved the wand under her nose, summoning up a magical mask that would filter out the worst of the smell, and kept advancing, looking all around for her prey.

"Come out, come out, wherever you are," she whispered as she looked to the right and left. The charm she'd cast over the stores should have driven out the rustroaches that had been causing trouble inside. Now she had to catch them before they found their way out of the alleyway.

It was a morning of intermittent clouds, with the dull light casting muted shadows. Lucy peered into the gloom underneath the dumpsters, prime ground for magical vermin-like rustroaches. They must be around here somewhere, but there were a lot of places to hide.

A sound made her look around. Something fell off one

of the dumpsters farther into the darkness at the back of the alley. Something must have dislodged it, perhaps even the roaches. Lucy crept that way, wand at the ready.

The Shadow Stalker flowed from the shelter of one dumpster to another, never taking his gaze off Agent Lucy Heron. The trick with the rustroaches had worked better than he could have hoped. The Griffins had sent one of their best agents to deal with the problem, a target more than worthy of the magic that would bring about the Shadow Time.

He moved around behind her and slowly drew his blades. He had done things right at Gruffbar's office, but the ambush had still gone wrong, thanks to the skills and observation of his opponents. He had grown careless, practicing his craft on mundanes and low-level magicals. Against people of skill and power, he needed to work harder. He needed to be the best hunter he could be.

The agent crept farther into the alley, her wand raised, looking to the right and left. She didn't look back. Why would she when she was stalking vermin?

The Shadow Stalker looked back over his shoulder, just in case. There was nobody there.

Time to do this.

The faintest of sounds made Lucy look to her right. She felt as if she had seen something move, but now it wasn't there. No rustroaches crawling between the garbage or gnawing on the pipes. No movement at all.

Then she saw it out of the corner of her eye, a moment of movement, a dark and pointed shadow shifting against the ground.

She spun and raised her wand as the Shadow Man swept his blade around. The knife hit the wand in a shower of magical sparks.

"Stupefacio!" Lucy snapped.

The Shadow Stalker twisted, and the spell shot past him. He swung his knife again, but Lucy cast another spell and a magical baton extended from her wand. She caught the knife on it. The two of them shoved and strained, pushing against each other, a battle of strength and will.

Lucy didn't see the kick coming. It was hard to make out the movements of the Shadow Stalker, here among the shadows of the alley. The blow hit her in the stomach as if from out of nowhere, doubling her over in pain. She crumpled, and another blow hit the back of her head as the Shadow Man brought his fists down together. She fell to the ground, pain shooting through her skull.

The Shadow Man sank to his knees, grabbed a fistful of Lucy's shadow, and slashed at it with his knife. The shadow detached from her at one of her feet.

A wave of dizziness swept through Lucy, a sense of weakness and of the world growing more distant. She lifted her wand, but it was as if she wasn't quite there—like she was watching the alley from a distance and herself in it.

"Stupefacio," she mumbled.

The stun spell shot from her wand, but her aim was off.

The magic missed the Shadow Man and spattered futilely against the brickwork.

The Shadow Man lashed out, knocking the wand from Lucy's hand. Although reality felt distant, she still felt connected enough to know that was a very bad thing. She rolled over and stretched for the wand, but it was out of reach. She crawled toward it, but the Shadow Man yanked at her shadow, hauling her back. With a final effort, she flung herself across the ground and grasped her wand between the tips of her fingers. She rolled over, ready to cast a spell.

The Shadow Man's blade came down, severing Lucy's shadow. The world of light and substance, the world she lived in, faded away.

The Shadow Stalker looked down at the famous Agent Heron, lying on her back in the filthy alleyway, her wand limp in her hand. Her eyes stared vacantly into the sky, but he knew that she would see no clouds. She wasn't here anymore. Her mind was gone, severed from her body by the same blows that had severed her shadow. Magic had cut her apart.

He slung the shadow over his shoulder. It was a shame that they had lost the Shadow Steward, and not only in the way that it was when any of the Shadow Men fell. The Shadow Stalker had respected the Steward's way with figures and records, but the man had been getting ideas above his station. There had been a delight in putting him in his place. Turning up with a prize like this, then forcing the Shadow Steward to record it in his ledger, would've been a powerful reminder of who the real hunter was.

Never mind. There were other Shadow Men still. The Mage would thank him for his efforts. The Sentry would understand that this had been a tough fight and acknowledge the Stalker's skills.

Still, he missed the Steward. What was life without someone to channel your bitterness against?

The Shadow Stalker slung Lucy's shadow over his shoulder, pulled up a utility hole cover, and descended into the world where darkness reigned.

Lucy sat in her Rivian outside Ashley's school. Buddy was in the passenger seat next to her, his feet on the dashboard and his tongue hanging out as he watched gummy worms rain down outside the window.

"I used to love the school run," Buddy said. "It was a great chance to get out of the house, stick my head out the window and feel the wind blowing my ears about."

"Sorry," Lucy said. "It got too complicated, bringing you along while picking up all three kids. You understand, right?"

"Oh, yeah." Buddy licked his paw, then sat back in his seat. "Things change. Like that rain is changing."

Sure enough, the gummy worms had turned to silver snakes that rattled metallically on the roof as they fell.

"Oh, Ashley." Lucy laughed. "She's even got her robots into the rain clouds. That girl is so smart."

She turned the key and started the engine. She had a

case to solve in the next street over. Something urgent for her and her partner. In the seat next to her, Jackie let go of a pigeon, and it started flapping around their heads.

"Weren't you Buddy a moment ago?" Lucy asked.

"Things change," Jackie said. "Shadows fall. The world moves on."

"I guess."

Lucy started to pull away from the curb, then stopped. Where there had been a school and houses, there were trees now, ones she had seen on a trip to the New Forest when she was a kid. Something wasn't right. What had she forgotten?

There was a tingling in the tips of her fingers, a tingling that cut through to the calculating, analytical part of her mind.

"This is a dream, isn't it?" she said.

"How could you tell?" the pigeon asked.

"I'm not sure, but I have power in dreams, don't I? I've beaten bad guys in them."

"You certainly have," said Mr. No's voice from the pigeon's beak.

"Well then, I can do it again. I step into the space between dreams, right? Something like that..."

It was hard to organize her thoughts, to remember what she could do and how. It was as if pieces were missing, and without them, the rest wouldn't quite fit together.

"I can do this." She pushed on the car door, willing it to open onto somewhere else. When she stepped out, instead of emerging into the darkness between dreams, she was in her kitchen with bags of flour floating all around her. "This isn't where I'm supposed to be. It isn't somebody else's dream, is it? I'm still inside my head."

"Perhaps," one of the bags of flour said. "Does it really matter?"

"Of course it matters!"

"Except you can't wake up. You're not asleep."

"Of course I am. Otherwise, I wouldn't be dreaming."

"Oh, sweetheart," the flour said, "it's not that sort of dream, remember?"

Then she did. The memory hit her like a punch to the brain. Creeping down the alley. The movement behind her. The attack. That knife, as insubstantial as breath and as deadly as poison, slicing her shadow away. She gasped at the grim reality of it all.

"They got me," she whispered. "I'm in a coma, like the others."

The bags banged against each other, making a round of applause. Loose flour clouded the air.

"No, I don't accept this," Lucy said. "This might not be normal, but I'm still in the dream realm. I still have power here. I only need to find it."

"How are you going to do that?"

The memory had become part of the dream. Lucy stood over herself, lying on her back in the alley, no shadow under her, staring blankly at the sky. Her wand lay loose in one hand.

Lucy's fingertips tingled.

"Here's how."

She took hold of her unconscious counterpart's hand and closed limp fingers around the wand. As she did so, the tingling in her fingers increased. She held out her hand, and the wand appeared in it.

"Surgit," she said, and magic spilled from the wand. "Wake up." Power tugged at her, but the dream held her firm. "Wake up." The power intensified, and she felt as if it was pulling her in two directions at once. "Wake up!"

The power rushed in, the alleyway crumpled, the flour bags screamed, and the world around her vanished.

Lucy woke with a start in the alleyway. She sat bolt upright, her wand in her hand.

A rustroach stared at her from under a dumpster, then scurried away. There was no sign of the Shadow Man.

Lucy forced herself to her feet and looked down. Though sunlight was shining brightly down the middle of the alley, she cast no shadow.

CHAPTER THIRTY-ONE

It shouldn't have felt weird for Charlie to be walking into Gunther's auto shop. After all, he'd been there dozens of times over the past few weeks, working on cars with Ringo and Max amid the sounds and sights of the other mechanics at work.

Today was different. Today, he wasn't rushing in at the end of the afternoon after a day at work. He wasn't turning up on Saturday morning to spend his day off rummaging around inside a machine. He was in the shop first thing on a weekday morning, so bright and early that almost no one was around. Because today, for the first time, this wasn't a hobby or a side hustle. It was his job.

He walked up to the corner where Green Machine Conversions did their work. To his surprise, he wasn't the first one there. Max was sitting on a folding chair, a laptop perched on his knees. He smiled and waved hello.

"You're early," Max said.

"You're earlier," Charlie pointed out.

"I'm used to working lawyer's hours, and sometimes

they get insane. Plus I wanted to get some admin done before it gets noisy in here."

Hunched over his laptop like this, Max looked a little like a vulture, shoulders hunched and head hanging down. It couldn't be healthy.

"Isn't there somewhere better you can do that?" Charlie asked. "Maybe we could fit a desk in here somewhere..."

"Really?" Max raised an eyebrow. "And what would we get rid of to make space for it?"

The two wizards looked around their workspace. In the few months of its existence, Green Machine Conversions had acquired a whole heap of specialist parts and equipment from welding torches to exhaust filters to jars of fairy dust. The racks that Charlie and Ringo had built along their stretch of the wall were increasingly crowded and increasingly hidden behind other boxes full of supplies. There was barely space to fit in the cars they worked on, never mind extra furniture.

"Okay, maybe not. Can't you do the admin work at home?"

Max frowned. "Yes and no. Kelly's supportive of all of this in theory, but seeing me working on company business reminds her that I'm working with you, which reminds her of Lucy, which puts her in such a bad mood that I can't get anything done."

"Ouch." Charlie winced. "It's not that bad at my place, but it's still a thing. Lucy tenses up any time I mention you or Kelly."

"It feels more than a little unfair." Max closed the laptop. "I mean, we're left walking on eggshells because they're not getting on."

"Is there anything we can do about it?"

Max shrugged. "If there is, I haven't thought it up yet, and I've been trying."

They got into their overalls, checked the list of the day's jobs, and started getting out the necessary tools and components. They were looking at information about one of the cars, trying to decide how to approach its exhaust, when Ringo strolled in, already in his overalls.

"Hey, guys." He slung his bag down in the corner. "First day working together full-time. You all ready for this?"

"Not only ready but enthusiastic," Charlie said. "I might not have slept much last night."

"So that's why you're both here so early."

"It's not that early, is it?"

Ringo pointed to the clock on the wall. "First client's not due for fifteen minutes, and you've already got all this stuff out. That shows an unsettling level of enthusiasm."

"Well, if we have fifteen minutes..." Charlie rummaged in his bag and took out a tub of cookies. "These are a first-day treat, baked by Lucy last night."

He and Max exchanged an awkward look, but a reminder of their wives' feud wasn't going to stop them from enjoying the cookies.

"Those should last us a while," Ringo said, looking at the heap of treats.

"They're not only for the three of us, but I figured we should get one first before I put them in the break room. I can't imagine they'll last long around Gunther's crew."

They each took a cookie and stood waiting while the other mechanics arrived.

With a roar, a black Harley Davidson rolled in off the

street and up to its parking spot close to the Green Machine Conversions working space. Gruffbar climbed down off the bike, hung his helmet over the handlebars, and secured it with a solid chain.

"Morning, man." Ringo nodded at the dwarf lawyer.

"Would you like a cookie?" Charlie asked, holding out the box.

"Sure, why not." Gruffbar took one. "Your wife's work?"

"Of course."

"She should be a baker."

"They are good, aren't they?"

"Yeah, and it would make life easier for some of my clients."

Gruffbar and Max exchanged a small nod, as much greeting as they'd managed in the past few weeks. It was a reminder to Charlie of the other awkwardness Max faced here. It had been Gruffbar who beat him in court, wrecking his legal career. The auto shop's personnel couldn't have been comfortable for him to be around, and yet Max kept turning up, his enthusiasm for their work undiminished. It was impressive, in a sad sort of way.

Gruffbar looked up the steel stairs at the back of the building to his office door.

"Cleaners have been in." Ringo's voice was quieter than usual. "Gunther says they've gotten rid of the, um..."

"The bloodstains," Gruffbar said firmly. "No need to dance around that. It won't be the first time I've worked where I've seen people die." He talked with confidence, but he still didn't approach the stairs, just stood looking at them and the door at the top.

An idea struck Charlie. "Hey, Gruffbar, could we maybe

sublet the office from you when you're not using it? It wouldn't have to be anything too formal, but Max could do with office space, and we can't exactly set that up here."

"Sure, why not." Gruffbar stroked his beard. "Hells, you can probably have the office. I'm thinking of leaving town anyway."

"Really?" Max looked stunned. "After your success against Nuada, surely half the clients in L.A. want to hire you?"

Gruffbar shrugged. "Sure, I guess. The sort of practice I've got going here, I'm not sure it's the sort I want. Too many bad people doing bad things."

"Isn't that your bag, man?" Ringo asked. "I mean, no offense, but you ain't exactly been good people yourself."

"What can I say? You law-abiding losers are rubbing off on me."

"So you're changing your ways?"

"Modifying them slightly, to see how it feels. That'll be easier without the weight of L.A. hanging around my neck." Gruffbar drew a deep breath. "You know what, it was only an idea before. Now that I say it out loud, it feels right. Thanks."

"And the office?"

"I'll let Gunther know I'm leaving and suggest he talk to you. He'll be happy to get a new tenant so quick, especially one he already knows." At last, Gruffbar headed for the stairs. "I'm not gone yet, though. Looks like it's time to get to work."

With the dwarf gone, the wizards turned back to their schedule for the day.

"What have we got first?" Ringo asked.

"An interesting new challenge for you guys," Max said.

"Interesting how?"

"Like that."

Max pointed at the entrance, where a camper was rolling in. Directed by one of the other mechanics, the driver steered it carefully up to the Green Machine Conversions space, then brought the looming vehicle to a stop.

"You haven't done one of these before, have you?" Max asked.

"Nope." Ringo grinned. "Should be fun."

The driver opened the door and climbed down. He was a slightly portly wizard in flip-flops, baggy shorts, and a Hawaiian shirt. His red face was half-hidden by a sun hat and aviators, but even after he took off the shades, it took Charlie a moment to recognize him.

"Roger?" he asked. "That's a very different look."

"Charles, always a pleasure to see you." Roger Applegate beamed. "I'm trying on my retirement outfit today. It doesn't feel right to drive this thing while dressed in a three-piece suit."

"I didn't know you had a camper."

"I didn't. Wouldn't have had time to make use of it. Now..." He patted the side of it. "Once I finish at the Griffins, I'm going to tour the country. I want to see the Grand Canyon, Yosemite, Mount Rushmore, all the sights. Might even head up into Canada and explore the wilderness."

Charlie stood stunned. This was as far as he could imagine from Lucy's smartly dressed, desk-bound manager. He would have expected Applegate to be a luxury hotels and ocean cruises kind of guy, not one for living out the back of a vehicle.

"Is your wife going with you?" he asked.

"Oh, yes. For some of it, at least. She's not as keen on fishing as I am, but she'll get to go birdwatching while I relax by a river somewhere and watch the world go by. After the hectic year we've had at the Griffins, I can't imagine anything better."

Gunther's auto shop didn't see a lot of vehicles like this, and a few mechanics had wandered over to have a look. When Ring opened the hood, half a dozen figures in overalls gathered to peek inside.

"Can you clean up her emissions?" Applegate asked. "If I'm going to spend my retirement enjoying the beauty of nature, I don't want to destroy it with fumes at the same time."

"I'm sure we can." Charlie accepted the vehicle's keys. "It might take a while, though. This is the first camper van we've converted, so we'll be working it out as we go along."

"No rush. I've not quite hit retirement yet."

"I'll give you a call when it's ready."

"Marvelous. I'll be in the office, but nobody is going to mind if I leave early. After all, who would they complain to, me?" Applegate laughed.

"You're going in like that?" Charlie tried to imagine the Silver Griffins' reactions.

"Certainly not." Applegate waved his wand and his casual clothes transformed into his familiar suit. He stowed the wand away inside his jacket, straightened his tie, and headed for the door. Behind him, Charlie and his colleagues settled down to work.

CHAPTER THIRTY-TWO

"Is it me, or does the phrase 'cream cheese wontons' just not sound right?" Ellis asked, staring in confusion at his menu.

"Sorry, what was that?" Sarah looked across the table at him, her gaze coming back into focus.

"Just saying that cream cheese wontons seems kind of odd."

"I suppose." She smiled. "Now that I think about it, they sound intriguing. Maybe not very authentic Thai cuisine, but very Los Angeles."

"Well, if you're interested, do you want to split some as a starter?"

"If we can share some vegetable tempura too." She licked her lips. "I love tempura."

"If you want it, we'll have it." He reached across the table and squeezed her hand. "Given how hard you've been working lately, you deserve all the battered vegetables you want."

"You say the sweetest things."

They laughed and went back to reading the menus. Ellis was glad he'd been able to drag Sarah out for date night. She'd been so busy over the past few days, her hours filled with hospital shifts and tending to the coma patients at Silver Griffins' HQ, that they'd barely had a minute to themselves. Seeing her pass in the corridor at HQ didn't count. They could hardly have a cozy, intimate moment with messenger pigeons squawking past and other Silver Griffins butting in.

Of course, a restaurant wasn't a private space either, as Ellis remembered when the waiter turned up with their drinks and took their food order. At least a waiter knew to get back out of the way, unlike those pigeons. And here, nobody was going to try to talk to them about work.

"How's work going?" Sarah asked.

Ellis laughed. "Sorry, I was thinking about how we'd gotten away from work for once."

Sarah laughed too. "I guess it follows you, especially if you have the sort of job where you can be on call."

"Or the sort you care about. I know folks I grew up with; they wound up in office jobs they don't care about one way or the other. They step away at the end of the day, and that's it. Come the weekend, and they go two whole days without considering what's waiting when they go back."

"Sounds healthy."

"Maybe, but is it really healthy to spend half your waking life doing something you don't care about? Something that matters so little you can leave it behind like that?"

"When you put it that way, I guess not." Sarah raised her glass. "A toast: here's to jobs that won't let us go."

"To those jobs."

They *clinked* and drank. Ellis glanced out the window, half-expecting the conversation to have summoned a messenger pigeon calling him into action, but for once his luck was holding. Maybe tonight, they would be left to their own devices.

"You wanna go see a movie at the weekend?" he asked. "I hear there's a new *Fast and Furious* film out. Course, there's almost always a new *Fast and Furious* film out, but that don't mean we can't enjoy it."

He looked at Sarah, but she only stared at the tabletop.

"Or we could find something more to your tastes," Ellis continued. "There must be some cute animated thing out, like those Disney films you showed me. How about it?"

"Hm?" Sarah looked up. "Oh, yes, that sounds great. Disney. Yes."

"You okay there?" Ellis raised an eyebrow.

"Sorry, I got distracted thinking about my patients. It's like we were saying, the downside of having a job you care about."

Their starters arrived, and the conversation was interrupted while the waiter laid plates out on the table. As the waiter departed, Ellis picked up one of the wontons and examined it.

"Guess it's time to give this a go." He took a bite, then smiled. Cream cheese wonton wasn't the atrocity he'd feared. "This is good. You should try one."

Sarah's gaze had grown distant again.

"Sarah?" Ellis waved a hand in the air. "Seriously, you

should try one. Or maybe go for some of that tempura instead?"

"What?" She shook her head. "Sorry, bad day for this."

"You sure you're okay?" Ellis looked at her with concern. He was used to her getting distracted occasionally, everyone did that, but this was on another level. She was barely even in the room with him.

"I'm fine, yes. A bit tired, perhaps." She dipped a battered mushroom in chili sauce but didn't get as far as taking a bite. "It's these poor people in the comas. I can't get them out of my mind."

"The ones without shadows?"

"That's it. I want to make them better, but nothing I've done so far seems to work. The best I can do is make them comfortable, but now they've started dying, and anything I do feels like delaying the inevitable." She sighed. "It's all so dispiriting."

She finally put the mushroom in her mouth and chewed on it, mechanically, joylessly, as if her favorite food meant nothing to her.

Once again, Ellis reached across the table. This time, he took her hand gently, feeling the softness of her skin, a miracle in itself given all her hard work, making that touch a reminder to her that he was there.

In some ways, he wanted to distract her, to take her mind off of what was causing her this strain. To lighten her spirits and make her smile. To bring back the happy, light-spirited woman he'd fallen in love with.

Still, even if he could've made her laugh, it wouldn't have been real. It would've been a cover for the strain that was dragging her down. They needed to fix this, not sweep it aside. That was how it worked when you made your job the heart of your life.

Under the table, he pulled out his wand and cast a discreet spell. Now, their words would be muffled to the other diners and passing staff, removing any risk of being overheard and leaking stories of magic into the mundane world. He put his wand back in his pocket and turned his full attention to Sarah.

"Talk to me about it," he said quietly.

"Don't be silly." She shook her head. "It's hardly date night stuff."

"It's part of the world that connects us. It's something we can both understand. It's something we're both passionate about. There ain't a better topic for date night."

She gave a hollow laugh and squeezed his hand.

"All right, you asked for it."

Slowly at first, but with increasing animation, Sarah talked about the condition of the patients and all the different approaches she'd taken to try to understand what was wrong with them and to make them better. There was a lot of medical jargon that Ellis only half-understood, but he didn't interrupt. His role wasn't to provide a solution. It was to let Sarah get this off her chest and to help her think through a situation that was far more her area than his.

When they got onto magic, he understood it better. None of the spells Sarah had tried had worked so far, indicating the magic that had cut away the victims' shadows, put them into comas, and seemed to be drawing them slowly toward death, was more powerful than anything she was throwing at it.

Even understanding that shadow magic had proved

difficult. The condition of the patients was too unfamiliar, too different from the magic that witches and wizards worked with.

"The patients are still deteriorating," she said. "It's only a matter of time before more die. The only sign of hope is what happened with Lucy."

"How she woke up despite losing her shadow?"

"Exactly. I've examined her, and it looks like she's going to be fine, for now at least. Weaker than usual, physically as well as magically, but she's not dying."

"You can't do whatever she did for these other folks?"

Sarah shook her head.

"Lucy woke up because she has more power in dreams. She has ever since she got that wand. There's a connection between them that let her pull the wand in to help her. With her power over dreams, and the wand on her side, she woke herself up, but I don't think anyone else could do that."

"Not even if you gave them the wand?"

"Not even if they had it in their dreams. They don't have Lucy's power or connection."

"Shame, 'cause we could have got the wand into their dreams."

"Really?"

"Sure. Remember when Lucy took down Mr. No? Part of it was using that magical pillow Jenkins came up with. You put something inside it, and that something goes to the person who's sleeping with their head on the pillow. You can use it to arm a dreamer."

"Huh." Sarah leaned back in her seat, tempura and

cream cheese wontons forgotten. "We don't need to arm these patients. They're not under attack in their dreams, but they are stuck there..."

"You have an idea." Ellis smiled with pride.

"Maybe." Sarah tapped a finger against the table. "Assume that all our patients are dreaming while they're in their comas and those comas are magically triggered. Perhaps getting into their dreams could be a way around the shadow magic, a way to deliver medicine or magical items that would help them."

"So you'd send them dream medicine?"

"I don't know." Sarah pressed her hands against her head. "When you put it like that, it sounds ridiculous."

"No, it doesn't. It sounds like it could be a breakthrough. I mean, sure, we probably don't need to send them aspirin, but there must be something that can help, right?"

"Must be? No. But maybe..." Sarah pulled out her phone. "I should call the infirmary and let them know."

"I've got a better idea." Ellis pulled out his phone. "I'll call transport, get them to portal us back from the nearest alleyway."

"But it's date night!"

"Whatever we do, you're gonna be thinking about your coma patients all evening, and now I will be too. So let's cut to the chase and see what we can do for them. I can't think of a better date for us than saving lives." He popped a wonton into his mouth. "Plus it gives me an excuse to come back for more of these later."

The waiter approached, bringing their main courses.

"Can we get that to go?" Sarah tossed payment onto the table. "Sorry to mess you around, but my boyfriend and I have lives to save."

CHAPTER THIRTY-THREE

"Thanks for this." Lucy sipped her tea. "Work's been so hectic. I needed someone to make me sit down and take a rest."

"No problem." Charlie leaned back and looked out the window of the coffee shop. "What's the point of running my own business if I can't take a long lunch break with my wife when I want it?"

"Well, I thought the point was saving the world, but this is good too. Though isn't it a bit early to start slacking off? You've only been working there full time for a day and a half."

"Today's the day when the kids are busy and neither of us needs to keep an eye on them. What better time for this?"

"What are the kids up to today, anyway?"

"Probably out with their gang, busy saving the world."

"I suppose it runs in the family."

As she stretched out her legs, Lucy couldn't help noticing the absence of her shadow. She wouldn't normally have noticed its presence, but without it, she had a disconcerting sense of things being incomplete. Something she never typically paid attention to had become the only thing that she could think about.

It didn't help that the Shadow Man's attack had left her weakened. She got tired more quickly than usual, could only make it halfway around her regular running route with Jackie and Sarah, and had diminished reserves of her typically impressive magical power. It was all incredibly frustrating. It was also part of why she'd been willing to take a break like this. She needed the rest.

"Are you all right?" Lucy asked. Charlie seemed distracted, repeatedly looking out of the window, his attention not on her or his coffee.

"Yeah, sure," he said. "I just... Someone else is going to join us. I hope that's okay."

"Sure, of course," Lucy said. "Who else is—"

She stopped mid-sentence as the door opened and Kelly walked in, Max closely following.

"Oh, this place is adorable!" Kelly said. "Thank you, Max, it was very sweet of you to—"

Kelly also stopped talking as she noticed Lucy.

"Sweetheart." Lucy looked at Charlie. "Did you do this on purpose?"

Charlie looked at Max, who gave him a little nod.

"Yes," he said. "Max and I thought it would be a good idea for you two to sit and talk."

"Good is not the word I would use for this idea." Lucy gritted her teeth. "But I suppose we're here now."

By the counter, Max had a similar conversation with his wife while they waited for their coffee.

"I am not sitting down for a coffee with her." Kelly folded her arms firmly.

"Please, sweetie," Max said. "It's one coffee, twenty minutes tops."

"I have to put up with her enough at work. I'm not doing it elsewhere."

"Maybe if you didn't think about it as putting up with—"

"Seriously, Max, how could you spring this on me?"

Max drew a deep breath. "You might not need this, but Charlie and I do. You might not want to sit down with the Herons, but I do, and I hope you'll join me."

He picked up his coffee and walked over to the table where Charlie and Lucy were sitting. Kelly reluctantly followed him.

"Good to see you both," Max said as he sat.

"And you." Charlie smiled at Kelly as she sat next to her husband. She didn't smile back. "I think it'll be good to sit and talk."

Kelly snorted at the idea. Lucy laughed slightly and shook her head.

"This is a waste of time. I'm sorry, but if Kelly and I can't sort this out at work, where we're under pressure from above and have cases to solve, what makes you think it'll work here?"

"Us." Charlie pointed at himself and Max. "Being caught between you two is bad for anyone, but it's especially tough for us. We're friends, we work together, and we can't talk about our home lives without it getting awkward. Max can't work at home because of the stress it causes. It's driving us both nuts. We need you to at least try to clear the air."

"I agree with everything Charlie said." Max turned to his wife. "Honey, I know you don't care about getting on with Lucy, but you care about me, right? If you do, can you please at least try to sort this out?"

"Fine." Kelly scowled. "We'll try, but don't get your hopes up. And don't think you're sleeping anywhere but the couch tonight."

"So, why don't you tell us what this is all about?" Charlie asked. "Why are you so mad at each other at the moment?"

"She tried to sabotage my computer," Kelly said.

"She sabotaged my car," Lucy responded.

"She undermined me in front of the other Griffins."

"She messed with my cases."

"She keeps telling me how to do mine."

"She said that she was going to make my life a misery."

"She makes my life a misery!"

They sat glaring at each other, hands clutching the arms of their chairs tight.

"How does Lucy make your life miserable, Kelly?" Charlie asked quietly.

"She's constantly undermining me," Kelly hissed. "Making comments about my work and my attitude. Making fun of me with her friends in the office."

"This is absurd," Lucy said. "It's not high school. You can't act out because you think the mean girls are spreading rumors about you."

"Oh, can't I? What else am I supposed to do? Start other rumors with the people who won't talk to me because they listen to what you say?"

"The only reason I say anything is because you act like

such a petty cow. I mean, you added a stink spell to my brownies at the PTA bake sale, for goodness sake."

"You can't seriously still be mad about that."

"Of course I'm mad about it! It was disgusting, it was undermining, and it was a completely irresponsible misuse of magic. I should've reported you to Applegate."

"Oh yes, bring him in against me too." Kelly leaned forward, eyes narrowed. "I see what you're up to, trying to turn the whole office against me so you can steal the manager's position."

"It's not yours for me to steal. That job should go to the best candidate."

"It won't because you keep undermining me."

"Have you ever considered that you might not be the best candidate?"

"Look around that office. Of course, I am."

"What about me?"

"You? Ha!"

Charlie and Max exchanged a look.

"Maybe you could tone it down a little," Max said with the calm, reasonable tone of a professional lawyer. "It seems like you're both getting wound up against each other."

"Don't you start," Kelly hissed. "You're my husband, and you can't even take my side when we're dealing with her."

"It's not about taking sides."

"Of course it is."

Charlie leaned forward. "Kelly, Max is just trying to—"

"Charlie, stay out of this," Lucy said firmly. "You've done enough damage already."

"Huh?"

"This is between Kelly and Max."

"But I—"

"We're going to have a similar conversation when we get home. I can't believe you thought this was okay, forcing us together like this."

"Exactly." Kelly glared at Max. "Our relationship is not for you to fix. Do you realize how it would look to other Griffins if they heard about this? Our husbands going behind our backs to interfere in our work?"

"How would you feel if we turned up at the garage and started telling you how to interact with your colleagues?" Lucy added.

Charlie shrugged. "I suppose it would be weird."

"And if we didn't back you up in an argument with them?"

"Well, I..."

"Exactly." Lucy exchanged a look with Kelly. Both witches shook their heads. "I understand why this might have looked like a good idea, but you can't treat us like bickering kids. We have to sort our lives out for ourselves."

"Precisely." Kelly nodded firmly. "We put up with enough men telling us what to do elsewhere. The last thing we need is to face that in our marriages."

Charlie hung his head. Max did the same.

"Sorry," they both mumbled.

"I should think so too." Lucy looked at Kelly, one eyebrow raised. "What do you think we should do with them?"

"They treated us like children. I think we should do the same in return," Kelly said. "Coffee shop privileges revoked. You don't get to sit here and enjoy your drinks." She whipped their cups away from in front of them. "Now playtime is over. You should both get back to work, and while you're there, you should think about what you've done."

"Maybe Ringo can offer you some advice on how to get this right in future," Lucy added.

"Ringo, relationship advice?" Charlie asked, incredulous.

"Right now, he can't be doing worse than you two." Kelly made a shooing motion toward the door. "Now scram, both of you."

Charlie and Max walked out of the coffee shop, both with shoulders slumped and heads hanging.

"That did not work like I hoped," Charlie mumbled.

"Me neither." Max sighed as they walked slowly away. "At least we tried, and when they get back to feuding, we can say that we did our best to avoid it."

"Yeah." Charlie glanced back over his shoulder. "Um, Max, don't look now, but I think it might have worked."

"Huh?" Despite Charlie's instruction, Max looked back. Together, they stared through the coffee shop window at Kelly and Lucy, who were chatting and laughing over their drinks.

"Hey, they're eating my cake!" Max said indignantly.

"Let them have it. We got what we wanted, right?"

They turned, and with brighter steps than before, walked in the direction of the auto shop.

"They were right though, weren't they?" Max asked. "We shouldn't have done that."

Charlie shrugged. "I guess. Live and learn, eh?"

CHAPTER THIRTY-FOUR

The Mini Griffins sat hidden in the trees, watching the same playground that had been the site of their most recent victory. Ashley and Tommy had modified tablets in their hands, while the others had wands at the ready in preparation for trouble.

"I get that the trolls are coming back," Mia said. "If I'd managed to escape on the way to Trevilsom Prison, I'd probably want to come home too. What I don't get is how you know they're coming back now?"

Ashley looked at the data on her screen. The tablet was wirelessly connected to her computers back in the lair, which had far more computational power. What she was looking at was nothing more than a mirror of what those computers had worked out.

"It's not about coming home," she said. "They're coming back for revenge. This playground was where they got caught so they're planning to trash it."

"But why now?" Dylan asked. "Or, I mean, how do you know that it's now?"

"The behavior of individual trolls looks chaotic," Ashley said, "but as groups, they're surprisingly predictable. Professors Meldberg and Horowitz have done extensive mathematical modeling, grounded in ethnographic research by Talbot, Talbot, and Jones, which reveals a surprising amount about how trolls organize their lives and how they understand that organization. Based on that, we can foresee their likely patterns of behavior, in a manner not dissimilar to the science-fictional mathematics of Asimov's *Foundation* series."

She paused for a moment to let the others stare uncomprehendingly at the data, then pulled up a different screen, showing discussion boards on the side of the Internet.

"Plus, they keep telling everyone what they're going to do."

Sure enough, there were whole threads of poorly spelled messages littered with emojis, pictures, and gifs, which someone could, with a lot of concentration and some creativity, decode into a conversation between trolls about how they were going to come back and smash up a playground.

"We don't know that these are our trolls," Dylan said. "What if there's another group in another city who got in trouble for trashing a park? It's the sort of thing they would do."

Ashley zoomed in on a photo that one of the trolls had posted. It was a picture of the very playground they were looking at.

"Okay," Dylan said. "It's them."

"How did you get the police tape?" Tommy asked.

The police tape had been the first thing the Mini

Griffins did when they arrived at the playground at the start of the morning. They had taped off the whole area so mundane kids wouldn't start using it. They didn't want anybody else getting caught in the middle of what they were doing.

"I predicted the behavior of a pack of wild sentient monsters," Ashely said. "After that, do you really think getting hold of some tape would be difficult?"

Wind rattled the tape, making a loose end flap against an empty slide. It was strange seeing a playground deserted like this in the middle of the day, and several of the Mini Griffins felt an urge to play if only so the swings didn't look so lonely. Instead, they waited patiently while Tommy and Ashley directed the string robots out to cover the terrain and keep an eye open for arrivals.

"There," Tommy whispered, pointing at his screen.

In footage from one of the robots, long grass was stirring. A spike of bright orange hair appeared, turned and tilted as the troll looked around, and hurried past. Two with purple hair followed, one with green, another with orange, and more, as the whole gang of trolls streamed past.

"There are more of them than last time," Dylan whispered.

"That's what happens when you advertise your plans on the Internet," Mia said.

The trolls reached the edge of the playground and stopped again to look around. Apparently content that they were alone and utterly oblivious to the ring of robots they'd passed through, they ran out. Some of them leaped on the swings, which swung wildly back and forth. Some clambered up the slide and shot down it. Others scrambled over the climbing frame. For a minute, it seemed like a scene of innocent fun.

Then the lead troll shouted, a noise that didn't mean anything to the Mini Griffins but that was the signal to attack. As one, the trolls started hitting, kicking, and biting the equipment they were playing on.

"All right, gang," Dylan said quietly. "Everyone ready?" The Mini Griffins nodded. "Then let's go."

They dashed out of their hiding places and straight toward the playground. As they approached, the trolls looked up. Some of them turned and ran in panic, only to be stopped by a swarm of silver string robots with electric zappers at their tips. Other trolls braced themselves and started to grow, ready to take on the Mini Griffins.

"Stupefacio!" Dylan chanted. A bolt of magic shot from his wand and hit the largest troll right in the face. It stopped growing, swayed for a moment, and fell to the ground with a *crash*.

In moments, the Mini Griffins were in among the trolls, using their wands up close to target their spells more accurately. Trolls that weren't in the middle of growing instead leaped on the young witches and wizards, clinging onto them and dragging them to the ground.

Three trolls got hold of Mia's legs and dragged her under the climbing frame.

"Don't worry, I've got this," Tommy said.

Tapping at his screen, he re-directed some of the string robots. Practicing with Ashley, he'd gotten pretty good at controlling the robots, and a small swarm wriggled across the ground to the climbing frame. They approached the trolls in pairs, electric sparks jumping from underneath the cameras on their heads.

One troll jumped into the air as the sparks jolted it. Dylan hit it with a freeze spell, and it stuck to the climbing frame. With it gone, Mia's wand hand was free, and she used it to stun the next troll that the robots shocked off her. The third and final troll clung to her arm for a moment, a look of doubt on his face, then leaped off and ran for the edge of the playground.

"Oh no, you don't." Mia steadied her wand with both hands. "Agglutino."

Glue appeared around the troll's feet, sticking him in place. He strained against the ground but couldn't break free. Remembering his one biggest advantage, he started to grow, going from a few inches high to a foot, two feet, three feet...

"Stupefacio!" Dylan said, and a bolt of magic hit the growing troll. It stopped growing, swayed for a moment, and fell on its back, feet still glued to the ground.

A few trolls were still upright, but the Mini Griffins and the robots had them cornered around the slide.

"You're probably thinking of growing," Ashley said as she approached. "You think that if you get bigger, you can fight your way out." She pointed at one of the larger unconscious trolls. "As you can see, that won't work. So, please sit down and wait while we call the Silver Griffins. It really will be easier for you all."

The trolls seemed convinced. Muttering and grumbling, they sat down, surrounded by the robots, while the Mini Griffins went to sit on benches at the edge of the park. Occasionally, a troll would stand, ready to make a run for it, only to be deterred by the sparking of the nearest robots.

Dylan took out a phone. "Should I call Mom about picking these guys up?"

Ashley shook her head. "She's busy today. Try Auntie Jackie."

While Dylan made the call, Tommy came to sit next to Ashley. He held out the tablet he'd been using.

"Thanks for letting me control your robots," he said. "That was awesome."

"You're welcome." Ashley didn't take the tablet. "You should hold onto that and some of the robots. That way, we'll have some in a different part of the city for emergencies."

"Thanks, but I'm not going to be in the city for much longer." Tommy looked down and sighed. "My mom got a job in Maine, so we're all moving across the country."

"Oh. When?"

Tommy shrugged. "Soon. They keep talking about dates, but it's complicated with sorting out Dad's job too and somewhere to live and the moving people and..." He shrugged again. "Anyway, if I'm leaving L.A., then I have to leave the Mini Griffins, so you should keep that."

Ashley looked down at the tablet, then back at Tommy. While he saw the end of something he loved, she saw an opportunity.

"You don't have to leave the Mini Griffins," she said. "In fact, you have an incredible responsibility: to set up our first branch on the East Coast."

"Huh?" Tommy looked at her, a little confused.

"You should start your own Mini Griffins in Maine. I'll

send you the equipment you need and tell you how to set it up. I can't help much with recruitment, but I'm sure you can find some kids to help you."

"Really?" Tommy's downcast expression was gone, replaced by a massive grin.

"Of course. The whole world needs protection. Why just make it about L.A.?"

Ashley pulled a bag out of her backpack, picked up half a dozen string robots off the ground, and put them in the bag before handing it to Tommy. "Enough to get you started. I'll send more when I have spares."

"Wow. Thanks, Ashley, this is the most awesome thing ever."

"It really isn't when you consider the amazing things that have happened on this planet, never mind in the rest of the universe, but I appreciate the sentiment."

A portal appeared in the middle of the playground. Jackie and Twylan emerged, dragging a wheeled cage behind them.

"Heard you have a pest problem," Jackie said. "Who wants to help me load them up for a trip to Trevilsom?"

"Me, me, me!" said half the Mini Griffins at once, sticking their hands in the air.

"Great." Jackie opened the cage. "Everyone grab a troll and let's get started."

Tommy looked at Ashley, who held out her hand.

"I'll hold the tablet for you," she said. "Go arrest a troll. You'll need practice for the ones in New England."

CHAPTER THIRTY-FIVE

"I don't like to say I told you so," Jenkins said as he checked the sensors attached to Old Rambler, "but I did tell you that these devices would be useful."

Sarah pressed her fingers against Old Rambler's neck. The graying Willen was the weakest of the coma patients. That made him both the one most in need of extra help and the one most likely to show changes if her idea worked out.

She felt a little guilty about turning her patient into a test subject, but there seemed to be no other way forward, and his family had agreed. So here they were, strapping him up to Jenkins' sensors and preparing to use other experimental magic on him.

"You didn't tell me that your devices would be useful," Sarah said. "That would've involved having a conversation. You just started using them on my patients."

"Well, either way, it's worked out, hasn't it?" Jenkins smiled. "These sensors will detect the tiniest fluctuations in the patient's condition as we test different variables on him. I mean, assuming that the sensors work correctly on a Willen, which I am ninety-four percent certain they will."

Sarah decided not to ask about the other six percent. It wasn't like she had access to any other super-sensitive sensors or any way to get through to her patients without Jenkins and his magical technologies. She had to take a chance.

"You've got this." Ellis squeezed her shoulder.

Sarah smiled. Working with Ellis had been one of the pleasures of the past day and had helped her keep her anxiety under control. It turned out that combining their professional lives wasn't such a bad idea. Having him there to lean on had made it easier to get through the hard work of refining and implementing her plan and to cope when it hadn't immediately worked. His presence, his encouragement, and his practical help had made it possible to get this far.

"It's still not working." Swallowing her disappointment, she retrieved the magical pillow from under Old Rambler's head and removed the wand inside. It was the same model as Lucy's, an Australian wand with a leaning toward dream magic, but if it had helped Rambler in his dreams, it didn't reflect in his health. His body and his magic were both fading as he slid inexorably toward death.

"It was a long shot, trying to replicate what Lucy did," Ellis said. "Most folks don't work like her. But there's still a chance we can find something to help him."

"I know." Sarah sighed. "But what? We've tried protective charms, we've tried bandages and medicine, we've tried a range of different wands. Assuming that Old

Rambler uses the things we send him—and that's a big assumption—they're not proving at all useful to him."

"I don't suppose we have any way to generate data on what is happening in his subconscious?" Jenkins asked.

"You mean, do we know what he dreams about?"

"Exactly."

Sarah considered that for a moment, then took a phone from its cradle on the wall and called reception.

"Hi, this is the infirmary. Do you still have coma patients' relatives there, waiting for news? Great. Are there any Willen? Fantastic. Can you please find out which of them knows Old Rambler best and send that one down? Thanks." She hung up the phone. "It has to be worth a try, right? Better to light a candle than to curse the darkness."

Jenkins' eyes went wide.

"That's it!" He leaped out of his seat. "Darkness and light. Dr. Smith, I think you've inadvertently found the solution we've been seeking."

"Really?" Sarah smiled. "Could you tell us what it..." Jenkins was already out the door and rushing off down the corridor. "Never mind."

"You get used to him after a while," Ellis said.

"Must I?"

She checked Old Rambler's vital signs again and made a few notes about his condition. Then there was a knock at the door, and another Willen walked in. It was the same one who had brought Old Rambler to Sarah in the first place.

"Hi, Tibtib," Sarah said. "Have you come to talk to us about Old Rambler?"

"Yes, yes." Tibtib clutched something square and leathery in his hands. "What do you want to know?"

"What did he dream about?"

"Dream?" Tibtib blinked. "You mean his hopes and goals?"

"No, the other sort of dreams. What came into his head while he was asleep?"

Tibtib sat on the edge of the bed, one of his paws still clutching the leather square, the other taking one of Old Rambler's paws.

"Dreams..." Tibtib hesitated. "Honestly, Dr. Smith, I don't know. He talked about other people more than himself. His dreams aren't something he would mention."

"Never?"

"Maybe once or twice. There was the time he dreamed about being eaten by a blueberry pie. I remember because I was young when he told me, and it made me laugh because people eat pies, not the other way around. Although he might've made that up to entertain us because we were kids. Oh, and during the election, he dreamed that he was being crushed to death by a giant tangerine."

"That's two food dreams," Ellis said. "Maybe. Could that help?"

"It's tenuous," Sarah said. "But any idea is better than nothing right now. Maybe we could put a snack in the pillow or a fork to help him eat whatever he faces."

"In a pillow?" Tibtib looked confused.

"We're trying to use a magical artifact to keep Old Rambler alive. It has to do with dreams."

"To keep him alive." Tibtib swallowed. "So he is dying."

"I'm sorry. We're doing what we can, but..."

"But those Shadow Men." Tibtib's face turned into an angry snarl. "If he dies, I'll catch them and gut them all."

Sarah had seen this too many times before, grief hardening into anger. It wasn't good for anyone.

"What's that you've brought?" She pointed at the leather square.

"It's, um..." Tibtib looked uncertainly at Ellis. "I'm not sure I should say."

"It's okay, nobody's going to punish you for anything right now, are they, Ellis?"

"No, ma'am."

"Then, um..." Tibtib laid the object on Old Rambler's chest. It was a wallet, worn at the edges from extensive use. "The very first pocket I ever picked, that's what I got. Old Rambler was so proud of me that he kept it as a souvenir. I was picking up things at his place, and I saw it, and I just..."

His voice trailed off as he looked sadly at the dying Willen.

The door burst open, and Jenkins burst in.

"I have it!" He held up a back velvet bag the size of his fist.

Given Tibtib's delicate state, Sarah would have preferred a more understated entrance, but asking Jenkins to tone it down would only trigger a long conversation, which would make matters worse.

"What is it?" she asked quietly, hoping that he would take the hint.

"The solution to our patients' shadow problems," Jenkins proclaimed loudly, then whipped away the black velvet to reveal a brightly glowing crystal sphere. "An everlight. Light to drive back the darkness and cast a shadow when the original is gone. It's what we should put in the pillow."

"That's a great idea." Sarah held out the magical dream pillow. With Old Rambler on death's door, there was no time to waste. "Put it in here."

Jenkins placed the everlight in the pillow, then Ellis and Tibtib carefully lifted Old Rambler's head and shoulders while Sarah slid the pillow into place. As the older Willen's head settled back down, Tibtib looked at him expectantly.

"This could take a while," Sarah said. "Would you like to wait with him and see if it works?"

Tibtib nodded. "If that's okay."

"Of course."

They all sat around the bed, watching and waiting. Jenkins made notes on his phone and occasionally prodded at his sensors. Sarah repeatedly checked the patient's breath, pulse, and other vitals for any sign of change. Ellis fetched coffee and snacks for all of them. Tibtib just watched Old Rambler's face.

After an hour, Sarah got up, tapped the side of the sensor device, and looked sadly at the display.

"No improvement," she said. "I'm afraid it's another failure. We'll have to try something else."

"I'll fetch some other light sources," Jenkins said, leaping out of his chair. "I'm still convinced that my hypothesis has potential if we can get the variables correct."

He strode out of the door while Ellis lifted Old Rambler's head and Sarah took out the everlight.

"It's not going work, is it?" Tibtib said, tears at the corners of his eyes. "He's going to die."

The worn wallet fell from his paws, and he clutched his face as he shook with grief.

"I'm sorry." Sarah laid one hand on his shoulder, while with the other she picked up the wallet. That artifact of the Willens' relationship felt more real somehow, more solid than anything else in the room. Anything except Tibtib's grief. Without stopping to think about what she was doing, she slid the wallet into the magic pillow under Old Rambler's head.

"What are you doing?" Tibtib sniffed.

"Giving him a reminder," she said. "A reason to cling on."

She looked at the monitors. Some part of her expected them to change immediately, as Old Rambler received the wallet, remembered the people he loved and found the will to cling on. But nothing happened. She had been deluding herself.

Jenkins burst back in, with Nigel behind him. They were clutching armfuls of assorted lights, both magical and mundane.

"I suggest we start with a flashlight," Jenkins said. "Then a Light Elf wand. After that, perhaps—"

"Wait!" Ellis grabbed Jenkins' hand to stop him from reaching for the pillow. "Look!"

The readings on the monitor had changed. Old Rambler's heartbeat was growing more steady, his magical aura stronger. He didn't wake up, but one of his paws clenched into a fist as if clinging tight to something of value. Sarah pulled back the sheet at the bottom of the bed and saw the tattered end remnants of his shadow coalesce, like a wound scarring over. The shadow wasn't back, but he wasn't dying anymore.

"It worked." She stared, stunned. "It worked. She started laughing. "It worked, it worked, it worked!"

"Thank you, thank you, thank you!" Tibtib hugged her. "I have to go tell the others."

He rushed out of the infirmary.

"I suppose these aren't needed," Jenkins said, looking at his armful of lights. "Back to the lab, Nigel."

The Special Equipment wizards headed off, leaving only Sarah, Ellis, and the unconscious patients.

"Ellis, it worked!" She flung her arms around him and kissed him hard, overcome with elation. "I couldn't have done it without your support."

"Yeah, you could." He smiled. "I'm still glad I was here to help."

She smiled at him. He was her rock, the person who kept her going no matter what. Without him, she might've fallen apart in the past few days. Instead, she'd found the energy and inspiration needed to save their coma patients, to keep them alive while Lucy and the rest dealt with the Shadow Men. She'd known Ellis less than a year, and yet she felt like she'd known him forever. She couldn't imagine life without him.

Ellis looked at her like she was the most amazing thing in the world.

"Marry me," they both said to each other at once.

They laughed.

"Yes," they both said.

They kissed again.

CHAPTER THIRTY-SIX

The late afternoon sun was shining as Charlie headed into the back yard of the Heron family house, an ax in his hand. It turned out that working with his hands on cars was a lot harder work physically than sitting at a desk programming, and he was already feeling tired, but if a job needed doing, it was worth getting it over and done with.

Buddy ran in circles around Charlie's ankles, barking excitedly.

"Don't worry, Buddy." Charlie bent to pat the dog's head. "Once I'm done with this, I'll take you for a walk."

At the sound of the word "walk", Buddy got even more excited, jumping up and down on his little legs. Ideas like "later" and "after this job" didn't matter to him: there was a walk to be had.

Charlie approached a maple tree near the bottom of the garden. It had been on the property far longer than the Herons, possibly even longer than their house. It was weatherworn, scarred by the attentions of dogs and cats, and grown around in places with the vines and tendrils of other plants.

Its branches had held a small tree house when Dylan was young before Charlie had decided the tree itself might not be strong enough. A single plank from that construction was still attached to an upper branch.

Sadly, the tree was also dying. Its leaves were wilting prematurely, and several branches had become pale and dry. Whether it was old age or some sort of infection, the maple's time had come.

"Sorry, old man." Charlie laid a hand against the tree. "Your legacy will live on."

He pulled the ax around, then swung it at the base of the tree. There was a satisfying *thud* but not much of a mark on the bark. He swung the ax again and again, and a little of the wood started to chip away. Charlie wiped his brow. This had looked easier on YouTube.

"Dad, what are you doing?" Ashley peered out of her treehouse in one of the garden's other, sturdier trees.

"Chopping this old maple down," Charlie said.

"Cutting down trees is bad. We need them for the environment."

"It's okay." He pulled a little plastic bag out of his pocket and held it up for her to see. "We saved some seeds from this tree last year. It's going to grow its replacement."

"Like you and mom having us?"

Charlie hesitated, not sure what to make of that slightly morbid thought.

"Sure, honey, like having you guys, except with more leaves and fewer robots."

"I wonder what sort of robots trees would make..."

Ashley climbed down from the tree, tablet in her hand, and came over to look at Charlie's work. "You haven't chopped much yet."

"Well, why don't you stand back then and I can show you how it's done."

He hefted the ax and, with renewed determination, swung at the base of the tree, but even after several chops, he still wasn't making much progress.

"Would you like me to help?" Ashley asked.

"It's good of you to offer, but I don't think you'd make more progress than me." Charlie grunted as he hit the tree again. "I know I'm not The Rock, but I have a few more muscles than you."

"Don't be silly, Dad. I wasn't going to do it that way." Ashley tapped the screen of her tablet, and a selection of silvery strings wriggled across the lawn, her robots in action. "The robots can chop it down."

Charlie took another swing. It didn't help that he kept missing the original spot. A solid foot of the bottom of the tree was now scarred from his blows, none of which had landed in the same place.

"How are your robots going to swing an ax?" he asked.

"They won't." Ashley tapped the screen again, and three snake-like robots raised their heads, revealing small red lights on the front. "They'll use their lasers."

"Lasers?" Charlie, the ax back for another blow, stared at the robots. "Since when do they have lasers? Is that safe?"

"I added them today. It's a new facility I'm experimenting with, so they can cut their way into inaccessible spaces or help prepare components for construction."

"That doesn't sound safe."

"It is. No individual robot has enough power to do any damage. It's only when they work together that they can cut things."

Charlie considered his options. He was going to have to talk with Lucy later to work out a house rule about the kids arming themselves with lasers. For now, though, he wanted this tree gone, and if that meant he got to see how safe or not these robots were, then surely that was good parenting?

"Okay," he said. "Give it a go."

Directed by Ashley, the robots gathered at one side of the tree. Light beams emerged from their heads, all pointing at the same spot. There was a smell of burning, and a black line scored its way across the trunk, digging deep into the wood.

A second line followed, and a wedge of wood slid out, leaving the maple with only a slender piece of trunk holding it up. One of the robots wriggled around the trunk, stretched up, and tapped the tree. With a *creak*, the remaining wood gave way, and the tree crashed down on the lawn.

"Wow." Charlie clapped. "Well done, honey."

Buddy joined in the applause, jumping and barking, then grabbed the maple in his teeth and tried to drag the gigantic stick away. He didn't get anywhere, but he seemed to be having fun.

"What happen to tree?" Eddie ambled down the garden to join them, a plastic dinosaur trailing from each of his hands.

"We've chopped this tree down," Charlie said, rolling the maple aside with help from the robots. "Now we're going to plant a new one." He stopped and stared at the stump. "Okay, so maybe we won't be planting it quite yet." He prodded the stump with the tip of his boot. "Ashley, I don't suppose your robots could dig this out, could they?"

"Maybe." She contemplated the stump. "I'd need to come up with a digging program and possibly some new tools for them..."

"I do it," Eddie announced.

The air around him shimmered, and a large mole replaced the small boy. He thrust his spade-like paws into the ground beside the stump and started digging. Dirt flew through the air, showering Charlie and Ashley, and within moments Eddie had disappeared.

Charlie and Ashley watched for several minutes. From time to time, a lump would appear in the ground close to the stump, or dirt would spray from a new hole. After a while, the trunk itself moved as if jostled from below. Then it lifted a little.

Charlie plunged his hands into the loosened soil and took hold of the stump. He pulled, and it easily emerged, seemingly unattached to the ground. When he lifted it, he saw that its longer, stronger roots had been severed, bitten through by animal teeth.

The mole emerged from the hole, covered in soil and waving his paws. He sat on the lawn, then the air shimmered, and he turned back into a little boy, still covered in dirt.

"Digged it!" Eddie declared.

"Yes, you did." Charlie smiled at him. "Thank you, and you're going to need a bath before dinner."

"Splish splash, I a fish!" Eddie waved his hands like flippers but had the good sense not to change into a trout without water around him.

"Now for the replacement." Charlie pushed displaced dirt into the hole where the stump had been and flattened it out with some help from the kids and the robots. When he was satisfied with the results, he took the bag of seeds out of his pocket, took a seed out of the bag, and thrust it into the dirt.

They all stepped back and stood looking at their handiwork.

"It grow now?" Eddie asked.

"Eventually, yes," Charlie said. "After we water it and compost it and wait for a year or two."

Ashley chewed on the tip of her finger. "This feels a little anticlimactic."

"Hey, my old treehouse!" Dylan walked down the garden toward them, then stood looking at the single plank on the felled tree. "I guess I hadn't climbed it in a few years."

"We grow tree." Eddie proudly pointed at the patch of dirt.

"Cool."

"It's a seed from your old tree," Charlie added.

"Cool."

"But now we have to wait for the miracle of nature," Ashley added. "Wait for several years."

"Huh." Dylan pulled out his wand. "I mean, we could do that, or..." He waved the wand. "Crescent plantae!"

Magic rippled across the surface of the churned dirt, then a slender green shoot emerged. It rose a couple of inches, its tip unfurled and leaves spread out to catch the sunlight. The plant kept rising, its trunk thickening, more leaves growing out, then a couple of slender branches. The whole time, Dylan's eyes remained narrowed, his wand hand trembling, as he focused on controlling the power he was using, not letting it get away from him.

"Better stop there," Charlie said softly, once the sapling was a couple of feet tall. "We don't want to have to explain to the neighbors how we got a full-grown tree into our yard without them seeing."

The magic stopped, and Dylan lowered his wand.

"That was really good," Charlie said. "Well done."

"Thanks, Dad."

Lucy emerged from the house, carrying a tray of cookies and lemonade.

"How's the work going?" she asked as she approached the gathered group, then she saw the new tree. "Oh, wow. That's fantastic."

"Dylan made tree grow." Eddie waved a muddy hand.

"Well done, Dylan," Lucy said.

"Eddie and Dad dug out the stump," Ashley pointed out.

"Then well done to both of you. That's hard work."

"We couldn't have done it without Ashley," Charlie said. "She was the one who felled the tree, using the lasers on her robots."

"Lasers, huh?" Lucy raised an eyebrow. "We might need to chat about that later. For now though, well done, Ashley, and thank you to all of you."

Buddy yapped.

"And of course to you." Lucy took a dog biscuit from

her pocket and threw it to him. "I'm sure you played your part."

They sat together around the new tree, eating cookies and drinking lemonade.

"A new tree." Charlie smiled. "Growing because of us."

"A family tree," Lucy said. "Our family tree."

CHAPTER THIRTY-SEVEN

The voices of the Underfoot Brigade echoed around the tunnel behind Twylan and Leontine as they made their way toward the newest forest cave. They had directions from the Tolderai, but this was the first time they'd been to this location.

"Do you think it will be like the other ones," Leontine said, "or will they use a different layout this time? More fir trees, perhaps?"

Twylan smiled. A year ago, she never could've pictured Leontine as a gardener. It still seemed a little incongruous although she'd seen him up to his elbows in the mud, planting trees and digging out weeds. It was nice how their work with the Tolderai had softened him and brought out his nurturing side.

He wasn't the only one. Many of the Underfoots had found a spark of green-fingered creativity they never had before. It was amazing what could come from hands-on experience of supporting life and seeing it grow.

"I expect it'll be pretty similar," she said. "I talked to

Heather, and there are some constraints on what plants they can use to grow the roots and branches that hold up the ceiling. That affects what other plants they put in the forest because of how they interact as an ecosystem. Nothing's out of bounds, but some things are easier than others."

"That makes sense." Leontine nodded. "I've been thinking I might like to learn more about this, maybe take an online college course or something."

"That's fantastic." Twylan squeezed his arm. "You should do it. See where it takes you."

She was sure that Leontine could learn far more about plants from the Tolderai than he ever could from a college, but it was great to see him developing ambitions for himself. Maybe one course would lead to another, and he would find things that he was interested in. She hoped so. With the Silver Griffins, she had found a purpose beyond the Underfoot Brigade, and it was time for Leontine to do the same.

They emerged into the warm glow of the Tolderai forest lights. The new cavern was bare, not a single plant in the dirt yet. A sturdy weave of branches and roots held up the ceiling and provided somewhere for the lights to sit, and there was a pool in the center of the artificial cavern, but otherwise, the space was bare. It made Twylan realize just how large these caverns were and how impressive.

The Tolderai stood near the entrance to the cavern, talking quietly to each other. They fell silent as the Underfoot Brigade walked in.

"Is something the matter?" Twylan asked, seeing the serious expressions on their faces. "Are we late?"

"Nothing is the matter," Heather said. "The opposite, in fact. We have an opportunity to offer you."

"An opportunity?" Twylan and the other Underfoots looked at each other in confusion. "What is it?"

"Well..." Usually direct and to the point, Heather seemed strangely reticent, almost as if she was nervous. "As you know, we've been making changes among the Tolderai. Renting out our ancestral art for people to see. Investing in solar energy. Setting up a company to manage all of this. It's not the sort of work we're used to, but it's the best way to continue our tribe's purpose in the twenty-first century."

"It's amazing," Twylan said. "The things you're doing, the way you're adapting, it must be difficult."

"Thank you. It is difficult. That's part of why we wanted to talk. We don't have all the skills we need to do this work. We don't even have people suited to learn all those skills. They come uncomfortably to us.

"The size of our tribe was right for our purpose in the old days, when our mission was simpler, when all we did was to stop people chopping down trees or setting fire to our beloved forests. The same is true of our habits of thinking. They worked for the old ways, but the times have changed, and we must change with them."

Heather wasn't the only one of the Tolderai looking uncomfortable. Many of them had eyes downcast, and Mackam seemed to flinch from her words.

"This sounds bad, but we've found a way to turn it into something good," Heather said, her voice lifting. "We want our tribe to grow, both in numbers and in the diversity of what it represents, its skills and its people. To do that, we need to find people we can trust, people with good hearts and a gift for the work the natural world needs." She smiled and held her hands wide. "So we invite the Underfoot Brigade, all of you, to join the Tolderai. You will become members of our tribe with all the support that provides. We will raise you out of the tunnels if that is what you want. You will have the support, the shelter, and above all, the purpose that a strong tribe can provide."

Twylan stood speechless. This wasn't a turn of events she could ever have predicted, despite all the hours she'd spent around the Tolderai. Now they were looking at her and the other Underfoots, expectant expressions on their faces, and she needed to react.

"Can we..." Twylan drew a deep breath. "Can we have a minute to discuss this?"

Heather's expression remained steady, but hurt and confusion were clear in the faces of some of the other Tolderai. Mackam muttered something, and Carol slapped him on his shoulder.

"Of course you can," Heather said. "We will wait by the pool."

Following her lead, the Tolderai walked away.

The Underfoot Brigade gathered around, with Twylan and Leontine at the center of the group.

"What do you all think?" Twylan asked. She recognized that the invitation was intended as a kind one and that the Tolderai thought they were helping the Underfoot Brigade escape life trapped under the ground. But the Underfoots had built a life for themselves and were used to living as a group. This offer could change their whole world. She wasn't sure how she felt about that.

"I like the Tolderai," Kix said. "I think this could be fun. Plus, we do good things with them, right?"

"With them, yes," Leontine said, frowning. "But that's different from being swallowed up by them. I'm proud of being an Underfoot. I don't want to give up our gang for someone else's."

"We'd be safer and more secure. We could keep learning from them."

"Turning into them," Leontine growled. "Do you want to give in to someone else's way of living? Remember how we were before we found each other, how the surface world has treated people like us. Do you trust anyone, truly trust them, to follow your best interests when they have charge of you?"

Twylan felt some of the same defensiveness Leontine did, but for her, it wasn't about trust. It was about giving up who they were, being absorbed by something bigger and more powerful. What Heather had offered wasn't a joining of equals.

What if it could be?

"I have an idea," she said. "A way to have the best of both worlds..."

She started explaining, and the Underfoot Brigade listened. Slowly, one by one, frowns turned into smiles, uncertain expressions into nods of approval. At last, even Leontine agreed.

"All right," he said. "You can suggest it, but I bet they say no."

With Twylan in the lead, the Underfoots walked over to where the Tolderai were waiting.

"Well?" Heather asked.

"We think you're right that we could achieve much more as one group," Twylan said. "But not on the terms you gave us. We're proud of what we created down here, and we don't want just to be absorbed. If we join together, it shouldn't be the Underfoot Brigade becoming Tolderai. That implies you would be in charge, that we would be expected to become like you.

"Instead, it should be the Tolderai and the Underfoot Brigade joining together on equal terms to create something new, something that's as much about who we are as it is about who you are."

"What would this new thing be?" Heather asked.

"I don't know yet, but I think it will be satisfying to work that out. Together."

Heather glanced at the other Tolderai. "This is a big decision. Now we must ask for time to talk."

Again, the two groups separated as the Tolderai went off to discuss Twylan's suggestion. Their conversation took far longer than the Underfoot Brigade's had.

"What do you think they're saying?" Kix asked

"I don't know." Siltor stretched his neck to look over the others' heads. "Mackam looks pretty wound up."

"He's stubborn," Leontine said. "He won't accept this."

"You did," Twylan pointed out.

"And what's that supposed to mean?"

At last, the Tolderai returned. Under the magical light of the cave, Heather stepped forward, with Mackam at her side.

"The Tolderai have stood for centuries," she said. "Bound together by custom and tradition, made strong by the ways in which we did not change.

"But nothing can stand like that forever. Joining our traditions with the youthful spirit of the Underfoot Brigade is the chance to make something even stronger, not to lose what we had but to gain something more." She held out her hand. "We accept."

Twylan shook Heather's hand. For a moment, there was silence as the two groups took in the enormity of what they were doing. Then the silence was replaced by chatter as they rushed forward to greet each other. Members of the two groups hugged, exchanged words of welcome, started talking excitedly about plans for the future.

"I have not met many chiefs who can lead their tribes with true strength and wisdom," Heather said, still clasping Twylan's hand. "You are impressive."

"I'm not a chief," Twylan pointed out.

"One day, you will be."

The lights flickered, and the babble of conversation stopped as the gathered magicals looked around. Before, the lights had always returned to their original brightness when the interference passed. This time, they remained dimmer than they had been.

"This is bad," Heather said. "If the other lights falter, the forests will grow sick."

"Then we have our first project for our new group," Twylan said. "Let's work out where this is coming from."

CHAPTER THIRTY-EIGHT

The reception room of Silver Griffins HQ was bustling with activity when Lucy arrived. A wide variety of magicals were in the waiting area, most of them clutching bags or boxes. She had to weave her way through the crowd to get to the front desk.

"What's going on?" she asked as she pressed her wand against the security device.

"Your friend Dr. Smith invited them in," the receptionist said. "They're friends and relatives of the coma patients."

"And they're all going to visit them?"

"No, we don't have space in the infirmary for that. She asked them all to bring in objects of great sentimental value to the patients. Apparently, they'll help with treatment." He lowered his voice. "I've heard so many stories this morning about where these things came from and why they matter to the people who own them. I'm not normally heartless, but I swear if I hear one more cute anecdote about how a couple met, I'm going to puke all over someone's shoes."

Lucy laughed as the door behind her opened, and a gnome came in carrying a ring box. "Good luck with that."

The main office floor was almost as crowded. Lucy had received the same message as everyone else, telling them that it was all hands on deck today and that they should be in the office at ten for a meeting. It seemed that everybody had taken the message seriously, from the witches and wizards to the admin staff. The place was as crowded and noisy as a children's birthday party.

With pigeons flapping past her head, Lucy made her way to her desk. There were so many spare bodies around that her seat was only empty because Jackie had been guarding it like a hawk, chasing off any visitors with one of her sharpest glares.

"Thought you'd be in early for this," Jackie said. "You're normally the diligent one."

"I spotted a band of escaped sprites on my way back from the school run." Lucy flung herself down in her chair. "Had to chase them down. I'm knackered already and the morning's not even half done."

She shouldn't have been so tired, but the Shadow Men's magic was still having its effect. However much sleep she got, however much she crammed herself full of caffeine and sugar, she couldn't get up to her regular energy levels. Then there was her magic, which still worked, but without its usual potency. She'd never believed that she needed her magic to be herself, but feeling it fade away like this gave her doubts. Apparently, it was more fundamental to her sense of self than she'd realized.

Ellis, who had been typing an email when Lucy came in, leaned forward so he could hear them over the noise.

"What do you reckon this is all about?" he asked, gesturing around the crowded room. "It ain't every day we start with this kind of fuss."

"Probably the Shadow Men," Jackie said. "That's the big deal at the moment, right?"

"It's certainly the biggest threat." Lucy looked down at the torn edges of darkness where her shadow should have been.

"Have you made some kind of breakthrough?" Jackie asked. "Found a clue to where they are?"

"The only breakthrough we've had recently was Sarah, working out how to stabilize the coma patients."

"Maybe she's achieved more, then. She's a smart girl our Sarah." Jackie looked at Ellis. "Well, apart from her taste in men."

"I ain't gonna disagree." He grinned. "But I ain't complaining either. If she had better taste, she'd have done better than me."

Jackie snorted. "It's a lot less fun when you don't fight back."

"Really? I never noticed."

There was some bustle going on outside Applegate's office, admin gnomes scurrying back and forth with forms and folders of documents. Although the Silver Griffins had accepted the arrival of the twenty-first century and made whatever use they could of modern technology, the organization still had some very old-fashioned bureaucracy, right down to its paper record-keeping.

"You think this is about Applegate?" Jackie asked. "Plans for his retirement, that sort of thing?"

"Maybe." Lucy shook her head. "My money's still on Shadow Men."

"Look out," Jackie said. "Here comes trouble."

Kelly walked across the office toward them. Most people would have used pauses and side-steps to get around the sheer mass of people cluttering up the place, but not Kelly. She simply strode straight ahead, expecting everyone else to get out of her way, and given a choice between moving and getting trampled, they usually moved.

"What is this nonsense?" she asked when she reached them.

"How would we know?" Jackie asked sharply.

"Because you sit near Mr. Applegate's office and you're in the middle of everyone."

"Well, we don't know."

"We've got it down to two options," Ellis said. "Shadow Men or Applegate's successor."

Lucy and Kelly looked at each other. The intense hostility that had held between them for so long might've diminished, but that didn't mean they knew how to interact now.

"Oh." Ellis slapped his hand to his forehead. "It's gonna be one of you two, ain't it?"

"Got to be," Jackie agreed. "Which means it's Lucy."

"Could be either." Lucy held out her hand to Kelly. "Best of luck."

Kelly shook the hand. "You too."

The clock struck ten. The last of the gnomes scurried away from Applegate's doorway. After a moment, the regional manager emerged, straightening his suit. The whole room fell silent, except for a lone pigeon that kept excitedly cooing until someone stunned it with a spell.

"Thank you all for coming in," Applegate said. "I know you have work to get on with, so I won't keep you for too long.

"Since I announced my imminent retirement, other senior Griffins and I have been engaged in the process of selecting my successor. As you can probably imagine, this works a little differently for us than for other organizations. We can hardly run an open recruitment campaign."

That drew the sort of subdued laughter that was obligatory when a senior manager made a joke, laughter born as much from a sense of duty as a sense of humor.

"Some of you might have expected interviews within the organization, but we decided to take a different approach. We've been looking at all the witches and wizards in this office, considering their experience, qualifications, and character, and balancing their career prospects with the best interests of the Silver Griffins. I'm pleased to announce that, after much debate and consideration, we've come to a decision."

Applegate paused, and Lucy caught a glint in his eye. He was enjoying this moment, keeping them expectant and waiting for more. There was a mischievous side to her boss that she'd never appreciated before, and she wasn't sure that she did now. She wanted this over and done with, so they knew who was in charge.

"My successor..." Applegate paused again and cleared his throat. "Sorry about that. As I was saying, my successor will be Jackie Kowal."

Lucy and Kelly looked at each other, then at Jackie, who sat with her mouth hanging open, staring at Applegate.

"Huh?" Jackie said.

"Agent Kowal has impressed both the directors and me with her recent work," Applegate continued, "in particular in negotiating our relationship with the Tolderai, a delicate situation with a powerful group of magicals, and one that could easily have turned sour. I can think of no one better to lead this office into the future."

Applegate started clapping. Lucy joined in, then Ellis and Kelly, and soon everyone was clapping and cheering. Across the room, Jenkins gave Jackie a big thumbs-up.

Jackie shook her head, got to her feet, and strode over to Applegate, the applause still thundering around her.

"You must've made a mistake," she said, just loudly enough for him to hear, while the applause stopped anyone else catching her words.

"Certainly not," Applegate said, grinning. "You're the perfect candidate."

"I'm not a candidate."

"Everybody was a candidate."

"I don't want the job!"

"That's part of why you'll be such a good choice for it. You don't care about the position and the power. You just want to get the job done. That's exactly what this place needs."

"What about Lucy?"

"She's an excellent field agent but very busy, what with her family and voluntary work. You have more time and energy to commit."

"I have other things in my life, you know. I have a girl-friend now."

"Congratulations. I'm sure she'll be very proud of you."

"That's not what I—"

"Agent Kowal, I know you don't want to live up to your family's expectations of leadership and political ambition, but are you going to turn down this opportunity simply to spite them? Surely that would mean letting them restrict you as much as if you took the job for them."

"I... That's not... I don't..."

"Honestly, do you think anyone here is going to run the place with as much discipline and as little bullshit as you?"

His words, and the tone of them, caught her off-guard, but when she looked around the room, Jackie realized that he was right. She had a chance to get the place running smoothly, to cut out some of the nonsense and unnecessary bureaucracy, and if she had the chance to do that, she was going to take it.

"All right," she said. "I give in. I'll take the damn job."

Applegate shook her hand. "Congratulations, Agent Kowal. I'm sure you'll do us all proud."

Jackie raised her hands and her voice. "All right, you lot, shut up!"

The applause finally died away.

"If you don't know who I am already, you'll know soon enough," Jackie said. "I'm sure we'll have a big party soon to say goodbye to the boss and celebrate my promotion and blah-blah-blah team bonding.

"Right now, the Shadow Men are out there assaulting magicals, we've still got troll problems down by the coast, and I hear weird things are going on with the shifters, so stop standing around doing nothing and get back to work." They still stood staring at her, waiting for some final motivational moment. "Go! Now! Work!"

The witches and wizards looked at each other, then rushed out of the room.

"Nice speech," Ellis said when Jackie got back to their desks. "Real inspiring."

"I'd tell you where to shove it, but I probably don't get to say that now I'm the boss." Jackie slumped into her seat. "This is going to be a lot of work."

Sam appeared at her shoulder.

"Agent Kowal, do you want to come and work in your new office?"

Jackie looked up. "My office?"

"Mr. Applegate said you can have the office immediately, if you want it."

"Including his chair, the one with the really good lumbar support?"

"Including his chair."

Jackie got up, grinning. "Maybe leadership won't be so bad after all."

CHAPTER THIRTY-NINE

Dylan, Sofia, and Lance ambled along the street, their school bags on their backs.

"I'm just saying, I'd be a lot more motivated in math if we counted things I care about," Lance said. "Like superhero movies or chocolate bars."

"Your parents would hate that," Sofia said. "You had to come to my place just to watch the new *Spiderman*, and didn't your mom say the other day that she doesn't allow refined sugar in the house anymore?"

"Which is why I need to get it at school. Sugar is a necessary part of a balanced diet."

"No, vitamins and protein are part of a balanced diet. Sugar is what we get as a reward for putting up with a balanced diet."

"Whatever. My point is, we should be counting something fun."

"We're not five anymore. It's all multiplication and algebra and things like that. We hardly ever count anything."

"Then maybe we should, and I'd stop failing math tests."

"Dylan, what do you think?"

"Huh?" Dylan looked up.

"You were miles away again."

"Sorry."

"He's thinking about Mia," Lance said, drawing her name out. "Isn't that right?"

"What? No! I was wondering if you guys wanted to come around to my place now to hang out in the lair."

"Are you sure you're not supposed to be hanging out with Mia?"

"Lance, Lance, Lance." Sofia shook her head solemnly. "We've been through this before. Mia isn't his girlfriend. She's a girl he hangs out with. All the time. Instead of hanging out with us."

Dylan groaned. "Look, do you want to come around or not?"

The other two laughed.

"Sure, of course," Sofia said.

"What if Mia gets jealous?" Lance asked.

Dylan blushed. "Mia will be there too."

"Well, we wouldn't want to get in the way..."

"Oh for flip's sake!" Dylan flung his hands up. "You're my friends. I have something cool I want to show you. Can't you stop making fun of me and come see?"

Sofia and Lance huddled together like they were treating the topic to a serious and secretive discussion. After a few moments, Sofia stuck her head up.

"Will there be cookies?" she asked.

"Probably."

"Your mom's homemade cookies?"

"I can't promise anything, but probably."

"Interesting, interesting." Her head went back down, and the muttering resumed.

"You know what, I give up." Dylan turned his back and stormed off up the road. His friends, laughing, ran after him.

"Of course we're coming with you," Lance said.

"And not only for the cookies," Sofia added.

"Although there had better be cookies."

When they got to the Heron house, Dylan let them in through the front door. Buddy ran up, yapping excitedly.

"I thought we were going into the secret lair?" Lance said.

"We are." Dylan picked up Buddy. "This guy's coming with us."

"Here." Lucy appeared from the kitchen, carrying a tray of milk and cookies. "Take this down with you too."

"Thanks, Mrs. Heron." Lance accepted the tray. He licked his lips.

Dylan led them around the outside of the house, opened the hidden hatch, and levitated both Buddy and the tray to the bottom of the steps. Then the three children climbed down.

"This is still so cool," Lance said, looking around. "Makes me want to fight super-criminals, like Batman."

"Batman's only a rich thug in a weird suit," Sofia said.

"You sound like my mom."

"Spiderman is way better."

"Okay, now you sound nothing like her."

"My mom likes Batman and Spiderman," Dylan said.

"That's why your mom is the coolest mom. That and cookies."

They walked through to the magic practice room. Mia was sitting on a beanbag, levitating juggling balls.

"Hi, guys." She let the balls fall and waved hello. "Hope you don't mind, I let myself in."

"That's fine." Dylan set the tray down near her. "Mini Griffins are welcome here whenever they want, like the rest of my friends." He pulled more beanbags over so the others could sit. "Here, have a cookie."

Lance didn't need any more invitations and got straight to eating, but Sofia had other priorities.

"You said you had something cool to show us." She looked around. "I'm pretty sure this place hasn't changed since last time, which means it's not a new bit of the lair. What is it?"

"Well..." Dylan pulled a dog biscuit from his pocket and used it to lure Buddy into his lap. "Mia and I have been working on a new piece of magic. We're not one hundred percent sure it's going to work, but if it does, we wanted you to see it."

"Magic?" Lance sprayed them with cookie crumbs. "Awesome!"

"I guess that could be cool." Sofia pulled out her sketchpad. "Can I draw it?"

"Sure," Dylan said.

Mia leaned forward, looking at Sofia's sketchpad as she flicked through in search of a clean page.

"Oh my goodness, did you draw all of those?" Mia asked.

"It's my sketchpad, so yes."

"Those are brilliant. Who's the one with the bow?"

Sofia turned back a couple of pages.

"That's Siltor the elf," she said. "Not the real Siltor, who's this guy who lives in the tunnels, but a fantasy version of him I made. He's one of the heroes of my comic."

"And the lady with the glowing eyes?"

"That's Twylan."

"The witch who works with the Silver Griffins? We met her. That's such a good likeness."

Mia squeezed herself into the space between Sofia and Dylan, where she could look more closely at Sofia's art. Together, the two of them flicked through the pad, talking enthusiastically about the pictures Sofia had drawn and the stories she was working on.

"I thought we were going to see magic," Lance said.

"Can't that wait until after the pictures?" Mia asked. "This is way more exciting than spells."

"How can anything be more exciting than spells?"

"It depends on what you see every day," Dylan said. "The novelty of magic can wear off after a while."

Lance shook his head. "At least the novelty of your mom's cookies will never wear off."

He took another cookie and helped himself to a glass of milk.

They sat and chatted, the girls looking at drawings, the boys keeping Buddy entertained. At last, when Mia had seen everything in the sketchpad, some of it several times over, she let Sofia turn to a blank page, ready for what came next.

"All right, magic time," Dylan said.

"At last!" Lance set his glass aside.

"This is what we needed Buddy for," Dylan said, putting the dog down between him and Mia.

"Buddy can cast spells too? Your family is amazing!"

"Buddy isn't going to cast the spell. He's going to be on the receiving end of it."

"Didn't you get in trouble for that last time?"

"Yes, but now I'm going to fix it." Dylan placed his hands on Buddy's back and looked at Mia. "Ready?"

"Ready." She laid her hands on his.

They closed their eyes and started to chant. The air between them glowed, shining points of light swirling around their hands, then down around Buddy, who peered at the bright spots with interest. The magic clung to his sides, his legs, and his face. It seeped into his fur and shone across his eyes. He *yapped* and licked his nose, trying to catch the sparks of magic.

There was a rustling sound as Sofia's pencil danced across her page, capturing all the details she could: the sparks, the dog, the looks of intense concentration on the faces of Dylan and Mia.

The points of magical light grew, flowed into one another, became a shining coat that enveloped the dog. He went quiet, his expression distant as if he was listening to a distant voice.

Then he started to change. His legs extended, his body stretched, and his face shifted. Wrinkles of skin appeared around his eyes, the point of his nose grew more rounded, and his cheeks sagged. As his legs grew, his belly rose away from the floor. His tail stretched out and started wagging back and forth.

The magic faded into the dog until the glow was

entirely gone. Where a dachshund had stood a few minutes before, there was now a bloodhound.

Dylan opened his eyes.

"It worked!" he exclaimed and threw his arms around Buddy.

If Buddy was at all confused or disconcerted by his change, he didn't show it. He flicked his tail, gave an appreciative *woof*, and leaned into Dylan's embrace.

"Ever since I accidentally changed him, I've wanted to make it right," Dylan said. "I didn't know how. I have a lot of power, but it can be really dangerous. You saw what happened when I tried to grow that plant at school."

"That was awesome," Lance said.

"But a lot of trouble," Sofia reminded him.

"Right." Dylan shook his head. "Anyway, I knew I had the power, but I was worried that I might hurt Buddy if I cast the spell and got it wrong. Mia's good at bits of magic I'm not so good at. Working together, we found a way to make the spell work, and now..." He squeezed Buddy tight. "We did it!"

"*Woof*!" Buddy said again, his face wobbling.

"How are you going to explain this to the neighbors?" Sofia asked.

"New dog again. It shouldn't be too hard to believe."

Buddy turned his head. He finally seemed to have registered what had happened to him. He wagged his tail, waved a leg, and shook his ears around. He barked, then burst out of Dylan's arms and went running around the room, stretching his long legs as far as he could.

"Someone's happy with our work." Mia smiled. "I think that might be the best piece of magic I've ever done."

"What else can you two do together?" Lance asked.

Dylan shrugged. "We don't know yet. We're trying to work this out, but we can do all sorts of things that we couldn't alone. That's part of why I wanted you guys here so I could ask you. This is magic. We could try to do almost anything. What do you think we should do?"

CHAPTER FORTY

The Tolderai and the Underfoot Brigade made their way through the tunnels, heading deeper into the ground below the city than either group had ever been before. It occurred to Twylan as they went that they would need a new name for themselves soon, now that the two groups were becoming one. That could wait for another day. Right now, they were looking for magic.

They'd already split up into several separate groups so they could follow any tunnel they found that seemed relevant. They carried lights from the forest with them, and each group had one of those lights. The light in Twylan's group, which Mackam was carrying, flickered in response to the magical interference. It was flickering more than ever, its glow gradually fading as darkness took hold.

"We must be getting closer to the source," Twylan said.

"Oh, yes." Mackam grinned. He had the light under one arm and a long knife in his other hand. The prospect of trouble seemed to excite him.

"What is it?" asked Leontine. He and Siltor walked

behind Twylan and Mackam, the only other members of their little group. "I mean, apart from magic? It can't be industrial magic, like the factory up top that caused trouble before. Nobody's going to build a factory down here."

"Maybe if it's a factory for something really dark, really secretive," Siltor said. "Something no one wants to admit they're making."

"That sounds like a lot of bother when you could set up in a building out of town," Twylan said. "I think this is something stranger. I think it might even be the Shadow Men."

"Interesting." Mackam looked at her. "It would fit them, deep down in the dark here, but it would fit other creatures too. So what makes you think it's the Shadows?"

"Two things. First, I saw one disappearing down a utility hole before, so I'm pretty sure they're living in holes under this part of the city. Second, the flavor of the magic around here, if that makes sense."

"Oh, it does." Mackam took a deep sniff. "There's a scent to these things, a flavor, a color. Something distinctive about each type of magic."

"Exactly!"

"And you smell Shadow Men..."

They reached a junction. Shadows shifted in the light cast by the artifact under Mackam's arm, by the floating orbs that Twylan had summoned to illuminate their way, and by the magic flickering around her eyes. Those shadows made her nervous. What else might be hiding in them?

"Do we split up again?" Siltor sounded as nervous as Twylan felt.

"No point," Leontine said. "We only have one detector." He pointed at the flickering light Mackam held. "So which way?"

"Down." Twylan pointed to a downward sloping tunnel. "They'll be as deep down as they can get."

A shifting shadow made her jump. Had it been one of the Shadow Men, or the way the light worked here? It was so hard to tell.

"Everyone stop moving," she said. "I need to check if—"

Something hit her from behind, slamming her into the wall.

"Shadow Man!" Mackam shouted. He dropped the light and dove forward as Siltor summoned magic to his hands and Leontine leaped in, fists raised.

In the shifting darkness of the tunnel, it was impossible to tell what was a Shadow Man and what was merely a shadow. Leontine punched at something but slammed his fist into the wall. Mackam stabbed one shadow, then another, but had no idea whether he'd hit an enemy. Siltor flung blasts of magic around wildly, hoping something would strike its target.

Twylan saw a shadow of a knife.

"Mackam!" she yelled. "Look out!"

He turned and raised his knife but was too late. The shadow blade thrust into his shoulder, and he fell back, clutching the wound.

Siltor flung a spell at the Shadow Man, but it turned, and the magic flew harmlessly past. Then it hurled itself at Siltor, slamming him into the wall. His head hit a rock, and he slid unconscious to the ground.

Twylan threw out spells of her own, but the Shadow

Man seemed to sense each one a moment before she cast it. Every time, it managed to dodge the spell.

Leontine grabbed the Shadow Man and even managed to take hold of its arm. It felt like nothing in Leontine's hand, but he tugged on it anyway, and the shadows fell toward him.

"Leontine, no!" Twylan screamed.

It was too late. The shadow knife lunged again, and Leontine staggered back, blood running down his side.

"Hurts," he whimpered as he fell against the wall. "Oh, that really hurts."

The Shadow Man turned to face Twylan. Even without a face for her to see, she could sense the malice radiating off of it. The creature was a force of pure menace, a being that wanted to wipe away the world she loved.

Twylan cast a stun spell, a glue, a freeze. Each time, the Shadow Man twisted, became a target so thin she couldn't possibly hit it, and kept advancing on her, knife raised. She held her hand steady, waiting for it to get so close she couldn't miss it. It was the only way.

Cold seized her wrist, shadow fingers clamping down on her skin. How had she not seen that coming? The creature had disappeared from view for a moment, but now it had hold of her wand hand and was twisting it away so that she couldn't target the spell. Next to her, the shadow knife rose.

"Got you," the Shadow Man hissed.

There was one last chance. Twylan opened her eyes as wide as she could and let the magic flow. It was the same magic she spent her whole life holding back, the magic she sought to contain, the magic that marked her out as a freak. It was the magic that meant she could never blend in with the mundane world. Maybe today, it could be the magic that saved her.

The magic burst from her eyes in a flare of light that would've blinded her if it weren't hers. The Shadow Man shrieked and staggered back, holding up his arms as if to protect his unseen face. His outline wavered as the light threatened to overwhelm him.

Twylan brought her wand around.

"Stupefacio!" she shouted.

The stun spell hit the Shadow Man, and he went limp. Twylan caught him as he fell. He was so insubstantial, he seemed like no weight at all, but if she let him fall among the other shadows, she didn't think she would be able to find him again. She flung him over her shoulder, put her hand there to hold him in place, and turned to her friends.

"Take him back," Leontine said through gritted teeth. "Quick, before he wakes up."

"You need help."

"We can help each other, but if that guy wakes up down here, we're all dead."

"Here." Mackam, still clutching his wound, pulled a seed from his pocket and pushed it into the dirt at their feet, then touched the ground with his wand. A green shoot emerged from the dirt, became a sapling, in seconds became a small tree. "Walk through the green, girl. You can do it."

Twylan called on the magic she'd learned from the Tolderai. The bark of the tree split, and she stepped in. There was a disconcerting moment of walking through the wood, which parted around her like shifting sand, then she emerged from another tree into daylight.

The Shadow Man shifted and groaned. He would wake up soon. Twylan looked around, pulled out her phone, and called the best number she could think of for such an emergency.

"Twylan?" Jackie said from the other end of the line. "What's up?"

"I've got a captive Shadow Man, but I'm not sure how long I can keep hold of him. I'm in Elysian Park, near the secret swing. Can you get me a portal?"

"Of course. Hang on. Help's on its way."

Jackie hung up. Twylan clutched the Shadow Man as he started to shift. If she stepped into bright daylight, would that help her hang onto him, or would it just make him struggle more?

The air shimmered, and a portal appeared.

"Quick." Jackie waved to her from the other side.

Twylan stepped through into the Silver Griffins' transport room. The portal closed behind her. Ellis and Jackie grabbed the Shadow Man off her shoulder, slapped magical manacles onto him, and flung him into one of the holding cells.

"Great work, Twylan," Jackie said. "Did you overcome him on your own?"

"Pretty much, but he hurt the others first. Leontine, Siltor, Mackam, they're injured and deep underground, probably near the Shadow Men's lair. They need help."

Jackie looked at Ellis.

"Put a team together and get on it," she said. "Make sure you take a medic."

"Yes, ma'am." Ellis saluted with his wand, then hurried away.

Jackie turned back to the cell.

"This is exactly what we need," she said. "More Shadow Men to question. More evidence of where they are. A chance to track them down in their base. Well done, Twylan."

"It wasn't only me. It was the Tolderai and the Underfoots working together, finding magic beneath the city, tracking it down."

"You're the one who found him in the end and caught him. This is why you're going to make such a great Silver Griffin."

Twylan smiled. "Thank you. One day, I hope I prove you right."

"Screw one day." Jackie put a hand on Twylan's shoulder. "Twylan, are you serious about wanting to be a Silver Griffin?"

"More than anything."

"You're one of the smartest, most gifted witches I know, and that matters more than any rules about how we do recruitment, what education you should go through, or how old you have to be. The Silver Griffins would be crazy to say no to you, and I'm not going to let them act crazy anymore. Twylan, I'm offering you the post of junior agent in the Silver Griffins. I assume you're going to accept?"

Twylan laughed. "Thank you for the thought, Jackie, but I'm pretty sure you don't have the power to do that."

"Haven't you heard?" Jackie grinned. "I'm the boss around here now. I have the power to do whatever I want."

CHAPTER FORTY-ONE

Lucy, Jackie, Heather, and Twylan stood around the edges of a meeting room in the Silver Griffins' HQ. In the middle of the room, a three-dimensional map hung in the air, a magical representation of the tunnels underneath L.A. It wasn't perfect, some parts being estimates and guesswork rather than accurate measurements of passages. With so many forgotten tunnels dug by humans or summoned into existence by magicals, it was certainly incomplete. Still, it was as accurate a representation as anybody in the city had.

"These are the locations of the Shadow Men's attacks." Lucy waved her wand. At the top of the map, where the tunnels met the streets, red dots appeared. "There's not much of a pattern, probably because they went after powerful magicals wherever they could find them, but everything is within this area." She used her wand to draw an orange circle around a section of the map. "That means their lair is probably under there."

Jackie waved, and the map expanded, peripheral details

disappearing from view to leave them looking only at the area Lucy had highlighted. Heather waved her wand, and two green globes appeared in the underground part of the map.

"Of the three of our forests that have suffered the most magical interference, two are inside that area. Their interference seems to be coming from below. According to Jenkins' sensors, it's within a mile of each one, as the worm burrows." She conjured a larger, fainter globe around each green one, then highlighted the area where they intersected. "Their lair is in here somewhere or underneath. The question is, where are the tunnels that lead to it?"

It was Twylan's turned to make a mark on the map. She added a blue point on the surface and a wiggly line farther down. She shuddered as she did so, remembering the sight of her friends lying stabbed in the darkness.

"That's the utility cover I saw one of them go through and the tunnel where they attacked us," she said. "It looks like they both provide routes to the Shadow Men."

Other tunnels and chambers lay close to the line she'd drawn, but without a complete map, it was hard to tell how they might connect. How many of them led to the Shadow Men, and which ones? Where were the opportunities, and where were the dead ends? Without answers to those questions, any trip into the darkness risked leading to the wrong place or straight into a Shadow Man ambush.

"What does our prisoner say?" Jackie asked.

"Mostly that the end time is coming," Lucy replied. "Plus a lot of other apocalyptic stuff about darkness and flatness and the end of the world as we know it. If he were human, I'd dismiss him as another nutter, but..."

"The Shadow Men are planning an actual apocalypse for the rest of us, and they've been gathering the power to do it." Jackie rubbed her temples. "What a week to become boss. I don't suppose we got anything from him about where they are or what they'll do next?"

"He tried to tell us that they were using caves outside the city, and that's clearly not true, so I think we should ignore any directions he gives. He did say that they got the last shadow they needed today and that the Shadow Mage's spell comes at midday."

"So it's all kicking off today, in about..." Jackie looked at her phone. "Two hours. Great."

"Casting powerful magic takes a lot of power and concentration," Heather said. "If we can catch the Shadow Mage during his ritual, he might be more vulnerable."

"Good to know, but with so little time left, it probably doesn't make much difference to our plans." Jackie stared intently at the map. "We need to get down there and stop them as soon as possible. But which way do we go in?"

There was a knock on the door and Ellis poked his head into the room.

"Sorry to interrupt y'all," he said, "but that dwarf lawyer is here to see Lucy."

"Gruffbar?" She frowned. "What does he want?"

"Said it's to do with the Shadow Men."

"Let me guess, he's representing them, and he wants to sue us for creating a hostile working environment."

"The way he said their name, I really don't think he's on their side."

"Send him in," Jackie said.

"You sure you want him to see all this?" Ellis waved at the map.

"If it turns out that he's on their side, we'll lock him up until this is over, then decide whether to throw away the key." Jackie grinned. "I can make decisions like that now, so you'd better not annoy me, cowboy man."

"No, ma'am."

Ellis headed out, only to reappear a minute later with Gruffbar. The dwarf was dressed in his biker leathers and had a bag over his shoulder that looked the right shape to hold an ax. He also carried a bag full of documents.

"Heard you were having some trouble with the Shadow Men," he said. "This is everything I have on them. Most of it's from when I worked for Zero, but there are bits from legal cases too, and some notes I made from memory."

He put the bag down on a table at the side of the room.

"Couldn't you have emailed us the information?" Lucy asked, pulling documents out of the bag. There were cardboard folders, fat box files, a couple of notebooks, even some loose handwritten sheets. She handed them to her colleagues, spreading them around so that they could skim through the collection as quickly as possible. "It would have been quicker and easier to search."

"Would you have opened a strange file I sent you?" Gruffbar asked.

Lucy thought about all the people Gruffbar had worked for and the terrible damage a virus could have done to the Silver Griffins' systems.

"Maybe not," she admitted. "At least not until someone very thoroughly scanned it."

"Which makes this quicker."

"Why are you helping us?"

"Because these bastards tried to steal my shadow. Because they killed a client I respected. Because I don't trust them not to screw up the world I live in."

"So you've not come over to the good side all of a sudden?"

Gruffbar snorted. "No thanks. It's all too sweet on this side of the law." He pulled one of the documents out of the pile. "Here, this is my thoughts on how best to hurt the Shadow Men, based on what I've seen them respond to. There's almost no point using physical weapons, but that's fine. You've got plenty of magic. Light spells aren't the instant win you might hope for, but they can weaken and disorientate them, and that will buy you time."

"Thanks, Gruffbar."

"Happy to help." He paused as if listening back to his own words. "I mean, happy to help when it also helps me." He looked at the magical image filling the air between them, then took a few steps forward into the middle of it, right into the area where they suspected the Shadow Men's base hid.

"This is the undercity, right? You're missing an old dwarf mine shaft here. Good access, well-connected to other tunnels, but most people forget it exists. Zero sent me to meet the Shadow Mage there a couple of times."

"This shaft, what's at the bottom of it?"

"Some old cave. That's why they gave up on the mine, I think. They didn't like what they found in the cave."

"Like a load of sinister shadows?"

"Could be." Gruffbar shrugged. "Either way, I'm out of here."

"You're not going to stick around and help? Looks like you came armed."

Gruffbar laughed. "By my beard, what kind of white knight do you take me for?"

"Not even to get revenge because they attacked you?"

"Revenge is for petty idiots. I'm more interested in survival." He adjusted his bag and headed for the door. "Good luck, agents. Try not to let the world end."

By the time the door closed behind him, the Griffins were already gathered around the spot on the map where Gruffbar had said the mine shaft was.

"That's it, isn't it?" Lucy said, drawing a line to represent the shaft. "Where the Shadow Men are coming in and out, and our way to get to them."

"Probably," Heather said.

"Probably will have to do," Jackie said. "We're running out of time, and it's not just the city that's counting on us today. It's the whole world. Heather, Twylan, go gather your people. Lucy, Ellis, come with me."

She strode out the door and along the corridor to the main office. The door slammed open in front of her, and she leaped up onto a table, kicking papers out of the way. Everybody in the room turned to look at her, even the pigeons.

"All right, you lot," she shouted. "We've got a Code Red emergency, or whatever we call it these days. End times are upon us, threat to the whole world, Silver Griffins to the rescue, you know the drill. I'd try to make it sound dramatic, but an apocalypse speaks for itself.

"Everybody to my left, you're in Lucy's squad once we get into action. Everyone to my right, you're with Ellis.

Anyone who's not sure, you're with me. Oh, and Sam, drag Jenkins out of his pit. We're going to need whatever crazy gadgets he has this week.

"Grab your wands, grab your weapons, and haul your asses down to the transport room. It's time for action."

She jumped down off the table as witches and wizards streamed past, pumped up and ready for action.

"Nice speech," Lucy said. "You're exactly what the Griffins need. I'm glad you got the manager's job instead of me."

"I'm not." Jackie laughed. "But I'll live with it. Now come on, Agent Heron, let's go save the world."

CHAPTER FORTY-TWO

The Shadow Mage stood in the center of the ancient cave. It was the heart of the space where the Shadow Men had lived, exiles from the world above, for so very long. At his feet, a bowl wider than an elf was tall and equally deep had been carved from the ground. One by one, the Shadow Men walked past, the Shadow Mage towering over them, and each one in turn flung a shadow into the bowl.

There were shadows of the rich, the famous, and the powerful. Shades of people of influence. Shadows from a hundred different magicals across L.A. Each one was full of magical power. It held the magical potential of the person it was harvested from and the magic summoned by the art of slicing a shadow away, by the small rituals of violence that had made this moment possible.

The shadows piled up in the bowl, souvenirs of assaults, ingredients for the most powerful spell the Shadow Mage had ever attempted.

He picked up a pole, eight feet long and carved from a

single piece of obsidian. There was little light in the cave, but what there was shone off its edges, accentuating the blackness beneath. He lowered the end of the pole into the bowl and started to stir.

More shadows went in. A Willen. A gnome. An Arpak. The Shadow Mage could smell the death on that last one and the extra strength it gave to the spell. Strange that there weren't more like that, where the shadow was severed live, and the person faded into oblivion. Those added an extra potency that he would've liked to make use of.

Why hadn't more of them died? Was this how the Silver Griffins were trying to stop him? If so, it was far too little, far too late. He had the shadows he needed. The end was coming.

The shadows swirled together as he stirred. Their edges started to break down, the power to combine. The darkness bubbled and swayed.

The last of the shadows were in the bowl. The Shadow Men formed a ring around the Mage. As he chanted, they echoed his words, dark and rasping sounds from before the dawn of human consciousness. His voice rose, and the chorus of the Shadow Men shifted, becoming different, a rhythm across which the Mage's spell played. Then the Shadow Men started to dance.

To an outsider, the movements would have seemed ugly and angular, legs flicking back and forth, arms jerking and twitching. To the Shadow Men, it was the most beautiful thing in the world. It was a coming together in which they danced out the pattern of their violence, a rhythmic imitation of how they'd stolen those shadows. Knives lifted and fists clenched. Some of the chanting turned to shrieking imitations of pain and howling cries of victory.

The Shadow Mage kept stirring, his magic flowing from his hands, through the obsidian pole, into the pool of shadow power. It shaped the magic, knitted it together, turned individual shadows into part of something far larger than themselves. The darkness crept up the sides of the bowl, then oozed across the floor, flowing between the feet of the Shadow Men.

One Shadow Man stood unmoving throughout. The Shadow Sentry held his post at the end of the cavern, watching even though his eyes were closed. He didn't only see the cave around him. He saw the world beyond and how it connected to this place. He watched not only the tunnels leading to the cavern, but the lives leading to this point, the movements in the magic of the world, the way pieces drew one another. He stood silent, watchful, aware.

The Shadow Stalker stepped back from the dance. Of all the Shadow Men, he had the least need for it. He was a true hunter. He lived the magic of violence. He didn't need to be part of this imitation to feel a connection or contribute his power to the spell.

"Is it working?" he asked the Shadow Sentry.

"Yes," the Sentry replied, but something in his voice caught the Stalker's attention, like the first trampled blade of grass that could become the clue to an animal's trail.

"What else do you see?" the Stalker asked.

"They are coming, the people of the light. They think they know what we are doing. They think they know where we are."

"Are they right?"

"Right enough to find us."

The Shadow Stalker didn't waste words on curses.

"Could they stop us?" he asked.

"Perhaps, if they are lucky and determined, they might stand a shadow of a chance."

The Stalker narrowed his eyes as he examined the Sentry. Around them, the chanting grew louder, the dancing more vigorous.

"You have been watching the upper people too long if you think that a shadow's chance is a weak one."

"I do not think that."

"I see."

"No, I see. You hear my report of it."

"You always were a frustrating pedant."

"And you always were a monstrous obsessive." The Sentry reached over his shoulder and drew a long two-handed sword made of darkness. "I hope you continue that way."

In the center of the room, the Shadow Mage chanted louder. Darkness flowed out of the bowl in ever-growing waves. It was more than an absence of light. It was a vile and clinging force, one that stuck to the rocks as it lapped over them, that coated the walls as it reached them, that snuffed out candles and lanterns until there was only enough light left to cast shadows by.

The Shadow Mage raised the obsidian pole, then slammed it into the ground. It shattered, black shards flying in every direction. They sliced through the darkness, tearing holes in its fabric, and more darkness bled from those gaps. It poured across the cavern and out into the tunnels, the caves, and along the abandoned mine shaft that ran up and away. It flowed and flowed without end, as a sea of shadow made and remade itself.

"Now is our day," the Shadow Mage bellowed. "Now is our hour. Now is our eternity. Now is our world. Now is the Shadow Time!"

The Shadow Stalker drew his knives and bounded up the steep slope toward the mine shaft, leaping from outcrop to outcrop of rock. If there was a chance for their time to come, he had to protect it. He wasn't the hunter anymore, he was the hunted, and he'd seen how prey could fight. Cornered. Desperate. Vicious.

The greater shadow swept past him, heading for the world above.

Heather and Twylan ran down the tunnel, the Tolderai and the Underfoot Brigade behind them. Magical lights floated around their heads, and Heather carried a light like the ones from the forest. It flickered in an ever more frantic and alarming pattern as they descended into the depths.

"This way." Twylan pointed past where the Shadow Man had attacked her. "Keep going down."

The tunnel ahead was dark as if they were rounding a corner and the light couldn't reach. Except that there was no corner, no bend in the path. Instead, there was a tide of darkness rising toward them.

"Lumen!" Twylan chanted and spread her arms wide. Light flowed from her, warm and bright. The shadow kept rising, thick and dark and toxic as an oil spill. It washed over them, and for a moment all light was extinguished. A terrible cold ran through Twylan, like ice grasping her flesh. Others cried out in alarm and Mackam swore so violently and energetically that Twylan wondered if her ears would ever recover.

When the front edge of the magical darkness had passed, a little light returned. The glowing orbs became visible again. The light in Heather's hands stuttered and pulsed. But gloom clung around them. None of the lights were as powerful as they had been.

Magicals stumbled as they tripped over unseen dips in the floor. The chill clung to them too, and the younger Underfoots wrapped their arms close around themselves to keep warm. Their shadows were longer and darker than they'd ever been.

"We keep going." Heather strode on down the tunnel. "The only way to drive back the darkness is to show it the real light."

Twylan hurried after her, and the others followed. As they ran, Twylan couldn't help wondering whether this was darkness they could ever drive back. Was there a bright enough light in the whole world, or was night about to wipe the day away? The only thing she knew for certain was that she wouldn't give in.

The darkness flowed up the tunnels, reached the sewers and cellars, flowed out through gratings and storm drains into the street. It rose like a miasma across L.A., pouring through the streets, clinging to everything it touched. The bright sunshine only accentuated the darkness.

The magic ran through the streets and alleyways, across rooftops, through windows, into offices and homes. Angelenos shivered and looked up in confusion as the darkness touched them. It spread through the city from its central welling point, out toward the outskirts, heading for the rest of the world.

"Cold," Eddie said as the darkness swept across the Herons' back yard.

"It sure is." Charlie looked up from watering the new tree. He couldn't see clouds, but somehow he couldn't see the sun either. The sky was a muted gray that seemed to be heading toward true darkness. He would've thought the night was falling, except that it was only midday.

"Dad, are you out here?" Dylan emerged from the back door. "Something's wrong."

Charlie hurried over, bringing Eddie with him.

"What's up?" he asked.

"My magic." Dylan held out his hand. A light shone there, but it was faint, not the sort of display Charlie expected from his powerful son. "Something's blocking it."

"It's not only your magic." Ashley appeared behind Dylan. She held up a string robot with a flashlight glowing feebly on one end. "Any source of light is failing."

In the distance, there was a squeal of tires as someone braked hard, then a crash. Charlie made a quick decision.

"Everyone inside," he said. "If it keeps getting darker,

soon we won't be able to see what we're doing, so I want to make sure we're together somewhere safe until this passes."

"What if it doesn't pass?" Ashley asked.

"Bad magic in L.A.?" Charlie forced a smile that was more confident than he felt. "Do you really think your mom isn't going to solve this?"

CHAPTER FORTY-THREE

Lucy's heart was racing as she ran down the last few hundred yards of the steeply sloping mine tunnel. Despite the magical lights around her, the darkness was so thick that she could hardly see where she was putting her feet. She almost tripped over an abandoned rail and a fallen rock but managed to keep going, despite her tiredness. What choice did she have? It was win now or lose forever.

Behind her, more Griffins were coming, wands in hand. Jenkins and Nigel were among them, carrying the most impressive gadgets they'd been able to grab from their arsenal. As they ran, Jenkins had a screwdriver out and was adjusting the settings on a magical light, trying to find a way to make it drive back the darkness.

Something shifted in the shadows up ahead, where the mine shaft opened into a wider cavern. Lucy's eyes were adjusting to the dark, but it still took a moment to realize what she was looking at: a Shadow Man barred their way, with a knife in each hand.

"Lumen!"

Lucy flung a bolt of bright light straight at the Shadow Man. He turned, and it shot past him, but as he turned back, her second light bolt hit him. He staggered, and for a moment, Lucy thought she had him beaten, but he straightened and raised his blades.

"The rest of you, keep going," she said. "I'll deal with this lad."

She flung herself at the Shadow Man, shoulder slamming into his midriff, arms wrapping around his waist. He was so light, there was nothing to absorb her momentum, and the two of them kept going, hurtling out of the tunnel mouth and tumbling down the slope beyond. Lucy clung tight as she took a bruising fall across rock protrusions and down to the floor of the cave.

The Shadow Stalker tried to bring his knives around, but he couldn't get a good angle to strike with Lucy holding him so close. He dropped the blades and grabbed hold of her, trying to pull her off.

The Griffins who had come with Lucy scrambled down the slope and into the cavern. The Shadow Mage looked up from his magic and waved.

"Stop them," he hissed.

The Shadow Men broke their dancing circle and went to the attack while the darkness flowed from the central pool. Spells flew, and lights flashed as the Griffins tried to take the Shadow Men down before they got close.

On the far side of the cave, the Tolderai and Underfoot Brigade emerged from the tunnel they followed. Leontine leaped into the air, spread his wings wide, and soared above the heads of the Shadow Men. He dropped high-powered flashlights into their midst, hoping that the brightness of those lights might slow them for a moment.

Twylan cast spells ahead of her, stunning some of the Shadow Men, using light to weaken others. Heather dropped the light she'd been carrying and summoned her ancestral spear before charging in to fight up close.

As she and the Shadow Stalker grappled on the ground, Lucy twisted her hand around and tapped her wand against the floor. A pre-prepared communication spell went off.

"Jackie, we're here," she called. "Target the area around me."

"Got it," Jackie's voice replied, distant and crackly but still firm.

A moment later, the air started shimmering in two different parts of the cave. Portals appeared, and Silver Griffins charged out of them, one group led by Jackie, the other by Ellis. There were dozens of them, every Griffin in L.A. and some summoned from farther afield, but their opponents still outnumbered them. This was the Shadow Men's home, and they were ready for the fight.

Heather lunged at a Shadow Man with her spear. He crumpled as the glowing blade hit him and collapsed to the ground, dissolving into the wider darkness. Then another Shadow Man stepped up. Broader and taller than the rest, he carried a double-handed sword, which he pointed at Heather.

"You shall not pass," the Shadow Sentinel said.

"You won't stop me." She swung her spear.

Across the cave, Jackie dodged and darted through the fighting, past witches, wizards, and Shadow Men. Any time one of the enemies came near, she flung a spell at them, using stuns, sleeps, and other distracting magic to throw them off-guard and give her friends an advantage.

She didn't use light. She didn't want to draw the attention that would bring as she headed for the center of the cavern. Someone had to stop the Shadow Mage, and as the leader of the L.A. Griffins, she saw one way to make sure that job got done: by doing it herself.

She walked up a rise in the rock floor toward the mage. As she did, he turned to face her, hands raised, dark magic flickering around them.

"I don't suppose you want to surrender and let me arrest you?" Jackie asked.

"Surrender, when the world is about to become ours?" the Shadow Mage hissed.

"That's what I thought." Jackie pointed her wand and let the magic flow through her. "Lumen."

Light flashed, and she jumped to the attack.

Near Heather, Twylan strode purposefully into a mass of Shadow Men, the Underfoot Brigade following her. She flung spells to the right and left, managing to take out some of the Shadow Men temporarily, but it never seemed to last. Their magic was too strong to be beaten while the other shadows were flowing around them.

Try as they might, the Underfoots struggled, several of them dragged to the ground by Shadow Men. Siltor was on the floor, a Shadow Man sawing at his shadow, while Kix tried to fend the attacker off with her spells.

Something more was needed. Something that would rob the enemy of their strength. Not for Twylan to beat any of them on her own, but to weaken them so her friends stood a chance.

She drew a deep breath and let her wild magic flow. It poured out of her, from her eyes, mouth, and hands, raw power that glowed as it ran forth, becoming brighter with every passing moment. Her whole body shone, and the power of it lifted her off her feet.

In the face of that radiance, the Shadow Men staggered back. Some fell to their knees. The flowing shadows rolled back for a moment, then flowed again. Light and dark battled for dominance across the cave.

As the light burst from Twylan, Lucy was lying on her back, the Shadow Stalker crouching over her. He pressed her down with one hand and raised a blade with the other.

"I don't know how you're conscious," he hissed, "but it's over. No prey of mine walks away to tell the tale."

Then the light came. It hit him from behind and tossed him around like a boat on a storm-tossed sea. He kept a grip on his knife, but his grasp on Lucy weakened.

She seized her opportunity, grabbed his wrist, and yanked him off her. He crashed to his knees, head shaking and shoulders trembling. The light had robbed him of his strength, but he only needed a moment to recover. The shadows always returned, no light could stop them, and he would return too.

Lucy thrust her wand into the middle of his face.

"Lumen." She threw all of her fading strength into the spell.

The Stalker's head evaporated in a blinding flash. For a moment, he still knelt in front of Lucy. She was afraid he would somehow find his strength again, that his head would grow back and he would attack her once more. Then he toppled forward, and his shadow dissolved into the darkness around them.

The same wave of light from Twylan hit the Shadow Sentinel as he swung his sword at Heather. She caught the blow on her ghost spear and twisted the shaft around, sliding his blade to the floor. He stepped back and raised his weapon to defend himself, but as he did so he stumbled. His body, which had at first seemed vast and muscled, now seemed ordinary. There were points of light in his face where others might've had eyes.

"I see it," he said. "The light is coming."

"The light just came," Heather said, her grimace lit by Twylan's glow. "And it's going to mess you up."

She lunged. The Sentinel knocked that blow aside and the next one after it. He stiffened as if pulling himself together and swung at her again, some of his strength restored.

"I see it," he said. "But I see my end as well, and it is good."

"I am your end." Heather parried his attack, then lunged again. She got the shaft of her spear between his legs and tripped him. He fell to the ground. She brought her spear up, and he raised his sword to block, but not fast enough. Her spear slammed into his chest, running him through. The sword fell from his hands.

"Good..." the Sentinel whispered. "Good to go down fighting."

Then the light flowed from his eyes, and his shadow body melted away.

By the bowl in the center of the cavern, Jackie and the

Shadow Mage flung magic back and forth, each countering the other's spells. The air crackled with their power, and the static of it made Jackie's hair stand on end.

"I love the mad scientist look," she said, "but it's time to end this."

"I will end you," the Shadow Mage responded, throwing a bolt of freezing magic at her.

"No chance." Jackie deflected the spell. "Your side's losing. Soon you'll all be gone."

"It does not matter. The Shadow Time is coming. We will emerge once more in its darkness and more like us. It will sweep you away, and the world will be ours."

"You like this Shadow Time so much; why don't you become a part of it?"

Jackie stepped forward. The Shadow Mage raised a fistful of magic, ready to deflect her spell. Except there was no spell. Jackie punched the Shadow Mage squarely in the jaw, knocking him into the bowl of shifting shadows. They swirled over him, and the magic he had put into the bowl seized his body, unraveling his boundaries, making him one with the darkness. He let out a final mad laugh as the shape that had been the Shadow Mage faded away.

Lucy stumbled up to the edge of the bowl and looked in.

"Did we win?" Jackie asked.

"I don't think so," Lucy said. "The darkness is still flowing out."

"But the Shadow Men..."

"They started something. We need a way to stop it."

Twylan stood between them. "What do we do?"

"The only thing we can." Lucy thrust her hand into the bowl. "Use light to drive back the darkness. Lumen!"

Light glowed around her hand. Jackie thrust her hand in and did the same. Heather joined them, then Ellis, and Jenkins, and Nigel with glowing devices instead of wands. They all thrust their hands into the pool and let light magic flow.

"It's not enough," Twylan whispered.

"It has to be," Lucy said. She thought of her family and a world where darkness swept them away. "It just has to."

"There's one way it can be." Twylan sucked in magic from the world all around and let it flow through her. For a moment, so much power poured from her that it looked as if she was made of pure light. Then she stepped forward and fell into the shadow bowl.

The others stared in horror as she vanished beneath the surface.

"Twylan?" Lucy called.

"Kid?" Jackie said. "Kid, get out of there."

Then the shadows shifted, slid back, and faded away. The darkness that had filled the cave subsided, and the blackness in the bowl sank like a puddle evaporating in the sunshine.

At last, all the shadow magic was gone from the cave and the Shadow Men with it. In the bowl, all that remained was Twylan, lying on her back with her eyes closed.

"Twylan?" Fearful of what she might find, Lucy took the young witch's hand.

Twylan opened her eyes. Magic still glowed there; its flicker made faint by her exhaustion. "Did we win?"

"Yes," Lucy replied. "Thanks to you."

"Look at this." Jenkins pointed at the ground behind Lucy. "You've got your shadow back."

"Really?" As she asked, she knew he must be right because she felt her strength returning and the full power of her magic with it.

Jenkins pulled a device from his pocket and pointed it close to Lucy's feet. "Do you mind if I run some tests?"

Above them in the streets of Los Angeles, the strange darkness faded, and daylight returned.

CHAPTER FORTY-FOUR

"Dinner time!" Lucy called as she set the lasagna dish down on the table.

"Yay!" came the shout from the living room.

The kids rushed through, but Buddy was ahead of them, loping into the dining room with long strides and a flick of his tail. He ran to the end of the room and rested his head on the table, his crumpled jowls spreading across the cloth.

Lucy laughed. "Is that how it's going to be, now that you can reach the table again?"

Buddy *woofed* and his tail wagged some more.

"All right, just this once." Lucy went into the kitchen. By the time she returned with Buddy's food bowl, the rest of the family were taking their seats. "Here." She set the bowl down on the table by Buddy, then patted his head. "Enjoy."

Buddy set to attacking his dinner with enthusiasm, while Charlie started dishing out lasagna for the rest of them.

"There's a lot of vegetables in this." Dylan peeled back a sheet of pasta with his fork.

"Do you not like them?" Lucy asked.

"Mushrooms, courgettes, eggplant... No, these are all things I like." Dylan let the pasta flop back down. "Just not what I expected."

"We're cutting back on meat, remember?" Charlie said. "For the good of the environment."

"Scientifically speaking, it's the right thing to do," Ashley said. "But you need to be careful. We need calcium and protein for our growing bodies."

"I'll try not to forget." Lucy laughed. How could she forget when they were all growing out of their clothes so quickly?

"I've been thinking more about the environment since we planted that tree," Ashley said. "Could we plant more?"

"Where would we plant them, sweetheart?" Lucy asked.

"In the garden."

"We can't fill the whole garden with trees. Eddie and Buddy need space to run around."

"In Elysian Park then. There are places there without much growing."

"It's not up to us to plant things without permission, but we could try joining a tree planting scheme again if you like."

"Yes, please."

If that failed, Lucy could think of another tree planting scheme Ashley might enjoy. Her robots would probably be a huge help to the Tolderai and the Underfoot Brigade if they could persuade the likes of Mackam to accept high-tech assistance in their wondrous caves. It might even be good to show Ashley more of the secrets of the magical world. While she was distracted, some of the other Mini Griffins could have a go at running their little gang.

"Have you read any of the articles people have written about the eclipse?" Charlie asked.

"No," Lucy said. "There doesn't seem to be much point in reading someone else's wild theories when I'm one of the people who know the truth."

"Still, those theories are interesting. Or at least, the way people talk about them is. It's amazing how all of these people have found a way to believe in an unpredicted eclipse so they can make sense of the world around them."

"Amazing."

Lucy smiled. It would have been even more amazing if it had happened without the Silver Griffins' help, but of course, covering up for magic was what they did, even when it was magic that could have ended the world. After returning from the Shadow Men's cave, they had cast a broad but subtle enchantment, one that encouraged ordinary people to look for an ordinary explanation to the strange thing that had happened, that wave of darkness across the city.

Of course, some people wanted to believe in the strange, and they were still out looking for magic or UFOs or government conspiracies. The vast majority had taken their lead from a secret wizard on the Observatory staff, who claimed to have spotted an asteroid that temporarily cast a shadow over L.A.

Now everyone from amateur stargazers to professional astronomers was looking for more evidence of this asteroid because it was the only thing that made any sense.

Meanwhile, the Silver Griffins could get back to countering everyday magic.

"How's work going, sweetheart?" Lucy asked.

"Pretty good." Charlie used his fork to sketch a shape in the cheese sauce on top of his lasagna. "We've come up with a new configuration for the filters, based on our experience fixing up Roger Applegate's camper. Ringo thinks it would let us convert heavy trucks more cost-effectively, which opens up a new line of business. Max is already phoning around the haulage and delivery companies, seeing if he can drum up some business."

"I thought you already had plenty of work?"

"We do, but it can't do any harm to find more. Getting into commercial work would help to boost our positive environmental impact, which is what it's all about."

Lucy squeezed his hand. "I'm so proud of you."

"Me too." Dylan smiled at his dad.

"And me," Ashley added.

"Me-me-me too!" Eddie said.

Buddy *woofed* into his bowl of dog food.

"I think we all have things to be proud of," Charlie said. "I mean, you saved the city again, Lucy. Heck, you probably saved the world."

"Just doing my job."

"Your amazing job! Dylan, look what you achieved." Charlie pointed at Buddy. "That is one happy dog."

Buddy *woofed* again and wagged his tail.

"The best part is, I think I could do it on other animals," Dylan said. "Or even people. We could all have a go at turning into something else like Eddie does."

Charlie and Lucy exchanged a look.

"You know that Buddy spent a year as a dachshund because your spell went wrong," she cautioned. "So maybe take it slow on trying to turn human beings into cats."

"Don't worry, Mom, I'm going to be careful. Ashley's helping me plan out a series of tests to make sure I do it right."

"We're going to have a control group," Ashley said. "And an escalating series of trials, starting with animal subjects."

"Buddy again?"

"No, not Buddy again. His previous transformations might bias the outcome."

"Okay. Can you please let us know what you're going to do before you do it?"

"You want to know more about my experiments?" Ashley beamed.

"Of course, sweetheart. We're very proud of you."

"I change too," Eddie said loudly, feeling a little left out.

"Of course you do." Lucy smiled at her youngest. "You change brilliantly."

"Proud of me?"

"Of course we're proud of you!"

Eddie pulled a thoughtful face. "What for?"

Lucy blinked. She hadn't been sure that Eddie knew what the word "proud" meant.

"For being you. Your amazing, wonderful self." She looked around at her family. "That would be enough to make me proud of any of you."

She wiped a tear from the corner of her eye.

"I thought English people weren't supposed to show emotions," Dylan said.

Lucy laughed. "What can I say? I'm a maverick."

"A maverick who keeps us all safe." Charlie leaned over and kissed her on the cheek. "Thank you, honey, from all of us."

"Happy to do it." Lucy blushed. "Now, it's dinner time, so it must be quiz time. Who's feeling wise today?" She glanced at Eddie as the air started to shimmer around him. " No turning into an owl at the dinner table."

Shadows stretched across the auto shop's floor as the last light of evening crept through the doors. Gruffbar watched the shadows, wary for any sign of movement, but they seemed to be perfectly mundane. No two-dimensional assassins or knife-wielding darkness.

He carried the last of his old files into Gunther's office and fed them through the shredder. There went Zero's debtor lists, Meredith Womack's educational contracts, and the details of companies he'd contracted for Blight's pollution work. Cases and clients, research and rambling ideas, all turned into paper ribbons, ready to go for recycling.

Gunther, holding a coffee mug the size of a small bucket, watched him from the corner of the room.

"This for real?" Gunther asked.

"I'm committed now." Gruffbar nudged the shredder with his steel-toed boot. "No going back."

"Bullshit. You could get a wizard to put those back together. Bet you know a guy already."

Gruffbar nodded. It was true. In L.A., he always knew a guy who knew a guy who could do the thing he needed, whether it was sourcing weapons, stalking informants, or finding the perfect croissant. That was part of what made this so hard.

"It's not the papers," he said. "It's the decision. I've made it, and I'm not going back."

"It ain't gonna be the same around here without you."

"Around here in the shop, or around here in L.A.?"

"Both."

"Thanks." Gruffbar stroked his beard. "This is my chance to start again. Ever since that business with Mr. No, I've felt the need to build something new. At first, I thought that meant rebuilding my bike or taking up sculpture, maybe even going back to the mines. Now I think I was wrong. What I want to build is a new life for myself."

"Pretty deep. How'd you work that out?"

Gruffbar thought of Lucy Heron, of all the times she'd thwarted him and the times they'd wound up on the same side. He thought about how the world changed around her and how people responded. She was building a better world every day, one that wasn't only morally righteous but functioned to help the people in it.

Hidden beneath all the heroic posing, all the cringe-worthy talk of love and family, there was craftsmanship in that. If he wanted to build something on a truly significant scale, that was the way to go.

It wasn't that he felt guilty or that he liked the idea of being a good guy. After all, that was for chumps, wasn't it?

"Someone's mom had a word with me," he said. "Made me see the error of my ways."

"Fine, don't tell me." Gunther set his mug down and

picked up the saddlebags sitting in the corner of the room. "Come on, let's get you out. I need to lock up."

They walked across the shop floor to where the midnight black Harley Davidson Deluxe stood. Gunther strapped on the saddlebags and double-checked that they were secure, while Gruffbar tied down his shotgun-ax, put his helmet on, and climbed into the saddle.

"By my beard, I'm going to miss this place," he said.

"The shop or L.A.?"

"Both."

"Sure you don't want to wait for tomorrow?" Gunther nodded into the fading light of the street. "Day's almost over."

"End of one day, beginning of another, it's the same thing, and leaving under cover of darkness seems like my perfect exit."

"Where you gonna go?"

"Up to Silicon Valley, for a start. It's supposed to be a good place for a new business."

"Over to the other valley, even?"

"Maybe. I've had a lot of weird adventures lately, so I'll stay on the mundane side this time." Gruffbar held out his hand. "See you around."

"I hope not." Gunther shook. "Hope you build something good enough to keep you away."

Gruffbar started the engine. There was a growl like a caged beast, and he rode out into the night.

Gunther pulled the shutters down and locked the door. He didn't bother with the magical padlock he used to add every night. L.A. was safe from magical trouble these days, thanks to Lucy Heron and the Silver Griffins.

The End

Did you enjoy this series? If so, more are coming from the Oriceran Universe. If you haven't checked out <u>THE LEIRA CHRONICLES</u> yet, you're missing out. It's the series that started it all!

Cheerios Chocolate Peanut Butter Cups Recipe

Ingredients:

Chocolate Cheerios
- 1 cup semi-sweet chocolate chips (or 6.5 oz. dark chocolate-finely chopped)
- 2 Tablespoons coconut oil
- 1 ¼ cup Cheerios

Peanut Butter Cheerios:
- ¾ cup peanut butter
- 3 Tablespoons organic brown rice syrup
- 3 Tablespoons organic coconut oil
- 1 ¼ cup Cheerios

Instructions

1. Spray 12 cup silicon muffin pan with cooking spray and set aside.
2. In a heat proof bowl set over a pan of simmering water combine dark chocolate and 2 Tbsp. of coconut oil. Stir until it's completely melted and smooth. Remove from heat and stir in Cheerios. (optionally you can melt the chocolate and coconut oil in the microwave or in a sauce pan over low heat)
3. In another heath proof bowl over a pan of simmering water combine peanut butter, dark corn syrup and coconut oil. Stir until it's completely melted and smooth. (optionally you can melt peanut butter, rice syrup and coconut oil in the microwave or in a sauce pan over low heat) Remove from heat and stir in Cheerios.
4. Cool both mixture to a room temperature stirring occasionally.
5. To assemble the cups, alternately drop spoonful of chocolate and peanut butter Cheerios in prepared pan. Tap the pan onto working surface to help the mixture to set.
6. Chill in the fridge or freezer until firm. Remove from the mold and store in and air-tight container in the fridge.

Get sneak peeks, exclusive giveaways, behind the scenes content, and more. PLUS you'll be notified of special **one day only fan pricing** on new releases.

Sign up today to get free stories.

Visit: https://marthacarr.com/read-free-stories/

This past Saturday, my sweet pittie, Leela passed away from complications of cancer. I had been on vacation in Big Sur, the first real vacation I had taken in over five years and got a message early Friday morning that something was going very wrong.

In a matter of hours, I had changed my flight and was rushing to a distant airport to get home two days early. The entire drive up the coast of California I kept whispering, "Please let me get there in time."

I didn't want her dying with strangers, wondering where I was in the end.

I got home after midnight and went straight to the animal ER where Leela was being kept comfortable. They laid a blanket on the ground in a small examining room. The same one where we had sat when she needed to get her leg looked at a few years ago.

I laid on the ground next to her and talked to her calmly, telling her it was okay. Go if you need to. She rolled her warm body back against my leg and shut her eyes and we stayed just like that for as long as they let us.

The next day, the Offspring and I went back and spent more time with her, and it was obvious where we had come to. Leela was struggling to do the simplest things. The cancer had gone far enough. We rubbed her back and told her we loved her, and she passed away peacefully.

It feels like there is a hole in the space around me that moves with me wherever I go. In the grocery store I passed by the watermelon chunks and pulled my hand back, realizing there was no need to get them anymore.

I still have another dog at home. My wild child, Lois Lane who is eighty-five pounds of rambunctious curiosity, always in motion. She gets up early to greet the day and goes to sleep late, always wanting to be in on the action. She's great for a game of tag or hide-and-go-seek.

It was Leela who hung nearby, staring up at me with brown eyes that looked like she was wearing eyeliner, waiting for some kind of response. She was the one who would sit under my feet at the desk or out on the deck in the warm air. Although if someone was using a mower or even better, an edger, Leela was happy to bark relentlessly at them through the fence, running back and forth. She was also the crafty one who would slip outside to greet other dogs or people walking by, never venturing much further.

Last summer, while the wild child was at daycare, Leela and I took endless walks around the neighborhood, five days a week, sometimes getting caught in a downpour. She would drag me up the street, trotting at a quick pace as we left the house behind us, and slow down to a crawl when a few miles later we were finally nearing home.

This past spring, when I had one ridiculous surgery after another and felt like I was hiccupping anesthesia, Leela was the one who wiggled close to me and laid her head across my legs. Lois ran circles in the backyard while Leela stayed right next to me.

This summer, while I have been going through chemo for a cancer of my own, often too tired by the afternoons to do more than sit, or my bones individually ached too much to walk down a hallway, it was Leela who sat next to me, keeping me company. Occasionally, around noon she would lift her nose in the air and howl for a treat. She was also good for a howl at dinner time and could even get Lois worked up. It was a noisy household at times.

My sweet girl was a rescue my son picked out the day before she was to be euthanized because she was on the list too long and no one else had picked her. The only time she jumped into a pool, she sank like a rock and the Offspring quickly dove to the bottom to rescue her. She came up sneezing and only slightly startled at the adventure.

The place echoes from the stillness now on the days Lois goes off to see her friends. Leela had too much anxiety at daycare and spent her days with just me, happy to be home.

The strange thing about loss and grief is it's in direct proportion to the love and connection we shared with those we lose. It's part of a life well lived in the company of others, including dogs who greet us as if they can only see the better versions of ourselves. Raise a glass when you can to the sweet pittie, Leela, who will be forever missed. More adventures to follow.

Thank you for not only reading this book but this entire series so far and these author notes as well.

You know, one thing Martha and I share is a dark sense of humor. We don't talk about it openly because it isn't polite.

However, there is one thing I won't joke about, and it is her love for Leela.

(I'll kid her about her son all day long, but not her dog(s)… Well, Leela. I'm not sure if I'll joke about Lois Lane yet–although I think I have already.)

We share some political points of view, we differ on others. We can laugh at jokes the other makes, even at our expense.

Especially at our expense.

But not Leela's passing away.

Oh, we have talked many times and had Leela barking at…God only knows what. I sometimes think she could see into the paranormal realm. Which would be ok; she was deaf. (Leela, not Martha. Don't get me started on Martha's hearing.)

But what always struck me was Martha's patience with Leela.

Now, I don't have any pets. The last dog the family had was sent to live with Grandmother (and is now famously spoiled by that same grandmother). Note that I said, "the family had."

I did not desire any dogs; they came with my wife. Marry wife, acquire dogs.

My stepmom is the same way. While my dad might bitch and groan about getting another damn dog, I roll my eyes because who do you think the latest pet snuggles up to? And who do you believe eats that affection up like the big, gray-haired teddy bear he really is?

That's right... My dad. Sir Anderle, the one who is ALL bark and no bite with the "not another damned dog."

So, having pets is a family trait. But, I've heard many bad pet stories and lived a few myself when someone else had a pet and I didn't have enough vetos.

Now that there are only two of us in the house–the kids are all gone–I merely have to explain to my wife that SHE will be the one to deal with the pet. If she wants one, the care and feeding are 100% on her. So far, no pet.

Also, we travel a lot. Have fun (I explain to my wife) trying to take a dog everywhere with us (France, Germany, UAE, Mexico, California...)

I know my wife has not given up on this discussion. It comes up about every 8-12 weeks or after a really cute puppy video. I've been steadfast so far. I really, really don't want another responsibility where I have to worry about a mouth to feed or a mess to clean up.

But if we end up with only one house...look out. I suspect a full-court press will occur. I might fake the need for hearing aids and claim the batteries aren't working as a cop-out.

Why? Because I know in my genes that if we get a dog, I'll probably be just like my dad.

May you have a great week or weekend, wherever you are!

Ad Aeternitatem,
Michael Anderle

Solve a murder, save her mother, and stop the apocalypse?

What would you do when elves ask you to investigate a prince's murder and you didn't even know elves, or magic, was real?

Meet Leira Berens, Austin homicide detective who's good at what she does – track down the bad guys and lock them away.

Which is why the elves want her to solve this murder – fast. It's not just about tracking down the killer and bringing them to justice. It's about saving the world!

If you're looking for a heroine who prefers fighting to flirting, check out The Leira Chronicles today!

<u>**AVAILABLE ON AMAZON AND IN KINDLE UNLIMITED!**</u>